p. 10

The Last Casualty

Cyn Mobley

The Last Casualty

Published by:

Radix Press, an imprint of Greyhound Books
2000 Stock Creek Road
Knoxville, TN 37920
865-405-3002
radixpress.com

ISBN trade paperback: 1-59677-014-7
First printing, June 2006

The first casualty when war comes, is truth.

Senator Hiram Johnson, 1917

Glory to you, beholding the depths
From the high vault of Heaven,
Glory to you.

Canticle 13

4

A Note from Cyn

This story has been on my hard drive for years now and it's walked with me through years of growth and changes. Researching it brought me back into the Episcopal Church and into EFM. By the time I'd finished writing it, I'd moved from San Diego to Knoxville, returned to karate and earned a black belt in Isshinryu, joined several new dojos, adopted eight more dogs and written around ten more books.

There are so many people to thank, starting with Father Bill Mahedy, now retired from the Veteran's Administration. Bill was the first person to get to know Lieutenant Dalt. His enthusiasm and encouragement included reading countless drafts and answering my endless questions about sacraments and post traumatic stress. As a lawyer, I looked for loopholes. As a priest, he looked for grace and taught me how to do the same.

Oddly enough, Fr. Bill had been reading my work for years. He now knows my secret macho pen names and has forgiven me for the deception. He's also the author of *Out Of The Night, Traces of Grace,* and *Living in Community.*

And more people to thank:

Canon George Dopp, of the Diocese of San Diego. When I first began thinking about writing this book, I knew I had to update my familiarity with the church I grew up in. I expected to be bored. Instead, he gave me the gift of a renewed faith in the church I'd left.

Chaplain Babs Meairs at the VA in San Diego and Fr. Ed Busch, of St. Columba's in San Diego, both Episcopal priests. St. Columba's is a small, vibrant group of people who know what it means to live in community.

Father Joe Ballard, of St. James in Knoxville, Tennessee, and his wife Bobbye, for making St. James the radically-special place it is and for showing us all how to grow from compassion to justice. Now if Fr. Joe will just let me get a collection of his sermons together....

The folks on the AOL Episcopalians message board and the Continuing Anglicans message board.

My EFM group, especially Marnie, who's been the mentor during my entire four years, and her co-mentors Mary R. and Ann. My fellow graduates, Betsy, Lucy and Joy, all of the Librarian/Wordsmith year. The rest of our Thursday morning group who've graduated or are still in: Ann, Jane, Carol, Susan P. and Susan S., Ellen, Flossie, Woodson, Trish, Elaine, Bobbye, Lynn, Virginia, Tomas, Diane, Mary S.

George Donahue and Michael Seidman, excellent editors. You know what for.

My very first editor, John Talbot, and his successors, Gary Goldstein and Tom Colgan. John read countless drafts of my first novel, *Rites of War*, and, along with Gary and Tom, put it on the *USA Today* bestseller list. Thanks, guys!

Of course, they wouldn't even have known about me without the work of star agents Jake Elwell and George Wieser and Olga Wieser.

My husband, Ron Morton, and my stepkids, Heather and Daniel. My brothers, Jack and Ed, and their wives, Pam and Sandra, and a special thanks to Pam for copy edits!

On the writing side of things—how does any writer survive without friends like Doug Clegg and Jana Costa and Ken Schaefer and Mark Clements?

Despite all of the wisdom and advice from the above folks, I've taken a few liberties here and there. Any errors, intentional or otherwise, are mine alone. All the characters are fictional, although they shouldn't be.

All my older titles will soon be back in print at radixpress.com and help support my work with At Risk Intervention, an organization that helps keep kids out of trouble through martial arts. You can also check out my dog stories at dogbooks.org.

Thanks for reading *The Last Casualty*.

One

No priest should know what I know: that the difference between murdering and killing is irrelevant. Oh, sure, theologians can go on forever about what the Sixth Commandment really forbids, but the distinction between the two breaks down in the translation from seminary to reality. It's one thing to parse Old Testament Hebrew looking for a loophole, another entirely to deal with the stain that taking a life leaves on your own soul.

Like most sins, this particular one can be a sin of commission or omission—something you do or you don't do. In theological terms, whether I shoot you myself or abandon you to die, I'm equally guilty, or at least that's been my experience. But those are human terms, as meaningless as the concepts of mortal, venial, and unforgivable. Sin, both in the committing and in the forgiving, is a calculus beyond most mortal men

I've tried to forget what I did on Muralis Island. That didn't stop the nightmares. Neither did confession, therapy or simply pretending it never happened.

Nothing works. The men I left behind four years ago are with me always, as alive as I am, if I'm any benchmark by which to distinguish between the quick and the dead.

Penance brings no relief, but I try. I stand *in familia loci* with dying men like Ben Alvarez, hoping that by some grace or magic my dutiful attendance at their sides will atone for deserting Sean Maltierre and Jeremy Forsythe.

Alvarez is swathed in morphine and wool blankets, unresponsive, his breathing ragged. He's a big-boned man, muscle running to fat, webs of broken veins on his nose and cheeks. He has blond hair and gray eyes. According to his chart, he is a retired Navy commander, age 58, widowed.

Over the last hour, the rhythm of Alvarez's breathing has deteriorated. It's now agonal, uneven and shuddering. It's taking him longer to die than it did Maltierre or Forsythe, but he's warm and in no pain.

Does he know how lucky he is?

An unworthy thought. A better priest would have more compassion for the dying.

No one was with Maltierre when he died alone and cold, splayed on rocks awash at high tide, dirt ground into his wounds. No sterilized sheets. No morphine.

The waves sucked Maltierre's body off the rocks and the surface currents took possession of what was left of him. He might have floated for a while, but after the gasses associated with decomposition leaked out of his body, he would have sunk.

Once he drifted down out of the surface currents, the mid-ocean currents would have carried him through the rich fishing waters surrounding Muralis Island. Later, much later, if anything remained, the cold dark Arctic current moving along the ocean floor would have swept him south. Absent a chance encounter with an upwelling somewhere, that's where he was now, reduced to particulate matter by the pressure, endlessly circumnavigating the globe with the bottom currents.

Oddly enough, I find some comfort in that thought. There is a cruel constancy to those bottom currents, unaffected by surface waters or weather as they are. They endure the passing of times and seasons with nary a fluctuation.

Alvarez groans. It's a reproach, a reminder of what I'm supposed to be doing instead of reliving the past.

I try to pray but have no sense that the words ever leave my own mind. Doctor Sarini saves me from further frustration when she strides into the room.

Sarah Sarini: lean, hard curves and angles inside faded green scrubs, a tall woman whose head comes up to my chin. She has a faintly exotic look to her, a marked contrast to my own nondescript blue eyes and brown hair. Her hair is darker than my buzz cut but almost as short, with a hard gloss to it. She would never burn in the sun the way I do. Her olive skin is tanned, the whites of her eyes stark with dark green eyes Botticelli could have painted—profound, enigmatic eyes that see everything and give away nothing, shuttered and noncommittal. I hope I'm as good at masking my own thoughts, because she would not speak to me if she knew how I thought of her.

I know a lot about Sarini and in the peculiar way of military friendships, we're close. We're on a last name basis, dropping ranks and professional titles when we talk, which is the military equivalent of civilians using first names. That's as close as it gets in the military—we would not use first names at work.

I've got a fairly accurate summary of her career and life to date, based on hospital gossip and what she lets drop at work. She went to undergraduate and medical school at Vanderbilt. This is her first duty station and she's been here two years. From here, she'd like to go to sea, perhaps on an aircraft carrier, although she worries about whether to rent her house out or not. She likes living near the beach and runs every morning when she's not on call. She paid $289,000 for a small house in Pacific Beach. Okay, so in addition to listening to the gossip, I did a little research.

The one thing I *don't* know is whether or not she likes me. I'm not alone in that, at least. There is a core of her that is untouchable.

Sarini's hands move over Alvarez, probing, inquisitive. She studies the color of his skin, takes in his smell, strokes the skin around his IV. Only after she's done that does she glance up at the monitors and reach for his chart. "No change," she says.

"No."

"Well, then." She touches his forehead with her fingertips as though trying to read his mind.

Two hours ago, the paramedics brought Alvarez to the emergency room. No blood, no wounds, no visible reason for him to be unconscious and dying. He is still an enigma. Sarini cannot help being fascinated by him, but at least she has the decency to try to hide it.

No, that's too harsh. It's not that she doesn't care that he's dying. I have watched her cycle from frustration to anticipation over the last two hours, flipping through the lab results, her forehead creased and upper teeth scraping her lower lip as she tries to unravel the puzzle. Alvarez is not conscious and his body is refusing to yield up his secrets. She is beginning to grow angry with him for not cooperating.

Sarini and I have more in common than either of us is willing to admit. We are both better at dealing with the dying than the living. We each have a specialized language to reduce the ineffable to the concrete, to define problems that can be dealt with, treated, corrected. I administer sacraments while she orders transfusions. I hear confessions while she reviews lab results. Science and faith: both approximations at best, deceptions at worst, but the best that either of us can do.

The double doors to the ambulance entrance open, saved from slamming against the walls by hydraulics. Sarini pats Alvarez on the hand before slipping out to see the new arrival.

I don't follow her. The organizational chart says the duty chaplain is "an integral, important member of the multi-modality treatment team", but the patients know better. They want sutures, x-rays and pain meds. I'm at the other end of the triage scale and they don't want to see me until they feel the pull of the bottom currents.

Alvarez is stripped down and in a hospital gown. He's wearing an intricately worked crucifix on a heavy gold chain.

I take his hand. It's cool, the pulse slow and unsteady under my fingers. "I'm Father David Dalt." Perhaps he hears me, perhaps he doesn't. It doesn't matter. "You're at the Balboa emergency room, and they're taking good care of you."

Did his pulse beat a bit quicker? I glance up at the monitor. Yes. This time, wherever he is, he hears me.

"I noticed your cross. I'm going to anoint you and say a prayer for healing." I trace a cross on his forehead with my thumb and say a prayer, hoping that the words will comfort rather than frighten. I hold Alvarez's hand a moment longer, promise him I'll be back soon, then go to check the tote board that tracks the wounded, dead and dying in the Balboa Naval Hospital emergency room.

The hospital is just east of downtown, wedged in between the city itself and two hundred acres of Balboa Park. It's one of the newest military hospitals, built shortly before base closures and consolidation drained funds out of building allowances. Its emergency room expands into the bowels of the hospital from a small reception area, curving around like a nautilus as it winds its way into the center of the hospital.

On the outer edges of the ER are the numbered rooms, the ones used to treat the less critical cases. Behind that, deeper into the hospital, is Sarini's domain, the critical ER area. Here, the rooms are assigned letters instead of numbers. There are more doctors, more nurses, faster access to the MRI just across the hallway. More people die in the lettered rooms.

Sarini has finished her initial assessment of the new patient. "Put him in B." She leads the way into a treatment room on the other side of the central nursing station.

The man stretched out on the gurney is older than most of the people that make it back this far, probably

11

retired for at least ten years judging from the look of his hands knotting the sheets.

Sarini and her acolytes crowd into room B. I stand just outside the door, out of the way of the people coming and going but able to see what's going on and immediately available if he starts to go south on them. The woman who followed the gurney in is standing next to me, her hands flat on the window, fingernails clicking on the glass, staring in. She's much younger than the patient, but the massive diamond on her left hand and the look on her face mark her as his wife. Soon enough, someone will gently herd her out into the waiting room, but for now she's got a ringside seat.

"Doctor Sarini is very good," I say. She turns to look at me and her gaze tumbles to the cross on my collar. "I'm David Dalt. What's your name?"

"Heidi Caermon." She's not sure she wants to talk to a clergyman right now. To do so means things are far more serious than she wants to believe.

Sarini's hands are on Caermon's exposed stomach, palpating, probing, seeing his guts through her fingertips. She watches his face, reading the pain. On the other side of the table, a nurse draws blood, filling up an array of vacuum tubes with different colored plugs, each one color-coded according to its purpose. Caermon is conscious enough to moan at some of the intrusions and push feebly at the hands, but not coherent enough to understand everything that Sarini is saying to him.

Finally, with a grunt of satisfaction, Sarini removes her hands. She draws the gown over his belly and smoothes the fabric flat, a peculiar gentleness to her movements. She glances over at the window, sees me standing with the wife. Her face grows still. She's deciding how much to say, whether to wait until the lab work comes back before she tells the wife what her fingers and experience have already told her.

She steps back from the table. I've worked with her often enough to know that her mind is already running through the list of patients in the ER, prioritizing, remembering what she wants to do next. Alvarez is on her mind, as is the nineteen-year old Marine Corps corporal in Room A who is still-living-for-now proof of the folly of trying to take on a tractor-trailer with a spiffed up ten-year-old Firebird. I have been to see him, wedging in between two nurses long enough to hold his hand and hear a quick general confession before being edged away by Sarini. Caermon will have her attention again when he needs it, but there are others just as critically ill that she is responsible for.

She's halfway to the door when I step in to the room to meet her. She turns her back on the window to prevent Caermon's wife from reading her lips.

"The liver, probably," she says, barely pausing. "I won't know for sure until the labs come back."

"Serious?"

"He's dying. I won't tell his wife yet." There's a trace of impatience on her face now. "They never believe you unless you can show them labs."

I believe her, even though her specialty is trauma rather than internal medicine. Her patients decide whether to live or die in minutes, hours, days, not the lingering long-term prognoses of medical cases. Although Caermon will be a medical case rather than a trauma one, her experience tells her what the prognosis will be.

"May I talk to him?" I ask.

"If you want. He'll be admitted tonight." This is her way of telling me that he's not going to die here, not on her watch.

"How long does he have?"

She shrugs. "Hard to say." What happens to Caermon after he leaves her domain is someone else's problem. She turns away, her attention already on those she can do something for, the traumas, the broken bones, the asthmatics and heart attacks. She pauses outside the room to speak to Caermon's wife then an orderly gently shuffles Heidi off to the waiting room.

I turn back to the table. Caermon is more responsive now than when he was brought in. Demerol is damming up the pain. His eyes are half shut and his face is relaxed. The sheets are pulled back up over him, curled around the one arm extended with the IV running into it.

"Mister Caermon? Can you hear me?" I lay one hand on his arm. His pulse beats thready and fast under my fingertips.

He turns his head slightly, his eyes focusing on me. "Captain."

For a moment, I think he's mistaken my Navy lieutenant bars for an Army captain's insignia but then I realize he's talking about himself. "Captain Caermon," I amend. "Do you know where you are?"

"Hospital." His eyes shut for a moment. When he opens them, there's a puzzled expression on his face as though wondering where the pain has gone.

"Yes, that's right. They've given you something to make you more comfortable. Your wife's here. She'll be in shortly."

"Who are you?" His eyes finally take in the small gold cross pinned to my left collar.

"Father Dalt. David Dalt."

"David Dalt."

"Yes, that's right."

Caermon's eyes close and his expression isn't nearly as relaxed as it was before. He's trying to work something out, fighting against the medication. For a moment I think he's drifted off to sleep and I start to leave. Then his eyes open, focused, alert, predatory.

"Scorpion."

The word stops me. I turn back to him. "What did you say?"

He smiles slightly. He knows I heard him.

"What did you call me?"

He should not know that name. Even my father doesn't know it. At least, I don't think he does. If he'd cared enough to ask, I imagine he could have found out, but I have a hard time imagining his caring enough.

"Go away, Dalt. Tell your father I'm not talking."

Many senior officers know my father. He's a three-star admiral, Chief of Naval Intelligence. From what I've heard, he's quite good at what he does. He never talks about it.

Then again, why would I expect him of all people to talk to me? He hasn't, not in decades, not beyond what the Navy would term logistical support: tuition, room and board, the obligatory gifts and cards on my birthday and at Christmas.

Caermon's eyes are closed but the pulse beats at his throat. The monitors indicate his blood pressure is slightly elevated, his breathing rapid and shallow.

Sarini comes back in, her gazed fixed on the monitor, frowning. "What did you say to him?"

"Nothing." Wrong question. It's what he's said to me that matters. "I'll leave."

"Good idea." Sarini's team flocks around her. Her hands flit over him, checking for any change in his condition.

Caermon's hand shoots out to grab her lapel. He tugs at her, pulling her head close to his. There's a frantic, pressured note in his whisper but I can't make out the words.

Sarini nods, her professional nod, the one that acknowledges that a patient is telling her something without admitting that it's got any validity. Caermon is so intent on what he's saying that he doesn't notice she's detaching his hand from her coat and pressing it down by his side.

An orderly starts forward with restraints but she shakes her head. She looks back at me, then nods and speaks soothingly to Caermon. A few moments later, the painkillers kick in and his eyes drift shut.

A nurse hands Sarini a sheaf of printouts. Sarini flips through them, pauses at one page and nods. Whatever she'd expected to see is there, and judging from her expression, it's not going to be good news for the Caermon family.

"Family. Come with me," she says briskly. She avoids my eyes.

"What did he say to you?" I ask. She ignores the question.

I follow her out into the hallway and down to the waiting area. Caermon's wife looks up, anxious. She thinks she's ready to hear the worst, but she's not. They never are.

Sarini and I are old hands at this, the coordinated way of delivering unbearable news. Sarini sits down next to her, her expression softer and grave. I take the seat across from the wife. I wish I could remember her name. "I'm afraid it's bad news," Sarini begins. "We just got the lab results back and I think there's something going on with his liver. They're taking him up for an MRI right now. We'll know more after that."

"His liver? Like what?"

"I suspect we're going to find either a tumor or another mass of some sort," Sarini says, her voice gentle but unable to mask the devastating effect of the news. "His condition is very serious."

"No." The wife is staring at Sarini. "He's been sick a couple of days, but—no, it can't be."

"We'll know more when the lab results come back." Sarini waits. I've seen her do this before, but I always find it profoundly moving. She stops the entire world to concentrate on one person, waiting for the news to sink in. Outside this room, there are patients that need her, orders to be given, lab results to be reviewed, but she has a peculiar reverence for those moments when she must tell someone that a life will be ending shortly. She would have made an excellent priest.

The wife turns to me now, her face pale, searching for a better future than the one Sarini offers her. The shift in her attention releases Sarini, who stands. Ten minutes from now, Sarini will not remember Heidi Caermon.

"I need to get back to your husband," Sarini says.

Not entirely true. Alvarez and the Firebird kid are taking up most of her attention right now, but Caermon's

16

wife is oblivious to the other families in the waiting room. She will find it easier to take Sarini's desertion if she believes it's for her husband.

Heidi Caermon's gaze fixes on me, my cue to take one of her hands in my own. "I'm so sorry," I say. "Is there anything I can do for you right now?"

She shakes her head, numbness setting in now. Whether she knows it or not, her mind has already processed the information and is reordering her life. Her emotions will take far longer to adjust, but the intellect is already at work.

"Do you belong to a church?" I ask.

"Anthony was raised as a Catholic," she says, her voice dull. "But he's not—I mean—."

Christenings, weddings and funerals, maybe Easter and Christmas, but that's it. "I understand. Is there someone I could call for you?" I ask.

"No. Can I—does he know yet?" She wants to see him, but she doesn't want to be the one to break the news to him.

"I'm sure Doctor Sarini is talking to him now. He's sedated, you understand. The pain."

She nods. "I want to see him."

I stand. "I'll take you back there." She stands and I ask, "I understand your husband is a captain in the Navy?"

"Was. He retired seven years ago." I'm off by three years in my estimate.

"What does he do now?"

She stopped walking and looked hard at me. "Why?"

We're standing outside his room now. Caermon sees us and screams, "Get away from her!" He swings his feet off the bed, moving unbelievably fast for someone so sedated. He's out of the room, his sheets on the ground behind him, and on me before Sarini can intercept him. His hands lock around my throat, unexpected strength in his fingers.

"Stop it." Sarini is on him, grabbing him around the chest and pulling him away, but his fingers are frozen solid on me. Dimly, I'm aware of his wife screaming besides me, of orderlies and nurses running, the clatter of metal as something is dropped, but I see nothing beyond Caermon's face.

Three years of seminary drop away as though they never were. I am left with only reflexes.

Caermon's weight drives me back and he follows, screaming incoherently. I turn so that I slam into the wall to break my fall and regain my balance. I step toward him, bring my left arm down hard across his elbows and twist out of the chokehold, letting my weight do the work. It's the simplest of hold breaks, one that they teach in every self-defense class. The trick is in practicing it enough so that it's automatic.

I haven't tried this in four years, but it still works. Caermon hits the wall chin first. I step in behind him, jerk him back, my right arm moving of its own accord around his neck into the beginning of a sleeper hold.

The orderlies swarm over us. I let them pull me off Caermon and hustle him away. His wife follows after him, but they shut the door on her and draw the curtain over the window. The last glimpse I have of Caermon is an orderly fastening a restraint around his wrist. His wife hammers on the door, crying, demanding to be let in.

Caermon's screams stutter, then stop. Sarini's work. Then Sarini comes out, all cool professional now, and puts her arm around the wife's shoulders, drawing her away from the room, murmuring quietly.

"I'll be in the duty room," I say finally. I stand there, waiting for some sign that I'm still part of the team, that this is Caermon's aberration, not mine.

No one speaks to me. No one even looks at me.

Two

The duty room for the chaplain is located in our office spaces in the west wing of the hospital. It's got a telephone and I have a beeper. If the ER needs me, it can find me.

The Chaplain Department shares a passageway with Social Services and Billing and we're intermingled with psychologists and social workers, with a smattering of nutritional, holistic and cultural programs fighting for space as well. The psychiatrists successfully fought being included, insisting that they be housed with their medical brethren to avoid the taint of our ilk. Their attitude was particularly offensive to the psychologists, since they regard their PhD as just as important as an MD degree. It's a battle the social workers gave up a long time ago.

The chaplain's office is the victim of committee remodeling. Nubby fabric-covered space dividers in mauve and teal and ergonomically-correct accoutrements replaced the homey place we used to have. It is very efficient. I hate it.

My office is down the passageway to the right of the reception area, then off a smaller passageway to the left. I'm not senior enough to warrant a window. I spent too many years out in the open to be comfortable without one.

But my life is supposed to be interior now rather than exterior, isn't it? It shouldn't matter to me whether or not I have a window. In fact, I should be grateful that I don't have a view that might distract me.

I should be. I try to be. But I'm still conscious that I'm trapped inside by inches of concrete.

Just as I turn down my passageway, the director of chaplains, Captain Farley Haynes, calls me. "David. Got a minute?" I've never asked Haynes how he always knows who's walking down the passageway. I suspect he's simply got a keen ear and has memorized our footsteps, but I'm not certain. He may simply *know*, just the way I used to know where every one of my men were.

"Yes, sir." I change course. His door is open and the light streams in through his floor to ceiling windows.

There are six chaplains assigned to Balboa Naval Hospital. We cover the spectrum of faiths, starting with our boss, Navy Captain Farley Haynes, a Southern Baptist, and continuing through Bert McCallister, Roman Catholic, Carla Testern, Methodist, Jack Johnson, Islam, and Bernie Green, a rabbi. I'm an Episcopal priest, walking the *media via*, the middle way between the Roman Catholic and the Protestant, both but neither.

Haynes has his computer cracked open on his desk and a grounded screwdriver in his hand. His face is all angles, the skin red and rough, dark salt and pepper hair clipped close to his head, far shorter than regulations required. Clear light blue eyes look perpetually surprised. A large nose dominates his face. Haynes is from Alabama, and his voice kept the soft vowels and sliding consonants.

Most people underestimated him. I made the same mistake once.

"Want some help?" I ask, settling into the visitor's chair.

He grunts. "No. I'd like to get this working this week." My technical incompetence and concurrent unwillingness to admit it were established early on in our relationship.

Silence for a moment, then, "I heard you had an interesting time this morning. You okay?"

Of course Haynes has heard. Balboa may be the largest naval hospital on the West Coast but it's a small community. The normal avenues of gossip and information flow can't be outlined on any organizational chart.

"I'm fine."

Haynes peers at me from over the computer casing. He's been in Navy for twenty-two years, served at remote duty stations as the only chaplain and at commands with scores of them. He's dealt with thousands of ministers, pastors, rabbis and religious leaders from every faith. He's a difficult man to lie to.

"Really?" Haynes' voice doesn't reflect the disbelief in his eyes. He puts down the screwdriver and leans back in his chair, his fingers interlaced behind his head. It's his open, nonjudgmental expression, an invitation to talk. "They said the fellow seemed to know you."

I shook my head. "I doubt it. Probably another priest some time, somewhere. Seeing the collar, he flashed back to it."

"Maybe. He didn't look familiar?"

"No, sir." *He didn't. But he knew my name.* I shrug, uneasy with the direction the conversation is taking. "Really. I'm okay. The orderlies were right there."

"The way I heard it, there wasn't much left for them to do."

I drain the last of my coffee, suddenly eager to be out of his office. Haynes knows my background, knows who I was before I was a priest.

Haynes sees the gesture and gives up. "Well, then. Busy day for us. Bill's out sick. Carla's going to take the general Protestant afternoon service and the cathedral's going to send someone over for the evening mass. Can you cover the Roman Catholic SI patients?"

The seriously ills, or SI patients, aren't expected to survive more than another day. They have to be visited.

"Yes, of course. What's wrong with McCallister?" I ask.

"Doc says some sort of crud, contagious as heck." Haynes slides a printout over to me.

I glance down the list without picking it up. Twelve more names.

"Wear your collar," Haynes says. A concession, but one with an ulterior motive. Haynes knows I prefer wearing black and clerical collar to my uniform, but he's never been entirely comfortable with it on an Episcopal priest. Roman Catholic priests, sure. But not Episcopal ones.

But Bert McCallister is a Roman Catholic priest, and Haynes figures the collar will make his constituency comfortable. Not fraud. Not exactly.

I pick up the list, hoping maybe one of the patients isn't RC and I can pawn him off on someone else. The last name on the list leaps out at me.

Caermon. Anthony Caermon.

Not Caermon.

Haynes, that wily old fox, is watching me closely. Of course he knows Caermon's name. Of course he knows Caermon is on this list. And of course he knows I know he knows. He's waited until now to give it to me in case I didn't want to talk earlier.

"It'll be fine," I say, answering the question he hasn't asked as I fold the list in half. I don't want to see Caermon's name, not right at this second. Let me get past Haynes first and then I'll think about it.

"If you're sure." Haynes pauses again, one of those infinitely patient looks on his face. Haynes wants me to talk more about whether I ought to see Caermon again. He suspects there's more that I want to know about Caermon and he's wondering whether I'll admit that another chaplain might be better for Caermon. It's a test, in a way. Am I able to put aside my own interests and focus on what's important to Caermon?

Perversely, Haynes' concern has the opposite effect that it should. I know Haynes' sort. Steel runs under that gentle expression. If I beg off on seeing Caermon, Haynes will say that he takes it as a sign of maturity—he'll even phrase it that way in my fitness reports—but he'll see it as a weakness. If I don't see Caermon, Haynes will go himself, and I'm not going to admit I need that much help.

"Yes, sir, I'm sure. He was pretty sedated earlier and that probably caused his delusion. They'll have him stabilized now. We can straighten things out, maybe relieve any concerns he's got about what he thought he saw. I think seeing me again will defuse any anxiety he might have about what happened in the ER."

It's not that I don't like Captain Haynes or that I don't trust him. I do, and I have a lot of respect for what he's accomplished and for how he runs the Chaplain Service. But there's a fundamental difference in our approach to God that has always led us to some—well, disagreements would be too strong a word, because it's not that. It's more of a mismatch of theologies that leads him to worry about my spiritual standing and me to chaff under what seems to be to be a suffocating preoccupation with God.

To Haynes, in his Baptist tradition, God is an immediate and personal companion. Challenges are nothing if you've got the Trinity strapped to your belt. He puts on the armor of God, the breastplate of righteousness, and he's dressed. If I wanted to take it to logical extremes, I'd say Haynes would pray about which pair of underwear to put on in the morning. I see him running a three-legged race with Jesus strapped to his leg.

Coming from the Anglican tradition, the *via media* or middle way, I have always been comfortable with a broader view of God, and with my own inability to understand Him. In essence, He remains unknowable, distant, a being beyond our ability to grasp. This is not to say that he's not present in daily life. He just expects us to be able to pick out our own underwear without His help.

Haynes resumes screwing the case of his computer back on. "You spend too much time down there, you know. If they need you, they'll call you."

Another bone of contention, but I let this one slide. Haynes suspects that I'm an adrenaline junkie, a holdover from my life prior to ordination. He's right, but not in the way that he thinks he is.

"See him first then. Get it over with," Haynes suggests. This is his way with any problem, to tackle the hardest part first. He's got a cavalry mentality rather than that of a commando. I tend to plan more, consider my options, and go for the more stealthy approach.

Yet there's a lot to be said for his way of doing things. Haynes is gifted with an astounding amount of discernment and a deeper understanding of people than I have. I tend to translate things onto a physical level, figure out my responses then translate back into spiritual action.

Haynes' computer beeps twice then settles into a long, piercing wail. He lays his hands on the monitor as though to heal it. I have no doubt he's praying for it. "Call me if you run out of time."

Onward Christian sailors. I'm dismissed.

As I leave, I can hear him unscrewing the housing again.

Three

We speak a different language, the dying and I. The surface waters of life no longer matter. In short phrases and elliptical comments, we plow through the darker, deeper currents running nearest to their souls, coming closer and closer to the bedrock. After medicine and science have done all they can, the questions that remain are the ones I know how to answer—when the dying are ready to ask them.

The families, though, are another matter. They're still on the surface, splashing in water warmed by the sun, rarely able to hold their breath long enough to get any deeper and unwilling to get their faces wet. They want what I cannot give—their lives restored, husbands, wives and children miraculously healed, damaged bodies put right. Sometimes I try to take them below the surface, but I'm inevitably left feeling frustrated. I lack Hayne's skill with the living.

I take my Bible, a small vial of holy oil, and the sacraments I reserved from yesterday's Eucharist, my tools of the trade. Will getting Caermon over with first free me up or suck me dry? I can't decide, so I follow Haynes' advice.

Caermon is in the west wing, second floor. I find Caermon's door, knock once then go in.

The smell hits me just as I step over the threshold. Hospital disinfectants can't eliminate the stench of decay as a body's systems shut down.

Caermon is propped up in bed, awake. Jaundiced skin hangs slack off his bones and the whites of his eyes are yellowed. In his prime, he had been a strong, forceful man. He's tall, large boned, but with delicate features at odds with the rest of his face. His eyes are dark, muddy brown, an odd tint of green just around the pupil. His pupils are pinpoint now, probably from the pain medication, emphasizing the green halos. He is, on balance, an evil-looking man, but one that you can imagine having a compelling charisma. He still has the command presence of a senior officer, even in his debilitated state.

"Good morning," I say, aware that I've been silent too long for politeness.

Caermon struggles to sit up straighter in the bed. "You again."

"Yes. I'm Father Dalt."

"I remember." Silence, then, "At least you look like a priest now."

"I had the duty last night, so I was wearing khakis."

He thinks I'm a Roman Catholic priest, just as Haynes intended. I should clear up the misunderstanding immediately.

But McCallister isn't available anyway. Why not let the collar work its magic? I'm part of the apostolic succession, fully versed in ministering to Roman Catholic patients. Besides, being available to him now will make up for the distress I caused him in the ER.

It has nothing to do with finding out what he knows about Scorpion. Nothing at all.

"Ensign Dalt." He's amused. I imagine him pulling the wings off flies.

"Lieutenant Dalt now." There's a chance that he doesn't remember what he said in the ER, but I think he might. And why does he think of me as an Ensign anyway?

If he doesn't bring it up, will I? Should I? I'm not sure yet.

But Caermon is focused on his own concerns. "I was a captain when I was on active duty. A *Navy* captain. Eight hundred men under my command. A captain, and now I can't even get one doctor to do what I tell her."

26

Caermon is finding it easier to focus on his frustration than on the fact that he's dying. "That bitch Sarini won't let me go outside."

"I'm sure there are medical reasons for it."

Caermon doesn't answer for a moment. Then he sighs. "Look, I've got some things on my mind and there's no privacy here. Please. See if you can take me outside for a while."

Please? From Caermon? Have I been wrong about him? Too focused on myself instead of on the needs of the patients? Maybe Haynes was right.

"I'll see what I can do," I say. "You'll need a wheelchair."

"Okay. But hurry."

It's early enough that the night shift is still on duty. Sarini has usurped the charge nurse's computer and is working her way through a stack of patient charts on the desk. Morning rounds, checking on the patients she admitted last night, making sure that they're being followed by the right specialties and that nothing has gotten lost in the transfer. Not all of the ER docs do this, but Sarini always does. I've asked her before why she does this when the others don't and never gotten a satisfactory answer.

"Good morning," I say.

Sarini jumps slightly. "You're always doing that. Make some noise when you walk, okay?"

"Sorry."

"What do you need?"

"I just saw Caermon. He wants me to take him outside."

Sarini shakes her head. "No. His chart says he's restricted to his room."

"Why?"

"It doesn't say." Sarini's forehead wrinkles for a moment. She's got one line that bisects her forehead vertically when she's puzzling something out. "We usually like them to move around as long as they're able to. And the order is signed by the hospital administrator, not an oncologist."

"Any chance I could take him down to the rose garden for a little while? We need to talk. Privately."

"For the sake of his soul? Forget it—he doesn't have one."

The vehemence in her voice surprises me. Sarini's used to difficult and terminal patients. Has she been here too long? Getting burned out? Or has Caermon managed to find a way to offend her? I'll try to find out later, but not now.

"Everyone has a soul. Even Caermon," I say, and I'm mildly gratified to find that I mean it. Perhaps there's hope for me yet.

She just shakes her head.

So he has managed to find a way to stand out of the pack. I'm not particularly surprised. All the more reason to talk to him privately. "I can call the director's office and get permission to take him out, if you like."

"Oh, yeah. I've been on call for thirty-six hours now. Answering the director's questions is just what I want to do." The line bisects her forehead again. "I'll log it as physical therapy. Have him back in half an hour so I don't have to answer any questions."

She goes with me back to Caermon's room and helps me lift Caermon into the wheelchair. Caermon's pajamas hang loose over his bones. He's far more wasted than he looks.

"Thirty minutes," Sarini reminds me. She watches us until we go around the corner to the elevators.

"You fucking her?" Caermon asks. "Somebody ought to. It'd do her a world of good."

He's waited until she's out of earshot, so I let it pass. If he's shared this observation with Sarini, that could account for her reaction to him.

"She's just concerned about you."

Caermon breaks into a deep, hacking cough. "Not a chance. She likes me even less than you do."

"You seem to think that of a lot of people."

That silences him for the ride down to the main lobby. The other people on the elevator wait until we get off. I wheel Caermon down a side passageway and then out onto the traffic circle and across to the rose garden.

The garden consists of winding concrete paths connecting sitting areas, each screened from the others by raised flowerbeds and bushes. One area at the end of the walk is reserved for smokers, and a few patients crowd around the ashtrays and garbage cans. Acrid cigarette smoke mixes with the scent of roses.

I nod to the men I recognize then veer off with Caermon to an unoccupied area. The other patients look relieved. My presence stifles the normal conversation of sailors.

Eucalyptus trees shade a green-slatted bench. I park Caermon in the shade then sit on the bench next to him. I wait.

His jaundice is even more noticeable in the sunlight. He slumps in his wheelchair and seems to drift off for a moment. I wonder whether it's been a mistake to bring him out here. Even in a wheelchair, the trip seems to have tired him more than he'd expected. I'm about to suggest we go back inside when Caermon speaks.

"Come closer, Dalt. So I don't have to raise my voice."

I slide over next to him until my ear is only inches from his mouth. His breath is sour and stale, distasteful against the skin just above my collar. I wonder if it will stain my collar. "Go ahead, Mister Caermon. Captain Caermon. No one can hear us."

"Bless me, Father, for I have sinned. It's been—oh, about thirty years—since my last confession."

"A long time."

"I had my reasons."

"Everyone does."

Silence for a moment. "That's not what you're supposed to say."

"I'm an Episcopal priest. I can get a Roman Catholic priest for you if you prefer."

Confession to a priest is not mandatory in our tradition. We find no necessity for an intermediary between God and a sinner. Still, we retain the ritual for use when a penitent requires assurance from a priest of the forgiveness that is God's alone to grant. This is a difference from Roman Catholic practice, where a priest is required to access the divine.

I hope he wants one of his own. I can call the cathedral, get someone to come down and hear his confession, be shut of him to continue on with my rounds.

"You'll do." Something seems to amuse him, a private joke. "Arcadia. Do you know anything about it?"

"It was a small village in rural Greece. Today it's shorthand for a simple pastoral life style."

"Yeah. That's why I picked the name. But Arcadia today is something quite different. It's a special program, Dalt, one that takes care of things nobody else wants to touch."

"What sorts of things?"

"Things that need doing." Caermon waves my question away impatiently. "The details don't matter now."

"What *does* matter?" The bottom currents—he feels them moving underneath him, trying to drag him down, and he's clutching for the life raft he was raised on.

Caermon doesn't answer immediately. There is often this moment before the confession itself starts, one during which the penitent decides just how much to say. Some people feel that as long as the sins aren't spoken out loud, they are somehow less real. For others, the sheer inertia of keeping sins secret for so long and the complicated web of truths and lies that they've told themselves make it difficult to know where to start. Since Caermon is Roman Catholic, he'll feel the pressure to talk more than an Anglican would.

"I was in a bind, Dalt. I want you to understand that. A new wife, trying to keep up with my neighbors, alimony and child support sucking up everything—hell, I was forty-three and money was tighter than when I was in

30

college. If there'd been any other way, I wouldn't have done it."

A cold knot forms in my stomach. Of all the sins that men and women confess, only a few start with this particular rationalization.

"Once, maybe twice a year, an opportunity would come up. Smaller operations. The money was good—I made more for a few bits of information than I made in an entire year, Dalt. And part of the deal was that nobody got hurt. I made them promise that." He wants me to believe that was important to him.

No more. No, dear God, do not make me hear this.

"Sometimes I even cancelled the operation, told them that it'd come from higher authority. But then that got too risky. These people—I thought I could control them, Dalt. But I was wrong." With the essence of his treachery now out in the open, Caermon is able to look at me. "After a while, I had no choice. I got them what they asked for."

I feel physically ill. Caermon's a traitor. Whatever dirty ops Arcadia handled were even dirtier because he sold out the people he sent into the field.

"So that's it. That's my confession." Evidently nothing else he's done in the previous thirty years rises to significant importance.

I lean back against the wooden slats of the bench. The sun is breaking through the morning low clouds and fog. In a few hours, it will be a warm, sunny San Diego day.

Hate the sin, love the sinner. But even now?

"A confession requires repentance." If Caermon's Catholic enough to want to confess, then he's Catholic enough to know what I'm getting at.

"Okay. I repent."

"True repentance requires turning from evil."

"I told you what I did. I confessed. Now do your part."

"Confession isn't a plea bargain, Mister Caermon. No promises other that the grace of God." Finally, I have him. Fear replaces his smirking grin. He wants very much to believe that he will not have to pay the price for what he's done, and I'm the one who has the power to grant that wish.

"Listen to me, Father." No hesitation using the title, a touch of desperation. "What happened to you on Muralis Island. They knew you were coming. They were waiting for you."

I should kill him now.

Six men swam ashore that night off the coast of Russia. Everything went wrong. Four lived, two died. We huddled in the black rocks cold with sea spray, waiting for the last pickup time, hoping that at least one thing would go right but knowing we'd probably die that night. We—I—left two men behind.

There are so many ways to kill a man. The human body is infinitely vulnerable to the right amount of force applied to exactly the right point. It can be done quickly, quietly.

I'm not that man anymore.

Am I?

Another long silence. "*Ego te absolvo*, that's what you're supposed to say next."

"No." I know the old Latin ritual well but I can't bring myself to say the words.

"You *have* to."

"No, I don't."

Caermon's face twists. "I know an awful lot about you, Dalt. And about your father. Things you might not want that fancy bitch doctor you've got the hots for to know."

His threats don't even touch me. Not where I am now.

That night, waiting for the submarine, I learned what it was to be alone. I hadn't thought it was possible to be so cold and still be alive. My skin was the same temperature as the rocks and the body I held. The men wedged into the rocks with me had been no warmer. I am still on the rocks, cold, almost dead. "Two of my men died because of you."

Caermon is desperate for what I'm withholding from him. "Okay, you want repentance? How about this? Muralis Island. Napier is going back."

"When?"

"Next week. They're staging out of Norway right now. I was supposed to—never mind." Caermon seems to finally understand how dangerous I am right now. "It's compromised, Dalt. All of it."

There are no words to express what I feel at that moment. There shouldn't be. Words aren't a survival skill and I'm back on Muralis Island, dying on the rocks.

"Hey! Chaplain!" Three orderlies accompanied by a security guard are heading for us at a trot.

Caermon groans. "No. Not yet. Say it, Dalt. *Ego te absolvo*. Say it." I turn away from him.

There's a small *pop*. The top rail of the bench I'm sitting on explodes into splinters. Reflex takes over. I dive forward, roll and end up behind the concrete trash can.

A second *pop*. Caermon's wheelchair slams into the eucalyptus tree, then spins around and dumps Caermon onto the ground.

Silence. I hunker down behind the concrete. Caermon's wasted body is splayed on the concrete path. The top half of his head is missing. Blood gouts from what is left for a moment then slows as gravity takes over for his heart.

Even the frailest patients in the rose garden have not forgotten their training. Old instincts stronger than the bodies they inhabit kick in. No panic, just immediate action. Those in wheelchairs break for the parking lot, intent on finding cover. The more mobile disappear behind concrete barriers, foliage, and into the trees.

The orderlies skid to a stop, then turn and run back into the hospital. The security guard takes one frantic look around and then common sense overrides duty. He follows the orderlies, holding his portable radio to his lips as he runs.

The shots sounded like they'd come from the knoll just behind the hospital. There's a retaining wall there, one that stands about two feet above the ground at the upper level. If I can get behind them, then I might be able to—.

To what? I'm an unarmed priest, not part of a SEAL squad.

Sirens in the background. A police car pulls up in front of the hospital, followed shortly by three more. SWAT will be on their way as well, but they'll take some time to assemble. The concrete is cold against my side.

I stay low and run from my position of safety to the line of cars nearby. Another shot, and my right leg spins out, bringing me down. I roll, ending up in a low crouch, then run a broken zigzag and reach the safety of the cars. A patient has taken shelter there, one of the men I know from the psych ward.

"That wasn't too smart, Father," he says. "Hold still—let me look at it." Rough fingers probe the wound. It will hurt later, but for now it is simply numb. "Just creased it. You're bleeding, but it didn't hit anything major."

"Thanks." The sirens converging on the hospital drown my words.

"You stay still," he says. "They're not stupid enough to come down here now."

They wouldn't have to. Not snipers.

How long has it been since the first shot? Maybe one minute, at the most. They're already gone. I would have been, in their position.

I pat the patient on the shoulder. "Stay down." He's not the one they're after, but there's no point in taking chances.

"Yeah."

I evaluate the cover, calculating my odds of making it to each little island of relative safety. The first is the concrete garbage can stand I'd sheltered behind earlier. From there, the open slat bench, then a short dash to the most tenuous of cover, a thick cluster of rose bushes. Then the final stretch, ten all-too-dangerous strides to a stand of eucalyptus trees.

Not ideal, not by a long shot. I move quickly, ignoring the pain throbbing in my leg, then head for the woods and the road beyond that.

"Hold it right there," a quiet voice says. "Don't move."

Not the sniper. If he were, I'd be dead now.

"Face down on the ground, arms away from your body."

I raise my hands, slowly, not wanting to panic anyone. "I'm a priest."

"Get down—face down," the voice orders.

I do as I'm told. The ground is soft and pungent with pine needles, still damp from the morning rain. I lay down, my arms stretched out from my sides, crucified on the wet ground.

There's a shuffle around me, then hands move over me, patting me down expertly, quickly. One hand pauses at my clerical collar. Another hand extracts my wallet from my back pocket.

"Roll over," the voice says. "Slowly. Keep your hands where I can see them." I comply.

The man standing over me is tall and wiry, but it is hard to be sure, looking up at him. He has dark hair graying at the temples and cold steel blue eyes set in a face of hard angles. There is no trace of emotion on the face.

"Who are you?" the man asks.

"Lieutenant David Dalt. I'm a chaplain here."

"What happened?"

"Can I get up? You know I'm not armed. You've got my billfold, so you've seen my ID card."

He considers that for moment then shakes his head. "No, not just yet. I like you on the ground better."

"Then who are you?"

"Special Agent Paul Wister, Naval Criminal Investigative Service."

"What are you doing here?"

"Asking questions. Not answering them."

"Then ask one."

"I did. What happened?"

"I was talking to a patient. Somebody started shooting." I see no reason to give more than the bare facts.

"Why were they trying to kill him?"

"How should I know?"

"That's the question. What did he say?" he asks.

"I don't have to answer that."

"You do if you want to get up." The pistol points unwaveringly at my gut.

I am long past the time when people should be pointing handguns at me. I revert to an earlier persona, interlace my fingers behind my head to form a pillow and shut my eyes. Haynes' pose, but mine before that. "Then I might as well get comfortable."

"Are you refusing to cooperate?"

"Our conversation is privileged."

"So Caermon was making a confession?"

Checkmate. He's not going to stop asking, I'm not going to answer.

Another agent runs up, a radio pinned to his shoulder, a shotgun at port arms. Wister sighs and surprises me by putting away his pistol. He holds out a hand to help me up. "We could continue the pissing contest for a couple of hours, I guess. But I don't see any point in it. Unless you do."

"Not really." I ignore the proffered hand and get up by myself. Dirt and pine needles cling to my black clothes and my clerical collar is loose. I run one finger around my neck and refastened the white circle. "I'd like to go get cleaned up."

"Okay." Wister points at the junior agent. "He needs to take some basic information, then you can go."

I don't understand his change of attitude, but that's all right. An aching need to get far away from this place overcomes me.

Something still bothers me, though. Since we're being civil to each other now, I ask, "How did you get here so fast?"

"I was in the area and heard the radio call."

"Ah." Civil, but not truthful.

I replay the timing, allowing for the fact that adrenaline distorts one's normal sense of time. Shots fired to sirens—maybe five seconds. Hardly enough time to pick up the phone and dial 911, certainly not enough time to tell a jaded dispatcher that shots had been fired.

Suppose I'm mistaken? What if it had been ten seconds? Or twenty? How about one minute?

No. Not enough time for Wister to have gotten here, assessed the situation, made a preliminary determination of where the shots had been fired from and get up here. Impossible

And we're inside the United States. NCIS doesn't have an emergency response team for this sort of thing.

So he's lying. But why? Does he know I know?

"Get his information and meet me at the security office." Wister trots off toward the hospital.

The junior agent takes down my address, telephone number, full name and date of birth then walks with me toward the main building entrance. I leave him standing the foyer and head off to the east wing. He's talking to hospital security, the chubby retired Navy now civil service fellows who guard our safety.

The foyer is full of cops. They check my hospital ID badge before letting me proceed.

It will be hours before they're all gone, if not days. There will be increased security, more badge checks, training seminars and memos. But there's no more danger here now. The snipers are long gone, and all this is just play acting, closing the barn door on empty stalls.

No danger, except to me. I punch the elevator button for my floor. My hand is rock steady.

The first shot was at my bench, not at Caermon. Caermon wasn't the primary target. I was.

No. This is not happening. I am Father David Alan Dalt, an Episcopal priest assigned to Balboa Naval Hospital, not Ensign Dave "Boomer" Dalt, leader of Charlie squad and usually attached to Seal Team Three.

I'm unarmed. For now.

Finding something with a sharp edge won't be difficult in the hospital and last night proved I still have a few useful reflexes. The security guards have a firearms locker. At least I'm wearing dark clothing.

I'll need to take precautions once I leave the hospital. Not now—they won't try anything here, not with the security and police still so evident. Later. When they can catch me alone. Vary my routine. Stay away from my house for a few days—I could even stay here in the duty room. Give Wister and his people a chance to do their jobs.

The security office firearms locker. How sturdy is the lock?

No. I am a priest. Priests do not contemplate stealing scalpels and breaking into firearms lockers. I am quite certain of this.

Muralis Island. They're going back. Of course they are. How could they not?

Napier is going back. Next week. It's compromised and he's already staging. He doesn't know that the other side knows every move he'll make, every code, every communications frequency. He doesn't know he's going to die.

I know what it's like, the days before, the waiting. The preparation. All of it. I was never so alive as I was then.

Caermon had no idea how impotent his threats were. Secrets? I've been keeping secrets since I was ten years old, and it would take far more than the threats of a dying man to worry me.

Four

Captain Haynes isn't in our offices, but Mrs. Agee, our receptionist, tells me he's expected back momentarily and wants to talk to me. She's all aflutter over the excitement and clearly dying to get the details from me, and is even willing to overlook the dirt on my shirt, although I know she sees it.

Mrs. Agee is a priest groupie. She's around fifty, a short, slim woman who dresses with a modesty that befits her assignment to our office and ignores any fashion trend since World War II. She delights in doing God's work for her chaplains, and has even grudgingly extended her devotion to Carla, our one female chaplain. She wears a WWJD—What Would Jesus Do—necklace and keeps us up to date on the details of her prayer circle and witnessing schedule. She tries not to play favorites, but it's clear she's itching to save the rabbi and bring me out of the shadow of Rome's sin. Father McCallister, a devout man with a strong faith, she regards as already lost.

I don't want to talk to Haynes. I don't want to talk to anyone. They're irrelevant distractions of the sort that can get you killed.

I flip the sign on my office door that indicates I do not want to be disturbed. It's usually used for counseling sessions, but is also to provide us a time for quiet reflection, study, and prayer—and time to fight off the impulse to arm myself. I feel naked without any weapons. The lack is excruciating as the adrenaline beats out a demand for one. The instinct for survival is coupled strongly in my mind with a certain weight on my hip.

I shut the door behind me then lean against it for a moment. The adrenaline is fading from my system now, leaving the jitters behind. The room feels safe, but far too small. No window.

If I stand on my desk, I can reach the acoustic tiling overhead. Past that, a maze of pipes and girders, the unseen web that is the real skeleton of the building. The flimsy nubby-fabric dividers are just window dressing.

God forbid that Haynes should find out that I already know which overhead beams will support my weight, but what was I supposed to do without a window? It's not safe, having just one way out of anywhere.

My leg is starting to ache. I pull up my pants leg and study the wound. Just a graze, not even bleeding now. I dab the blood that hasn't dried yet with a tissue. It will bruise, hurt like hell, and heal. No way to hurry that along so no point in getting medical treatment.

So what now? This isn't what it's supposed to be like. No one is supposed to be shooting at me or talking about Muralis Island. Not when I'm unarmed.

Come on, now. Priests shouldn't worry about whether or not they're armed. Our armor is the way Haynes sees it, the breastplate of righteousness and such, the body armor described in Ephesians. The sword of righteousness is our only offensive weapon. Not a Glock 27 .40 cal handgun loaded with Federal Hydroshock rounds stuck under our pillow. Priests don't worry about whether they have enough extra clips in the nightstand drawer. That was another life.

I do what a priest should do. I open my prayer book and look up the readings for the morning office. I scan the words, even read them softly out loud, but they refuse to sink in. Too much has happened today, the past intruding on the present.

The first shot—at me. The second shot—at Caermon. Wister hadn't asked me about the sequence of the shots. Did he already know? Or had it not occurred to him that it might be important?

40

Did the snipers screw up? Caermon, old sins—maybe someone didn't want him talking and he was the primary target. Maybe it was just a screw up.

No. Not the way I was dressed. There would have been no confusing me with Caermon, especially not through a scope. There were no wild shots fired.

So were they after me? Who exactly was "they"?

Well, start with the obvious: who wanted me dead? Someone who thought Caermon was talking out of school? Then why not take him out first?

Or someone from my past? Was it Napier? I hadn't taken his threats outside the Board of Inquiry hearing room seriously.

I should have. After all, it was his men I killed.

Two days before they were to deploy, Napier went med down with a hot appendix. No way to gut that out no matter how much you can bench press. My squad was on standby so I slid into Napier's spot.

Napier, nicknamed Naps, Maltierre and Forsythe's real squad leader, a classmate of mine in BUD/S, a fellow SEAL. Naps would never have left Maltierre and Forsythe behind.

But why now? Why not immediately after the hearing, during seminary, any other time during the last six years?

Maybe I should talk to Haynes, explain what has happened. I can't tell him the truth behind Scorpion, of course. Even if he's cleared for it, he doesn't have the requisite need to know.

I hear voices outside, but the rest of the world seems far away. I try to concentrate on the words in front of me, but Napier's face keeps intruding.

There's a knock on my door. The adrenaline surges, demanding that I get ready, the fear pointing out that I have nothing except my hands to protect me. That will be enough unless he has a gun.

The door opens. Wister is standing there, a bland expression on his face. Mrs. Agee is righteously indignant, but there's a hidden vindication in her eyes. This is my punishment for refusing to spill the details to her. "I told you weren't supposed to be disturbed, Chaplain."

"I asked her if you had someone in there with you," Wister says. "I figured you and God can talk anytime, but I'm on a tighter schedule."

It is an audacious move, one designed to unsettle me. Or is it merely boorishness? I'm not certain yet, but Wister doesn't strike me as a man who does anything without a purpose. Has he realized how much he's failed to ask me? Maybe I'm not the only one shaken up.

"I've got a few more questions," Wister says. "Shouldn't take up much of your time." I step aside to let him enter, sparing a moment to glare at Mrs. Agee.

"Nasty business out there," Wister says as he settles his bulk into one of my chairs. He takes his time, checking out the few mementos I have on the wall. "You okay?"

It depends on who I am right now, whether I'm okay or not. Besides, Wister has already lied to me once, about how he happened to be on scene so quickly. I'm not inclined to let him get any closer to me, physically or mentally, than I have to. "I'm fine. What do you want?"

"Most people might be a bit shook up," Wister continues, as though I haven't spoken. "I mean, sure, you're used to dealing with death—you see it all the time around here, right? But something like that, so violent, and you almost take a round yourself—you ought to take the rest of the day off or something, you know?"

"I appreciate your concern, but I'm afraid I've got a full schedule today." It doesn't jibe with my sitting in my office alone, but I don't care.

"Yeah, well. I guess maybe you have ways of dealing with things that most people don't," he says, his voice reflective. "But maybe not all from the seminary, huh?"

"You mean because I used to be a SEAL?"

He nods. "Unusual background for a priest."

"Not unheard of. Many Episcopal priests were something else before they were priests."

"But not SEALs, right?"

"Listen, Agent Wister, I'm sure we've both got a lot on our plates today," I say. I have a strong sense again of the missing weight on my hip. Wister must be armed. I force down the impulse to take his gun from him. "One of our chaplains called in sick—I've got to cover his patients today as well as my own. So if we could get to the point, I'd appreciate it."

He nods, apparently pleased by my directness. "Arthur Caermon—he was one of your regular patients?"

"No. He was Roman Catholic. Chaplain McCallister would have visited him if he'd been here." Let Wister find out on his own what happened in the ER.

"And that's pretty standard, then? You've all got your own assignments?"

"We do. I normally cover the psych ward, and Chaplain McCallister handles oncology, and we visit the patients of our denominations. But as I said, McCallister is out sick today."

"And you volunteered to see his patients?"

"No. The supervising chaplain asked me if I would cover them. Listen, I thought we were going to get to the point," I say, tired of the gentle probes. "What do you want?"

"What did Caermon tell you?"

"I've explained that those communications are privileged."

"Yes, you have. Barring that, I'd like to know how it is that you just happened to be there when Caermon was shot. It seems a little unusual, you see. Him not being your patient, you and that doctor violating orders allowing him outside, and him getting shot. And then a priest taking off after the bad guys—now, I know a little bit more about you now than I did when we first met, and I think I can understand your impulse, but it wasn't a very smart thing to do, was it? I think you can understand my confusion." Wister is a nibble-at-the-edges guy, not a shark like my father.

"Confusion, no. Suspicion, I think, is the word you're looking for."

He holds up his hand in protest. "Nothing like that. Like I said—I'm just confused."

"If reality confuses you, that's someone else's department," I say.

He's silent for a moment, but he's not pleased. "You're Admiral Dalt's son, aren't you?"

"What's that got to do with anything?"

"Your father, he's had an interesting career."

I stand up. "I'm afraid, Agent Wister—."

"Special Agent," he says. "Not just agent."

"Okay, *Special* Agent Wister. As I said, I've got a busy schedule today. And unless you're planning on getting to the point sometime within the next few seconds, this will have to wait."

"Scorpion. Is that you? Or was it?" he asks.

If he's planned to catch me off-guard and coax me into making some admission, he's going to have to do better than that. "Ask someone who can verify your clearance and your need to know," I say. "Not me."

"So it is you. What was it, an old name from the SEALs? A nickname, like a code name?"

"No comment."

"The Fifth?"

"No comment."

Wister sighs. "I was hoping you'd make this easy on yourself, Dalt."

"Father Dalt. Or Chaplain Dalt. I'll even answer to Lieutenant or Mister. A *Special* Agent ought to understand that."

"Okay, *Chaplain.* I hope you understand what kind of people you're playing games with."

"I'm not playing games with anyone, Special Agent Wister."

He shakes his head, disappointed. "Oh, but you are. You and I both know where that first shot was aimed. And unless you're a lot dumber than I think you are, you know why. Caermon talked—and he talked to you. Somebody's not going to like that."

44

I'm not the only one he talked to, but Wister may not know that yet. Should I tell him about that moment in the ER, Wister whispering to Sarini, her curious glance at me? What had Caermon said? I need to know as much if not more than Wister does.

"Why did you take him outside?" Wister asks. His voice is flat and level, the tone men use when they're determined not to show anger.

Another piece to the puzzle snicks into place. The response time, NCIS responding, the connections he must have to even guess what Scorpion meant.

Maybe it's a delayed reaction to Caermon's execution, but I'm now furious beyond all control. "You had his room wired, didn't you? Sound and video, or just sound? Both, I bet. And you were completely willing to eavesdrop on his last words to a priest, weren't you? Oh, you couldn't use them in court, but there's not much chance of you getting Caermon into court anyway, is there? Because he was dying—it was just a matter of time. But whatever it was, you didn't want him talking to anyone without your hearing it."

Wister is watching me closely now, his eyes giving away nothing. He reminds me of a cormorant stalking a trout.

"This is unspeakable."

"I wouldn't be too quick to go making accusations," Wister says, all traces of fake congeniality gone from his voice. "Not with who you are. Not under the circumstances."

"Are you threatening me?"

"Just pointing out the downside of refusing to cooperate."

"There's not a court in the country that would force a priest to reveal a confidential communication and you know it."

Wister is still studying me. "I'm not talking about courts. I'm talking about some real serious damage to this nation's interests. And if you know what I think you know, you'll understand what that means."

45

I'm sympathetic to his position. It's mine as well and if I could tell him, I would.

But I can't defy God like that, violate my vows. They're what keep me anchored in this life. Wister is asking me to give up far more than he knows. Being a priest is the only thing that keeps me sane and Muralis Island at bay.

"I can't help you," I say finally. I hope he hears the regret in my voice. "I would if I could, but I can't."

"You mean you won't." He leans forward and I smell peppermint on his breath. "Caermon's only the tip of it all, Dalt. What worries the hell out of me is the possibility that you're wrapped up in this somehow. And I swear to your God that if you are, I *will* find out. I will find out, and I will watch you prosecuted, convicted, and sent to prison for the rest of your life."

I laugh at that point. This has gone past annoying into lunacy.

"You've got a chance right now," Wister persists. "Tell me what you know. Cooperate. Is your father involved in this?"

"My *father*? Are you out of your mind?" My father's faces flashes into my mind. He's a hair taller than I am, built like a swimmer instead of a power lifter. I have his coloring but my mother's features. My father has an aristocratic, inbred look, a long patrician nose and high cheekbones. His eyes are a shade darker than mine, his hair lighter. On him, the combination is striking rather than ordinary.

Wister is still watching me closely. "Maybe. Maybe not."

"You actually believe this? That my father had something to do with someone shooting at me and Caermon?"

He shrugs. "You're not telling me what you know. "

I walk to the door and open it. Mrs. Agee is at her desk, trying very hard not to look like she's eavesdropping. "Get out, Special Agent Wister. Go play cops and robbers with someone else. All I did was talk to a dying man, and you'd like to elevate that to a capital offense."

Wister resists for a moment at the door. "Last chance."

"Wister, look—it's been a really shitty day," I say. "Why don't you just fuck off, okay?"

Mrs. Agee gasps. I've just confirmed her deepest suspicions about me.

Haynes comes in just then and he already knows what's happened. It would be hard not to, with police officers and security guards trotting down the passageways, the announcements over the intercom, and the general flurry of activity.

The hospital will be deploying the crisis team counselors. They'll find me soon enough, the young psychologists intent on having me process what has happened, defuse the inevitable psychic trauma by getting me to share my feelings. They'll tell me they understand and are here for me.

I'm on the same trauma team myself. The psychologists will find it particularly gratifying to treat a priest.

I have no desire to have noncombatants attempting to probe my psyche. What happened today is nothing new. I feel more a deep sense of disappointment at the violence rather than any sense of traumatic stress.

Wister steps forward and introduces himself to Haynes. Haynes studies him for a long moment, then turns to me. "I need to talk to you."

"Good luck," Wister says. "He's not in a talkative mood."

"I've told you all I can," I say.

"Which was nothing."

I shrug. Haynes touches me lightly on the shoulder. "My office. If you'll excuse us, Agent Wister."

"Special Agent," I supply as I follow Haynes down the passageway. "He's a *Special* Agent."

Behind me, I heard Wister chatting up Mrs. Agee, commiserating with the difficulties of her job. He's leaving his card for her, and if she hears anything, anything at all, he hopes she'll call him. He's making friends with the locals, establishing contact with resistance forces in hostile territory.

I start to turn around and bodily throw him out of the office. Haynes grabs my arm. "She understands," he says. "I know you two don't get along, but she's been here a long time. She won't tell him anything she shouldn't."

Haynes' computer is still disassembled on his desk and the monitor sitting on his chair. He takes a seat next to me in front of the desk.

Our conversation is short and to the point. He's concerned—I'm impatient. The list of patients I have to see is in my pocket and I feel the weight of it pressing on me. I do not want to talk about what happened. I do not want to even think about it. All I want to do is be a priest.

Haynes wants me to talk to the counselors. I demure, pointing out that I've got a bit of experience myself with this sort of thing and know that I'm okay. Haynes suggests that it's denial. I counter by calling it the grace of God. He's at the point of ordering me to participate in the crisis counseling session forming even now, when I stop him. "My patients. They have to be seen, sir. And frankly, it's best for me to stay busy for a while." Then I play the ecclesiastical trump card. "God will take care of me."

He can't argue with that. We're too short-handed and seeing the dying is a critical part of what we do. He doesn't want to, but finally he agrees.

But there has been too much today already that has tried to rip me from who I am now. I will not spend time whining to a psychologist when I should be visiting patients.

Before he lets me go, Haynes extracts a promise that if I feel the slightest uneasiness or reaction, I will hunt him down immediately. Not an easy task, since he'll be covering part of McCallister's duties as well, but I have his pager number.

I step back out into the wide hallways with a sense of relief. There's uncertainty in the air, in the knots of people clustered in the hallways, the nervous laughter, the presence of the police, but it doesn't affect me. Nothing can touch me right now. There's a euphoria you feel after narrowly escaping danger, a sense of soaring vitality and energy. Joy, even.

I remember this feeling from my SEAL days. And I remember now how much I miss it.

Five

FOr the next five hours, I speak only to the dying and their families. I pray, hold hands, hear three hurried confessions. I lay hands on the comatose, administer the rite of extreme unction, and comfort wives, husbands, parents and children. The holy oil seeps into my skin, dissolving my flesh until I'm no more than a channel between God and his people. There's a sense of agonizing transcendence that comes with this work.

In the moments between rooms, Forsythe's and Maltierre's faces comes back to me, cold and dead. Then Napier's, twisted in rage.

Later. I will deal with them later.

My next visit will be to Ted Singer, a man I know well, one of my own. A cradle Episcopalian, a strong Anglican. I have watched him deteriorate over the last weeks and we both know the end is coming soon. He is frightened but at peace.

I am paged just before I step into his room. I call the hospital switchboard from the nurses' station. The operator puts me on hold and a recorded pep talk from the administration comes on. It's supposed to make waiting more tolerable and tout a few new programs at the hospital. It seems to me that staff should be exempt from the cheerleading.

The line clicks and I hear my father's voice, deep and mellifluous as always. "David?" he asks.

"Yes."

"You're at the hospital?"

"Why wouldn't I be?"

I picture him at his desk, a large expanse of gleaming dark wood before him. The walls around him are bare, painted white. No windows, not in this security area, but the lack of natural light doesn't bother him the way it does me. He's listening to my tone of voice, evaluating my mental state, analyzing every bit of data from my word choice to how long it took me to pick up the page.

He ignores my question. "I heard about the shooting," he says. "There's an NCIS agent waiting to see me. Wister. You know him?"

"No, I'm not hurt. Thanks for asking."

Another silence. He's recalculating, deciding whether he made an error by not inquiring first about my well-being.

There were reasons he didn't ask me if I was alright, there had to be. My father does nothing without a reason.

Perhaps he thought that asking a personal question would simply open him up to cheap shots, just as not asking had. Perhaps he understood that there was no way he could say the right thing. Damned if you don't, damned if you do. How does it feel, dear old Dad, to be in that position?

"If you'd been hurt, I would have been notified. So why is this fellow here?"

"I don't know," I say. "Why don't you ask him?"

I already know why he doesn't ask Wister: because my father is never unprepared. Information and data are his life, as is reshaping facts into the truth as he sees it. He will want to know everything I know before he talks to Wister. If there are stories to be gotten straight, facts to be given, points to be reinforced, he'll want to know. It will not immediately occur to him that there's no need for a cover story.

"What did you tell him?" my father asks.

"That I can't tell him anything. Just like I can't tell you anything. I was talking to a patient and a sniper took him out. That's all I know."

"Who was the patient?"

For a moment, I'm tempted not to tell him. But that would be petty—he can find out easily enough through his own resources, and Wister will tell him as well. He may even already know. It wouldn't be the first time he'd tested me by asking for information he already has.

"Arthur Caermon," I say. "You know him?"

Silence. Information only flows one direction in my father's world. In, never out.

"And there's nothing you can tell me?" he says finally. "Nothing at all? Come on, surely not every conversation is completely privileged."

"Sorry." I'm not, and he knows it. "I don't have any written records, either. Just in case you're wondering."

"Now, David." His tone is faintly hurt, as if having my office searched for pastoral care notes would be far beneath him. "Did you sign anything? Make a statement?"

I don't have time for this, not if I expect to get through this day. I have work to do in deeper currents. Ted Singer is waiting. I tell him this, letting my anger show.

"You'll be a piss-poor priest if you're dead," my father answers. "I can't help you if I don't know what we're dealing with."

"I don't need help."

"They missed you this time. You won't be so lucky next time." He thinks it is a streak of stubbornness, that I'm holding out on him for my own reasons. That my vows could be more important than satisfying his need—no, his craving—for information will never sink in. "I'm coming over there."

"No. I'm busy."

"Make time. Five minutes. Is that too much to ask? You can take a leak or something while we talk. You still do that, don't you?"

I hang up on him. My hand shakes. For the next four hours, I ignore the hospital pages. I don't even wonder how he knew the first shot was aimed at me.

Hours later, I'm still deep in denial. I've seen the last of McCallister's patients. Sarini will be leaving by now, if she's not already gone. If she's running late, there may be a chance to talk to her.

If I ever had the slightest feeling that she saw me as someone besides a priest, it would have been a good deal easier. Most of what I know about her comes from others, even though we'd talked several times casually. I compare my state of mind now, as I try to work up the nerve to invite her to dinner, with my days as a randy SEAL. My old teammates would think me pathetic.

I've made sure that she knows I'm not Roman Catholic. I've mentioned my married priest friends, their families. I've tried to be open with her, turn the conversation away from patients and to her own life, but she resists all attempts to develop a personal relationship. You would think that God would make being virtuous a little easier.

As I get off the elevator on her floor, my father walks up to me.

He's not alone, of course. He rarely is these days. Two men in casual clothes are in the waiting room, watching.

"What a surprise," I say. It's not.

"We need to talk," he says, ignoring my pique. "Now."

I really have no choice. If I want to be churlish and stalk off, my father will simply invoke his status as a very senior officer and have the duty officer corral me. He could order me himself, of course, but he's not likely to. He knows the threat of making my chain of command aware of our disagreements will do more to persuade me than any appeal to my filial duties.

I see Sarini getting off the elevator. She raises one hand in greeting, assuming I'm occupied talking to the man I'm standing with, then disappears down the passageway. Now I'm really pissed.

My father, of course, sees all this. I can tell it amuses him.

"What do you want?" I ask.

"Can't a father stop by to see his son occasionally without wanting something?"

"Some could."

He blinks once, reevaluating the situation, then says, "I know you're not going to listen, but I'm going to talk to you anyway. And you're going to listen. Caermon is not the kind of person you want to be involved with. "

"Was," I say. "He's not any kind of person right now at all."

"Was," my father echoes.

"How do you know him?" I ask.

My father waves the question away. "I want you to come home with me. Stay at the house for a few days until we get this sorted out."

"No. There's nothing to sort out," I say. "I don't need a babysitter."

"Listen to me. You need protection. Anyone close to Caermon does right now. Yes, I want to know what he told you, but there are people out there who just as much want to make sure you can't tell anyone ever. They'll kill you before they'll let you talk, and they're not going to be impressed by this hocus pocus confidentiality privilege you seem to rely on."

"I can take care of myself."

He makes a small sound of disdain. "I was expecting you to say that God would take care of you."

That annoys me. "Of course He will."

"Then perhaps He sent me here to help you."

The men with him are watchers, not listeners. Still, I step close to him before I speak. It reminds me of that moment with Caermon on the bench, this trading of secrets not meant for anyone else.

I am tempted to tell him that Caermon knew his secrets. Surely that part was a threat, not part of the confession itself?

But if I start there, where do I stop? Down this slippery slope I must not go, because to treat this one part as not privileged would be to begin the process of eroding. And it is tempting.

This is the reason the seal of the confessional is a moral absolute. The men and women who hear these dark secrets are mortal, fallible. We cannot be trusted to apportion what a sinner says to God because we will subvert it to our own use. I see it in myself, as I am tempted to tell him what Caermon said merely to hurt him.

It hits me then, the real problem with my position. Napier and his squad in Norway, staging. One week. Back to Muralis with the whole mission compromised and everything I know locked under the seal of the confessional.

In truth, my father would be my best resource for stopping Napier. My father has resources, access to communications and the highest level of military planners.

So I will not tell him what would result in good, but I am willing to tell him what I hope will hurt him. Nice. Very nice.

Old grudges are easier than new ones. Instead of trying to hurt him with Caermon, I fall back on what I know works. Go with your strengths, I always say.

"You didn't save her. What makes you think you can save me?"

He starts to answer, but I'm already walking away when he says, "And what makes you think I didn't?" He and his men do not follow me.

When I was ten years old, my mother died in a boating accident. Death by misadventure, that was the official verdict. Not much of an adventure. Back then, coroners were a little more likely to find reasons other than suicide to put on the death certificate, and I'm sure my father's friends put some pressure on the process. Even then, he was marked for great things in the Navy, and they would have wanted to avoid the second-hand taint that a suicide would suggest.

We were on a sailboat, a smallish one rented from the Navy's recreation department. My father was a skilled sailor and we were within sight of Blacks Beach in La Jolla, anchored out overnight.

Sometime the second night out, my mother went over the side. My father heard the splash and went out on deck. He saw her briefly, and dove in after her, but she was out of sight by the time he got to her. I evidently heard the noise and went up on deck as well. I saw my father fully-clothed in the water and went in after him, figuring this was a night swimming party. I was a strong swimmer for my age and build, but there was a current running and it was a moonless cloudy night. My father shouted at me to get back to the boat.

Instead, I swam toward him. He made several more dives, still searching for my mother in the black water, then saw that I was starting to drift away. He took me back to the boat, ordered me to stay there, called the Coast Guard, and went back into the water to search for her. It wasn't until then that I knew anything was wrong. He continued searching until the Coast Guard arrived and took over the search.

That, at least, is his story and it is the legend that has wrapped itself so tightly around the rest of his life that I wonder if he can even acknowledge any other possibilities now. But surely he remembers that it was not exactly that way. If anyone had bothered to ask me what happened, I could have told him.

As the hospital empties, it is becoming less the haven that it was earlier today. It is time to leave, but I will do so carefully. I can't stop Napier if I'm dead.

One of the first things I did after I completed formal check-in procedures was to make a complete tour of the building and grounds. Not the cursory one that the indoctrination classes provided but a close, personalized look at the entire area.

I told myself it was just curiosity. I even laughed at my own paranoia. Yet still I knew I would not be comfortable until I knew the slope of the ground, the windows that were within reach of trees, the exits that were concealed by cover, even the configuration of the loading bays and dumpsters. It's the terrain that exists beneath the landscaping, the lay of the land that most people don't see because they don't look for it.

Because of the slope of the ground, most of the main hospital building is set back into a hill. The power plant and utility spaces are located in the basement. A massive boiler provides hot water for the entire complex, and the power junction boxes and telephone patch panels are also down there.

I make my way between steam lines and hot water heaters to the double doors that lead to the outside. Most of the hospital staff has never been down here, and I doubt any of the chaplains have.

Back behind two sets of fire pumps there's a half-window that opens up at ground level. It probably hasn't been opened since the hospital was built, and I'm not sure exactly why it is even here. Then I look again, and I see the plan—if the main entrances are blocked off by fire, this provides the only way out along this wall.

The bottom edge is just at eye-level, call it six feet above the floor. It's got a broad ledge and there are angled hand grips set along the edge, along with a metal toe bar at three feet set in the cement block. Whoever planned this understood what it was like to be trapped.

I grab the handhold and put my toe on the metal ledge. It's an easy vault up onto the broad ledge. The window is grimy, but I can see outside vaguely. I clean off a small spot for better visibility.

The window looks out just where I remember, onto a back storage area filled with dumpsters. The steep hill rises up behind, so there's not much clearance and the dumpsters obscure the visibility from the hill. A good exit—not perfect, since I'd prefer thicker bushes around— but better than waltzing out the front door.

The window itself proves to be a bit more difficult, though I get it open with more noise than I'd like. The bottom half finally pulls up, and I crouch down and duck under the top half.

Oleander bushes are planted two feet from the building in a solid row. They're only three feet tall and not entirely grown together yet, so it's possible someone can see me moving behind them.

I still haven't entirely decided what to do. The most convenient way to leave will be in my car. I'll ditch that at the airport, pick up a rental, and find somewhere to stay for a while.

But whoever was shooting at me may be watching my car. So I'm taking a look around, with a couple of backup plans in my mind, trying to decide.

I move around the back of the building and then down the west side of the building. The grounds in front of the building flooded by the spotlights. While parts of the parking lot are dark, surveillance cameras mounted high on poles survey the portions that are not. The cameras feed into the security station on the first floor. Sometimes the guards even look at them, and after what happened today, I'm certain they'll be watching them.

I pull my collar off. There was a time when I wouldn't have forgotten to remove anything white from my clothing. The black pants and black shirt blend well with the shadows.

Something moves on the high bank behind me, the rustling noise just barely audible over the traffic from the nearby interstate. I hold where I am. Movement gives away more than anything.

Someone shouts, and all hell starts breaking loose. I hear car doors opening, men moving all along the hill behind me. I can't see what caused it, but it doesn't matter. If I stay where I am, I'll be found.

I grab a handful of dirt and smear it across my face, doing that as I scuttle back the way I came. Back into the basement, into the hospital? No—I can't bear the thought of being confined right now. Better to be in a more natural environment. I'll have the advantage there.

But getting to cover is turning out to be a problem. I should not have tested the surveillance, I should have left while it was quiet. Stick to the mission, don't deviate. It was sheer hubris to do otherwise.

The noise is concentrated on the west side of the building, and I suspect that I'm the cause of it. Someone saw a shadow moving, something—I had not thought that the surveillance and protection would be this heavy this long, but I was mistaken.

The hospital sits on the edge of Balboa Park, an expanse of more than two hundred acres of woods, museums, and parks located in the center of San Diego. It's connected to a main road by a two-lane winding road that makes its way up the hill to the guard shack. Easy to block off, easy to control.

The north and west sides of the park are alive with noise. The entrance is to the south. That leaves the east as the best possibility.

Unless the noise is intentional? Am I being flushed out, driven before these people like quail before a good hunting dog? Possible.

The east is the most difficult terrain of the four sides, so perhaps they're relying on that to control access. It slops down at a steep angle to a rift running through the park. Some tall hardwood, but mostly brush, too thick and a fire hazard. From outside it looks impenetrable, but it is crisscrossed by animal trails. The brush merges overhead the tracks to form a canopy.

If they're using infrared gear, they'll see me, but otherwise they're going to have to try to distinguish between the movement the wind makes and my passage.

The dumpsters provide some cover—not enough, but enough to limit my exposure. I make it to the first one and there's no sign I've been seen. I take a quick look around then dart to the second one. My eyes are only partially night-adapted, and the shadows along the back of the dumpster are deep. As I come around the corner, now only thirty feet away from the edge of the brush, I run straight into Wister.

"Hold it right there," he says. He has his handgun out again, but it's pointed slightly to the side. The floodlights are in his face and he's not seeing much. Oh, but he hears, and he knows with that instinct that he's got that someone is here. He just can't pinpoint me exactly.

I should have known he would be here. There may be more.

I back up slowly, letting my feet settle on the ground carefully to avoid any noise. Wister speaks into his shoulder radio, summoning backup. I don't panic, but continue backing up until I'm at the corner of the dumpster again. Then I break into a run and head for the bush, zigzagging to foil his sight picture.

I hear the shots, too close. Good thing he's not using a shotgun.

I crash into the bush, then go low, crawling as fast as I can move searching for what I know is right around here somewhere. A random shot might nail me now, but unless they're using infrared, I'm clear of them. They won't know the trails, won't be able to find me. By the time they wade through the brush, I'll already be around enough people to blend in once I wash the mud off my face and hands.

Who do they think I am? The sniper, coming back for another try? Any illusions I have about that are dispelled by Wister's voice.

"Dalt. Come on out. We need to talk."

Talk?

No. If he's willing to shoot at a shadow, there's no way I'm going back.

Six

Balboa Park is surrounded by strip malls and long stretches of white stucco and red tile roof townhouses and condominiums. On the surface, it's a green haven carved out of a densely populated area.

Bottom currents: makeshift camps in the canyons. Trees and brush hide piles of belongings. Illegal aliens, the homeless, the desperate—they gravitate here, within easy walking distance of soup kitchens and social services but without the restrictions of organized shelters. Whether because of mental illness or sheer stubborn independence, they prefer their freedom.

They generally stay away from the trails meandering through the park, but I know they're watching. Small noises, smells out of place—one man cries out—they do not approach me.

Sixth Avenue forms the western boundary of the park, intersecting University Avenue to the north. It's mostly commercial, shops and restaurants serving both downtown San Diego a few miles to the south and the gay communities in Hillcrest. Ethnic and counter cultures collide, and it's not difficult to go unnoticed with the right camouflage.

Baggy shorts with deep pockets, a T-shirt and running shoes deplete my cash reserves by half. I change first then stop at an ATM before they can organize electronic surveillance. Even a few hours from now, it will be too risky.

Why was Wister waiting for me, staring into the brush, his gun searching the shadows for me? Why had he gone from asking questions to shooting? I'm not inclined to call him up and find out. Until I find out exactly what is going on, who wanted Caermon dead, I trust no one.

Trust no one—another lesson learned the hard way, first from my parents. My mother died and left me. My father might as well have gone with her. Then the Navy, surely big enough and strong enough to be trusted, had failed me. Cold, so cold—abandoned again, holding Sean Maltierre's body away from the current, barely conscious—it was at that moment I knew I would never trust another person as long as I lived.

What happened next is impossible to describe. Throughout the diocese discernment process and into seminary, I still have not been able to reduce the experience to words. I've worked out a way to describe it as a conversion experience, but that would fall short of what really happened. Suffice it to say that I came off the rocks of Muralis Island clutching the bare possibility that there might be something greater than myself that I could trust.

And then why not trust Him now? Turn myself over to Wister or the police, explain to them what happened and trust God with the results.

I cannot. Muralis Island taught me to trust my soul to God. My ass, however, remains my own responsibility.

I find a payphone and call a taxi. My need for a weapon has grown to almost panic. Returning to my house is a risk, but better than being unarmed.

What you don't know will kill you almost as fast as being unarmed. I see Sarini bending over Caermon, listening intently, the question in her eyes as she looked at me.

I live in Pacific Beach, a small community just to the north of San Diego itself. The streets are laid out in a convenient and well-planned fashion for the most part. North-south streets are named after minerals and the east-west ones are numbered. Alleys run conveniently behind many of the complexes and it's replete with short cuts and back entrances.

The inhabitants run the gamut from well-off stoners, surfers, and young professionals to old money right on the ocean and up on the hills. It's not difficult to fit in here, no matter who you are. There's a definite bent toward organic and natural New Age persuasions, but the beach culture predominates.

I give the driver an address on the street that runs behind my house. Ten minutes later, we're there.

"Park here. Wait for me—I'll be about five minutes." I hand him twenty dollars.

"That'll buy you a half an hour," the driver says.

"Plenty of time."

The art of camouflage encompasses more than face paint and jungle prints. It's about becoming part of an environment, moving unnoticeably through it. In my beach attire, I'm not noticeable. I walked purposefully down the street, signaling to anyone watching that I belong here. There's nothing about me that anyone would remember.

I cut down the alley then turn right. I'm two houses north of my own. One-car garages, dilapidated doors, front onto the alley. Plenty of reasons for someone to be back here this time of day.

Had I thought this out when I first rented this house? I don't remember doing so, but now I realize I must have. I couldn't have missed the approachability of the place, the multiple entrances and egresses, the availability of cover.

I jingle my car keys in my hand and walk on down the alley. I'm behind my house now. The man in the next house is in his back yard, sunning and smoking a joint. I have a feeling it's not a good time to be doing that. I ignore him—I doubt he'll recognize me. We've never spoken, but I've made it a point to know what the regulars in this area look like. I glance over into my back yard.

For moment, I feel foolish, paranoid. Even though it's just a rental, I've spent a fair amount of time on the small patch of dirt enclosed by the board fence. Bougainvillea flourish in the corners, and blooming hibiscus in blood reds and yellow grow tall along the fences. Even with the traffic noise, it's a haven.

Sunlight glints off metal in the southeastern patch of bougainvillea. I keep walking, just a casual inhabitant, hoping they haven't seen me. I can't run, not now. My patient cabby—if he's still there—will stop immediately if he's followed by flashing lights and a siren. I bluff.

Should I have the cab driver take me down the road outside my house to see if there was a surveillance van parked there? I could, if I really needed the confirmation of what I already know. I don't.

Who is hiding in my back yard, waiting for me? Wister and his people? Or the people who killed Caermon? Or my father's people?

At the moment, it simply doesn't matter.

I make it down the alley, cross over to the road, and back to my cab. I slid back into the back seat. "Airport, please." He's pleased—waiting time is good time for them, since they burn no gas, have a chance to relax. The airport is a profitable run as well.

I lean back against the cushion and position myself so that I can see out of the passenger side rear view mirror. If someone is following us, I'll know it.

I hit the ATM at the airport, withdrawing the rest of my available cash, then use plastic to rent a car. A trail, yes, but I won't need the car for long. If I use cabs, they may eventually trace my movements. With a rental car, all they know is that I'm mobile.

Sarini doesn't live far from me. It takes me twenty minutes to get from the airport back to Pacific Beach, and find her house. I cruise by it.

It's an unpretentious cottage three blocks from the bay. The small lawn in front is neatly manicured, climbing roses are trained up trellises, the lines of the flower beds bordering the walkway tidy with mulch spread around freshly planted annuals. An older-model Toyota is parked in the driveway. I see a splash of blue on the windshield, an officer's parking sticker. The bumper has a naval hospital parking sticker on it.

I see no indication that anyone's watching her place, but traffic is heavy. She's nearer the beach than I am, and the foot traffic is also considerably higher. There is no way to be certain that one of the cars parked along her street doesn't contain a surveillance team.

I drive around the neighborhood again. Planning the ingress is a bit more complicated than it had been in my own neighborhood, but the additional traffic, both on foot and vehicle, makes it easier to melt into the crowd.

I finally decide to approach her house the same way I had my own. There's no alley, and the lots are much smaller here, and the fences dividing them less imposing. There's a white picket fence in front of Sarini's yard, and from what I can tell, it runs back to the house behind her as well.

I park near the house in back of hers, leave the car unlocked. I walk into the side yard of the house behind hers, hoping to slip into the back undetected.

A woman is watching out of a kitchen window. I wave, pretending we are old friends and she smiles back uncertainly, unable to place me but certain that a burglar would not be so friendly. A bad assumption.

There's no fence between this house and the one next to it, but there is a low concrete block wall separating her yard from Sarini's. I vault over, and hear the back door of the house open. I turn, waved again, and say, "Sorry about that. Just taking a shortcut to Sarah's." It's part of the act, using Sarini's first name. I never do—I don't even think of her that way, even in my fantasies. Something military, perhaps, or just a way of keeping myself at a distance.

The neighbor looks doubtful, but goes back inside. I hope it was not to call the police.

I don't need much time, anyway. Just long enough to make sure that Sarini is at home, alone, and willing to talk to me.

There are two steps leading up to the house, which itself is set up on cinder blocks. I walk up to the back door.

Not good. Two deep marks are in the wood around the door latch. The door stands partly open.

Sarini would not leave a door open. Nor would the person who maintained the front yard allow a defect to remain on her door jamb.

I back off from the door and move quietly along the back of the house, staying out of view of the windows overhead. If the backyard neighbor is still watching, I undoubtedly look suspicious, but there is no time to worry about that now.

I hear low voices—a boyfriend? Another friend? What if they were—?

A moan comes out of a back window, then a sharp crack—a slap, by the sounds of it, followed by another muffled groan.

I shift my weight to the balls of my feet and move quietly up the stairs, keeping my weight on the outside edges to avoid creaking. The door is open enough for me to slide in to the kitchen. I pause and listened.

The sounds are clearer now, and, unless Sarini is into masochism, fall into the definitely not all right category.

A block of wood slotted to hold knives sits next to the stove top. I pull one out and heft it. Good steel, well-balanced—not much help against a gun, but I've got the element of surprise on my side.

From what I can tell, the sounds are coming from the room next to the kitchen, along the back of the house. Probably a bedroom. I can hear only two voices, that of a man, and Sarini's.

I move silently down a short hallway toward an open door. The sounds get more distinct. Finally, I am just outside it, but not close enough to see in.

What I heard before wasn't a moan of passion. It was a full-fledged scream choked off by a gag, high-pitched and keening. A man's back is to me, and Sarini is bound to a chair, gagged. Her shirt is torn open. Red welts and scorched flesh. A cigarette burns in the man's hand. A thin line dripping red runs around her neck.

"You can stop it any time you want to." His voice is calm and reasonable. "It's not your fault you're in this position. Tell me you're ready to talk, and this all stops."

Sarini's words are distorted by the gag but I can tell what she said: I don't know anything.

He sighs. "I don't like doing this, I really don't. But if you knew what was at stake—." Another high-pitched, muffled scream tells me what his body blocks from view.

I'm in the room before I can even think of it, grabbing him by the throat with one hand and jamming my knee into the small of his back. With the arm holding the knife, I pin his arms to his side.

I jerk back. The man lets out one muffled scream, astonishment rather than pain, and then crumples to the floor.

I drop, put the knife to his throat. Not necessary. The light's already fading in his eyes. I wait to make sure. A stench fills the room as he loses control of his bowels and bladder.

Sarini is silent. I pull the gag off. The duct tape leaves hard red marks on her pale skin. The knife slices easily through the bindings. She's starting to shake now, on the verge of passing out. As soon as I have her loose, I carry her out of the room and lay her down on her couch.

"You're okay now," I say. She touches the shallow cut on her neck then stares at the blood on her fingertips. "It's not deep. What did they want?"

She stares at me in disbelief. Her ordered world is gone, and it takes her a moment to place me out of my uniform. "Caermon—they want to know about Caermon. And you." There was no quake in her voice, no other indication of distress, but the tears coursed down her cheeks steadily, cutting lighter paths through the blood on her neck

Shock. I've seen this before. She'll be manageable for a bit longer, but then it will hit her. She shouldn't see herself like this—I'll wipe her face off before she can.

"We have to get out of here," I say, trying to sound gentle. "I know you don't feel like it, but whoever that was, he may have friends.

"Who was he?" she asks. "Caermon, I mean."

"I'll fill you in once we're safe," I promise. My sense of urgency is mounting. "But right now, we have to get out of here."

She reaches for the telephone. I catch her wrist, harder than I intended. "You can't call the police," I say. "Not yet."

"Why?" For the first time, her voice trembles. "Of course I'm going to call the cops—who else—?"

"No. They may be involved. There's more to this than I can explain right now. Please, just once—trust me. I'll explain everything, I promise."

Even badly shaken, Sarini is a professional. Her eyes assess me, and I can see the debate going on in her mind.

Calling the police is the obvious, law-abiding thing to do. But there is nothing obvious or law-abiding about the situation. Every second we delayed, my fear increases.

"Can you stand up?" I ask. "You look shaky."

"Shock," she says, all doctor now. She touches her throat and her chest again, then becomes conscious of the disarray of her clothing. She tries to pull the shirt together around her.

I turn my back. "Get something on." She doesn't go back into the bedroom—I should have thought of that, not tried to send her back into the room with the dead man in it. Instead, she heads for the kitchen. I hear her open a dryer.

Precious seconds tick by. Finally, she says, "Okay. I'm ready. But as soon as we're out of here, I want to know what the hell is going on."

"Can you walk about two blocks?" I ask.

She nods. "There's a possibility that I may pass out—keep your hand on my arm in case I go down." She starts for the front door.

"Not that way. Out the back—the way I came in. The car is closer that way."

70

We'll run the risk of the neighbor seeing us, but it's a chance we'll have to take. Given Sarini's obviously battered appearance will she call the police? Probably— she looks the type that would. Perhaps Sarini can talk her way out of it, but I suspect that the neighbor will believe she's under duress.

I let Sarini lead the way to the kitchen, then down the back steps. She stumbles then grabs the hand rail. I slip an arm around her waist. She doesn't object. I help her over the low concrete wall into her neighbor's backyard. The neighbor is nowhere in sight, and I breathe a sigh of relief. Just as we enter the front yard, we see her sitting on the front porch.

"Come on," I say and lead Sarini out to the sidewalk. By the time we reach car, Sarini is visibly flagging. "Where we going?"

"For now, a hotel. Somewhere you can get cleaned up, take care of the wounds, then I can explain what this is all about. After that—we'll see." *And after that, you'll tell me what Caermon told you. Because Napier is down to six days and I don't have time to wait.*

She gives me a sideways look and says nothing.

Seven

I head east on Interstate 8 to El Cajon, and then north to Lakeside. The area is dotted with small, no-name motels that expect cash for a room and don't ask for identification. I tell the clerk I am alone. He sneers, doesn't believe me, but doesn't care. I register as Henry Cabot. I have a driver's license in that name.

The room smells of stale beer and mold. Cheap gold velvet curtains sport thin spots where the plush has worn off. The TV is bolted to a metal stand.

"I'm sorry," I say. "It isn't much, but I think it'll be safe. What do you need to take care of those wounds?"

"Soap and water. Some band aids would be good."

"I imagine you want a shower. I'll go pick up some supplies, and then come back. Then we'll talk." She nods, her eyes dull and lifeless.

"Are you okay? The shock—should you lie down and elevate your feet, something like that?" I ask.

She shakes her head slowly. "No."

"Lock the door behind me and don't answer the phone."

She heads for the bathroom without acknowledging my request. I try the door and find it will lock on its own. I pull the blinds shut. The room closes in on me.

Thou shalt not kill. A bad translation, one that has haunted generations of English-speaking military men and women. More correctly, the commandment means *do no murder*, a term that excludes killings in self-defense and defense of others. I wonder whether Sarini knows that.

73

By the time I return with the bandages, she has showered and is sitting on the bed, combing her hair with her fingers. A soda is on the bedside table.

She's been out of the room. I hadn't told her not to, just to not answer the door.

"Medicinal sugar," she says, noticing my disapproval. "You brought Band-Aids?"

I hand over the brown paper sack.

"I'll be right back." She disappears into bathroom with the bandages, and returns a few moments later. "They'll heal best without any creams—open to the air, they'll dry out. In a few days, some aloe lotion or something to reduce the scarring."

She settles down on the edge of the bed. "So. Talk."

Where to start? I face the same problem with her that I had with Wister. I can't reveal what Caermon told me, yet understanding it is critical to getting her cooperation. Sitting here, pale, shaken, injured, she's got more of a right to know what I know than Wister did.

"Caermon was starting to feel his own mortality," I say slowly, thinking each sentence through before letting it past my lips. "There were things he needed to talk about—things I can't discuss with you."

"I understand why you *think* you can't."

I let that pass, and continue, "There are at least two groups of people who want very badly to know what Caermon said. The people who killed him and NCIS. And those are just the two I know about. That's why they came after you. Someone was hoping Caermon talked to you, or that you would know where I was."

"Why would I know where you were?" she asks. I notice she ignores the first part of the question.

"Did Caermon talk about anything out of the ordinary?"

"No." Her answer comes too quickly.

"Right after I talked to him, I saw him say something to you."

"He was asking for more pain medication."

"It didn't look like that."

"What did it look like?"

"Like he was telling you something about me."

"He wasn't."

I know she's not telling the truth but I'm in no position to demand that she tell me what she knows, not after I've refused to tell her what I know.

But that was different, wasn't it?

I tell her about the attack on Caermon and how I arrived at her house. "But why can't we go to the police?" she asks when I finish. "I still don't see why not."

I'm still unarmed, but she won't understand that as an explanation. Nor will she understand why Wister was shooting at me. I'm not sure I understand that yet, either.

"There are reasons that the government might not want what Caermon said to be made public," I say finally. "I think we're both in serious danger, and if we go to the police, we may be stepping right into the hands of the people who attacked you. Give me a day, let me check things out."

"Can't you get some sort of special dispensation to talk about it?" she asks.

"Not that I've ever heard of. It's a moral absolute— no balancing the lesser of two evils."

"How long have you been a priest?" she asks.

"Two years."

"Not long. Maybe you should get a second opinion."

I see her point immediately. "I could talk to the Bishop of the Armed Services—that's who I report to as an Episcopal priest. I suppose I could even asked Chaplain Haynes, but I don't think he'd be much help. And then there's the local Episcopal diocese—Bishop Oakes. Maybe they know something I haven't thought of."

"Pick one," she says. She yawns, the bones in her jaw cracking. "Look, I'm off right now. I just finished call, and if I don't get some sleep I'm going to fall over.

She has those instincts from her long residency and training. If there's nothing to do, get some sleep. What seem incongruous is normal for her and I know she's operating in a professional mode now. The emotions will come later.

Nobody's expecting to see me for another thirty-six hours. How about you?"

"My schedule's a little different."

"Will they be looking for us?"

"They'll go to our family and friends first," I say. "I registered here under a false name. The rental car won't be that difficult to trace—I had to use the credit card—but it's parked out of sight. They'll start in the Pacific Beach area, and work their way out. If we can lay low for a little while, it'll give us a chance to come up with a plan."

She yawns again. "Reaction to stress—adrenaline fade. Entirely normal." So is her voice, distant and professional, but that won't last.

"Sleep, then. I'll be back in a few hours."

She leans back on the bed, her eyes fluttering. I let myself out quietly.

Eight

Traffic is light heading back into town. By five o'clock, I'm downtown.

The diocese of San Diego is located next to Saint Andrews' cathedral and built of the same gray stone. I circle the complex twice then park on the street a few blocks away instead of in the diocese parking lot.

Sarini's question about some sort of special dispensation had lit a spark of hope in my heart. Three years at seminary can't cover everything, right? The church exists to deal with sinners and its canons predate most written laws. The Bishop has scholars on his staff, priests with law degrees, and clergy who have years of experience in dealing with the sort of ethical situations that a lone priest might face only once in a lifetime. If there is an answer, a way out, the Bishop will know it.

I've met the Bishop several times, talked with him at length once immediately after I reported in to Balboa. It's standard practice to check in with and develop a relationship with the local diocese. Not only are they closer and more immediately available, but they're also the entrance to a group of your peers, other Episcopal priests in the area. You get to know people, because you never know if you're staying in the Navy forever. Someday you may be back in the civilian diocese, and the transition will be easier if you already know people.

It's also another part of my earlier training. There's nothing quite as valuable as friendly locals when you're in country.

Getting into the diocese offices means buzzing the receptionist and asking to be let in. Too much risk. I go to the coffee shop across the street and take a table at the window. I have a good view of the diocese parking lot. I wait. Twenty minutes later, the Bishop leaves the Diocese office and heads for his car.

Bishop Steven Oakes is fifty years old but looks much younger. His hair is thick, dark and curly, only slightly touched with gray at the temples. From what I hear from the other priests, he's considered to be a tough, fair boss, one that understands the challenges of building congregations in a city growing as fast as San Diego, and one who is often impatient with bureaucracy. There is a sense of mission about him, of dedication, and it draws people to him.

I leave a five-dollar bill on the table and jog across the street to the parking lot. This is the most dangerous part of it, the time when I'm most exposed. If someone is watching the diocese office, I'm in trouble.

Bishop Oakes looks up as he hears my footsteps. He recognizes me immediately.

Not a good sign. I'm out of context. There should have been a hesitation as he tried to place my face.

"Bishop, I need to talk to you."

"I know you do." Oakes unlocks the car. "Get it and stay out of sight."

I slide into the passenger seat. "Bishop, I know this is highly irregular, but—"

"Not now."

The bishop pulls out of the parking lot, then turns north on Sixth Avenue. Two blocks later, he turns into Balboa Park and follows the main thoroughfare into the heart of the densely wooded area. He parks in a corner of the lot. "Let's go for a walk."

Rumor has it that the Bishop's early years were somewhat tumultuous. Before he was called to the ministry, he ran with a rough crowd. A gang, one story says, and hints that at one time he was a very dangerous man. Given his calm demeanor now, I'm inclined to believe the stories. I wonder if he still owns a gun.

I follow him down a crude path that leads into a stand of old hardwood trees. We walk perhaps a quarter of a mile before the bishop stops, looks around, and then takes a seat on a gnarled tree root poking up from the ground.

"You're in trouble," the bishop says. "There are people looking for you. And the stories they're telling me—before we talk any further, I have to know—did you kill anyone?"

"Yes." There's no getting around this one. I fill him in on what happened at Sarini's house, and conclude with, "I didn't have a choice."

The bishop nods. "This complicates matters badly, David. Now tell me the rest of it."

I walk the line between giving the bishop enough information to help me without revealing either the details of the confession or Caermon's identity. I bring him up to date, with the attack in the rose garden, the encounter with Wister, and why I had run.

I wonder again about his background as I watch him soak up the details, nodding when I answer a question before he's asked it. We think alike, the Bishop and I. That worries me.

I finish with, "I thought maybe—Bishop, is there any way out of this?"

The bishop sighs. "I was afraid of this. First, how certain are you that this was a valid confession? Are you convinced that he was seeking to reconcile with God, or was he trying to manipulate you in some way? Put aside your own ego for a moment—looking at it objectively, was he conning you?"

"I've considered that possibility," I admit. "He made very certain that we were speaking under the seal of the confessional and he kept telling me that he repented. I think in his mind he believed what he said was a sufficient confession. Near the end, he insisted that I grant him absolution."

"Did you?"

I look away.

"You withheld absolution, then."

"I was going to, but then—." I stop. "Yes, I did."

"But not because you were in doubt about whether it was truly a confession."

"Partially that, maybe. Mostly because I wanted to know whether he was responsible for something that happened before that."

"Something that concerned you personally?"

"Yes."

The bishop holds up his hand. "You believed it might be a valid confession, yet you withheld absolution for your own reasons."

I can't answer. Up until now, the bishop has been pruning away parts of my story to get to the heart of the matter. But now he's come too close. To explain *why* it mattered to me would be to reveal what Caermon had done and would go to the heart of Caermon's confession.

Then the bishop's point sinks it. During confession, a priest is a conduit for God's grace, not the ultimate decision-maker. A priest cannot know what passes through a man's mind during his last moments of consciousness or during a confession. It's not my place to judge that. I have screwed up badly. *Because I didn't want him to get off until I knew whether he was at fault for something that mattered to me.*

"And that was wrong." I feel his hand on my shoulder. "As were the choices you made after that. Running from the police, from the Navy. From your responsibilities."

I have no response. We sit in silence. I suspect the Bishop is praying for guidance. Finally, I ask, "What am I supposed to do now?"

"Go back to your office. Talk to your own bishop and let him know what's happened. Then Captain Haynes."

"Chaplain Haynes won't understand."

"I think he'll surprise you." So the Bishop knows Captain Haynes. Of course he does—they are peers, albeit different denominations, both senior clergymen responsible for sorting out messes that their juniors create.

I shake my head. "I can't, Bishop."

"Why did you come to me?"

"To ask you if there were any exceptions to the seal of the confessional."

"No. Not if you believe he was making a valid confession."

I had expected this, but it still hits me hard. "That's all I needed to know."

The bishop frowns. "You're not going back."

"Not now."

"Then you're abandoning your duties with the Navy. Do you really think that's the right choice?"

"I think it's my only choice."

The bishop picks up a dry leaf and runs his fingers over it. "This is what happens when it's no longer attached to the tree. It might survive for a short while on its own, living off the energy stored in its own body. But very soon it dies." He glances over at me, seeing if I'm getting his point.

"I've been alone before."

"Not like this." The bishop reaches into his pocket and takes out a folded letter. "The Bishop of the Armed Services called me. Unless you returned immediately to your duties, he's asked me to give you this. He faxed it to me an hour ago."

I unfold the paper. The subject line leaps out at me. It is a letter of prohibition, an order from my bishop that I am not to exercise my priestly powers.

"Do you understand the implications of this?" the bishop asks, his voice stern. "You're still a priest, of course. No mere letter can reverse your ordination and your acceptance into the apostolic succession. But you are ordered not to function as one on pain of excommunication from the body of Christ."

"I understand that," I say. An old joke comes back to me—if the church is the body of Christ, the bishops are His assholes.

"Then reconsider your decision. Report back to Balboa and cooperate with the authorities. No, I'm not telling you to reveal what you were told in confession. And you'll have to deal with your own shortcomings in how you handled the matter. But don't compound your earlier mistakes by ignoring—."

"I can't."

"You must." Oakes is losing his patience. "If you don't, the church will give the Navy and the police all possible assistance and cooperation. I don't think you understand what that means."

I have a momentary insane flash of black-cassocked priests searching the woods for me, Uzis carried at port arms, grenades hanging about their waists. "I can't."

"Well, then. There's nothing more I can do for you." Bishop Oakes stands, brushing leaves off his pants.

"There is one more thing," I say. "I'm unarmed. Are you?"

A long silence then. Oakes' face is still, impassive, but fire burns in his eyes. I have recognized something in him that he would rather keep hidden, that past that he carries with him as surely as I carry Muralis Island. "I will pray for you, David," he says, and then walks away.

I follow him without speaking through the woods to his car. He drops me off next to my rental car.

Nine

I stop for a pizza on the way back to the motel. Sarini is still asleep when I return. I put the pizza on the table, contemplate waking her up then eat three pieces myself. With hunger assuaged, exhaustion sweeps over me.

Not as tough as I used to be, am I? This wouldn't have bothered me six years ago.

But that was six years ago. Dalt today isn't nearly the man Dalt six years ago was, at least not in terms of being able to ignore pain, exhaustion and hunger. I lost those skills somewhere after Muralis Island.

There is only one double bed in the room, and I don't want to give the wrong message by stretching out on the other side. Besides, she needs sleep more than I do.

One hour. That used to be enough to clear the cobwebs. I stretch out on the floor. Sleep comes quickly.

Sixty minutes later, I'm wake. Sarini's still out but it's six o'clock—time for evening news. I turn on the TV, keeping the sound low and hoping not to wake her, but she moans and rolls over.

For a moment, confusion dominates her expression. She touches the bandages on her chest, then turns to look at me. "Dalt?" As she remembers where we are and what's happened, her face sags, looking much older. "Oh."

"There's pizza," I say, pointing at the table. "Holds up better than burgers."

She starts to get up then winces at the pain. "I should've expected this—it's going to get worse before it gets better."

"Anything I can get you?"

"Another soda. That one's hot."

"Can you wait for the commercial?" I ask. She nods.

The opening credits roll, then the teasers for the evening's stories.

"A killer priest turned kidnapper," a blond anchorwoman proclaims, a suitable look of deep concern on her face. My official Navy photo flashes up on the screen behind her, and then Sarini's. "Our story after this message." A commercial begins.

Sarini turns to me, shock evident on her face. "What the hell is that?"

"A cover story."

She rolls off the bed and stands. "That does it. We have to go to the police now. You're not a kidnapper, and as for the other part, they'll understand."

"Not a chance. Listen, if I'm going to get your soda, I have to go now."

"Fuck the soda. Damn it, David, this is insane!" She begins gathering up her things, slipping her shoes back on. "If you won't take me, I'm calling a cab."

"No. Listen, just wait until after the news, okay? Then give me fifteen minutes. If you still want to leave, I won't stop you."

Her face goes cold. "And you'd try to stop me if I don't?"

"No!" I have fouled this up badly. "Just fifteen minutes. That's not too much to ask, is it? Just the news, that's all. And no, I wouldn't try to stop you now."

"Why? Why the news?" She's not sitting down yet, but she's not bolting for the door, either.

I move away from the door, giving her a clear shot out if she wants to leave. "Whether it's true or not, it's what people are going to believe. They saw it on the news—it has to be true, right?"

"But it's not what happened. The truth is the truth." And it is to her. It's what she sees on a slide, what is recorded in a chart, what the lab reports say. Objective, verifiable, unchanging. Despite her experience with death, she knows nothing about the deeper layers and the bottom currents. Or at least she chooses not to know.

"It's the truth now. It's been on TV. That's all most people care about."

"And how do you know that?"

"My father. He's spent a lifetime creating truth. I don't think he's involved in this, but people like him are. I want to see what they're putting together." Her face is still unbelieving. "Please. Fifteen minutes."

The commercials are over and the lead story starts. The newscaster reads the chilling lead-in off her teleprompter again. Navy file photos of both of us flash up on the screen behind her. We both look younger, less real.

The next story is a fuller coverage of the murder at Sarini's house, filled with speculations about my involvement and my possible motives. When the anchor details my alleged obsession with Sarini, I feel my face turn red.

"Any truth to that?" Sarini asks.

"No," I say. "None at all." But I knew where she lived, what her schedule was.

She sits on the edge of the bed, a look of professional concern on her face, the same expression she used to calm Caermon's wife. "This can be straightened out. I think you're panicking needlessly. All we have to do is tell them what happened."

But the news isn't over. I shush her, and point to the TV screen. An overhead view of her house has replaced the two file photos. Then there's a quick cut to the front of a house—for a moment, I think it's Sarini's, but I see the frown on her face and I know it's not.

A yellow police tape runs around the small yard. There's a footpath down the side of the yard, the one I walked down to get to her house.

An airbrushed male reporter is transmitting live from the site. His name appears at the bottom of the screen. The screen is split between the anchor newscaster and him.

"Peter, what can you tell us?" the blonde anchor asks. His shot expands to fill the screen.

"Jane, I'm here at the scene of what police are calling a related tragedy. The house you see behind me is directly behind the kidnap victim's house. Two hours ago, Helen Smith's son came over for dinner and found her dead in the kitchen. The cause of death is apparently a gunshot wound to the head."

"What's the connection, Peter?"

"With me here is Detective Brady Harness, who will be heading up the investigation." A bluff, serious-looking officer steps into the picture. "Detective Harness, what can you tell us?"

"We're in the preliminary stages of investigation, of course," the detective begins. He's had some practice at this—he's coming across just right. "But we've recently come across some information that leads us to believe that our original theory was wrong. According to hospital officials, the alleged kidnapping victim, Doctor Sarah Sarini, has been under investigation for several weeks in connection with inventory irregularities and medications. As an emergency room doctor, she had access to virtually unlimited quantities of narcotics, and there are some questions about her in connection with them." The cop stops, well-trained to allow the reporter to appear to be a participant.

"Is there any indication she may have been using them herself?" the reporter asks.

The detective shakes his head. "No, not yet, although as a physician she would have known how to conceal her drug abuse better than most of us. However, the quantities of narcotics found in her house indicate that they were packaged for resale."

"So she was selling narcotics?"

"It's too soon to say for sure, but it looks that way." Both the reporter and the cop have grave, concerned looks on their faces.

Sarini has gone pale. I don't even have to ask.

"And the connection with the murder of Helen Smith?"

"It's just a theory right now, but it's possible that Miss Smith saw something she wasn't supposed to. As you can see, she's got a good view of Sarini's house from her back yard."

"And her connection to the priest, Father David Dalt?"

The detective shrugs. "We don't know yet. Perhaps he was buying them from her. Or he might have found out about it and come over to her house to confront her. There are too many possibilities right now, and we're keeping an open mind on it."

"The narcotics you found in her house—can you give us an idea of quantities, of what kinds?"

"Mostly morphine, all still in the packing it was shipped in. Demerol, Vicodin, Oxycotin, both in tablets and liquid form. A supply of syringes and other drug paraphernalia. About what you'd expect."

"Is it possible that Helen Smith was killed by Lieutenant Dalt and Doctor Sarini? Did she see too much? Or is this a simple drug deal gone bad?"

"At this point, anything is possible." The detective turns to look into the camera. "We need both of them to come forward at this point and clear this up."

From off camera, the anchor's voice: "Peter, what is the Navy saying about this?"

"There's been no official comment from the Navy as yet, but sources tell us that there may be a tie in with the shooting earlier today at Balboa Naval Hospital."

I focus on the background and see Wister. He is turned slightly away from me, as though to avoid the camera, but I recognize his profile and his sports jacket.

He knows I am watching. This entire charade of lies has been concocted purely for my ears, and his appearance in the background is no accident. He wants me to know he knows, and is convinced that he can drive me into his arms by showing me his resources.

An effective use of sixty seconds, but the news media isn't going to give him any more than that. I'm not

OJ Simpson, and there are other stories. As if on cue, the picture cuts back to the studio. Our blonde anchor is shaking her head. She turns to her compadre. "Bad business all around, isn't it, Carter?"

"It sure is. And speaking of business, a new venture in La Jolla just may be the ticket to the internet." The blonde anchor manages the segue easily, and they're off and running.

"I don't believe this," Sarini says. She's still staring at the screen. "How can they just make that up? I'll lose my license. I won't even be able to go into private practice, not after that."

"It's their story. Their truth."

She turns on me. "But it's *not* true. It's *not.* How can they get away with something like that?"

"They can. They will." I wish I did not know what I know about truth and its malleable nature in the right hands. "And they can undo it just as easily. But they've got to have a reason for it. Somebody's gone to an awful lot of trouble to make you look bad. That's why I have to know what Caermon told you."

"I told you. He asked for some more pain medication." She stares at me, angry, looking for someone to be responsible, to be at fault. I can't blame her—none of this was of her making, and yet now she's in as deep as I am.

I'm watching her, feeling an overwhelming reluctance to draw her any further into this. If it comes down to it, all I really need is her silence for a while, but even that will put her at risk.

But she's already in it. They've tried to find out what she knows once. If it's that important to them—whoever they are—then it's that important to me.

Caermon. Who wanted Caermon and anyone he talked to dead?

First, Arcadia itself. If Arcadia was certain—or even reasonably certain—that Caermon was the problem, they might have taken steps to eliminate the problem without a lengthy trial.

Second, someone Caermon betrayed. Someone like me. Justice by assassination.

Third, his foreign masters. Perhaps Caermon had doubled back and was providing misinformation in order to stay out of trouble with the American government.

Finally, another branch of the government, for reasons unknown. I hold no illusions about the working of intelligence agencies. Wister's already lying to me. Others will, too.

Why?

For the same reason Caermon was not allowed to leave his room. They were waiting for—for what? To see what Caermon said? To see if anyone approached him?

Wister—he's the enigma in all of this. Simply because he's an NCIS agent is no reason for me trust him more than anyone else.

But it does give me a reason to use him.

The first thing I need to do is clear the playing field. There are too many pieces in motion, too much confusion. Wister, my father, the Navy, whoever shot Caermon—all they can do is slow me down right now since I can't tell any of them what I intend to do.

But what about Sarini? She is my responsibility as certainly as Napier is. Until I know who's behind Caermon's assassination, I won't know who is after her. And if I don't know that, I don't know who can keep her safe while dealing with Napier. She'll have to stay with me.

I feel reborn, resurrected. No more groping around in the dark currents of men's lives. No more squeezing the transcendent into cold hospital rooms and crowded waiting areas.

This must be how Jesus felt at Gethsemane. Everything else peels away and you stand naked and alone confronted only with what really matters.

An odd peace descends on me. The metronome still beats in the background but the urgency has leached out of it. It's just keeping track of time, not laughing at how slow I'm moving. Now I know that seminary, ordination, the assignment to Balboa were all just six years of simply delaying the inevitable.

The first principle of special operations is to maintain focus on the objective. You do that with proper preparation and by eliminating distractions, using all available assets. The essence of special forces maneuver warfare is turning all elements of the battlefield to your advantage.

Father David Dalt, United States Naval Chaplain Corps, currently assigned to the Veteran's Hospital in San Diego, isn't quite sure what all that means. "Boomer" Dalt, Navy Seal, aka Scorpion, knows exactly what has to come next.

The enemy of my enemy is my friend. I have to stop my father.

Ten

Finding Wister is no more difficult than finding Bishop Oakes had been. NCIS doesn't expect fugitives to lurk outside its building watching people come and go. When Wister returns from lunch, I know what he drives. It is a simple matter to jimmy his door and crouch down in the back seat to wait for him.

I wait until he is well clear of the base before I rise up. "Pull over." He does so. I move from the back seat to the passenger seat.

Wister sighs. "Dalt, you're in a hell of a lot of trouble." He turns slightly toward me and the light catches him at a new angle. I look him over again, trying to take his measure.

He's in his mid-forties or so. Fighting to stay in shape, taking care of himself. The lines along his jaw are starting to blur a bit and he's got a rough, wind-burned look to his skin. His eyes are the most expressive part of him, I suspect, when he will let them be, which isn't now. Now he's simply pissed, maybe a little scared, too, but he's not going to let on.

I answer with, "Last time we talked, you mentioned my father. Why?"

"Why do you think?"

"You tell me."

"It's classified."

"So?"

Wister studies me for a moment and apparently reaches some decision. "There've been a few operations that haven't gone off as they were supposed to. Booby-traps, ambushes, that sort of thing. CinCPac thinks there's a leak."

"And you think my father is responsible for compromising classified material?"

"No. Not really. But he does know something he's not sharing. With him," Wister spreads his hands, a gesture of frustration, "you get close, you get lost. You follow me?"

I do. My father is the ultimate Teflon man. "So you need some hold on him. Some way to make him cooperate." Wister would be better off just telling my father what the problem was and letting my father solve things his own way, but that won't happen, not with inter-agency warfare the way it is in the intelligence community. At the level my father plays the game, Wister would be a toddler.

"If we had some way to get him to cooperate," Wister says, "it'd make things go a lot easier."

"Some dirt on him, maybe."

Wister gives me a speculative look. "That might do it. Depends on what he's done."

I let the silence stretch out a bit. This is harder than I thought it would be and there's no going back from it. Wister's good. He waits. Finally, I say, "Murder good enough?"

"Caermon?"

I ignore the question. "What's in it for me?"

"The thanks of a grateful nation."

I laugh.

"Immunity, if you need it," he continues, descending from the sublime to the practical.

"The man at Sarini's house—it was self-defense. I don't care what bullshit story you're putting out, you know that's the truth."

"Up to a judge and a jury, determining the truth." Wister senses that this is the wrong thing to say. "But if Sarini's story backs you up, it'll go away. Speaking of Sarini—."

"She's fine."

"I'm supposed to take your word on that?"

"Come on, you know she doesn't really matter."

"What are you doing here?" Wister asks, and I see honest curiosity in his face. "If you know something about your father, you're doing the right thing. But fathers and sons—well, it's got to be difficult." And he slides a bit into technique, trying to draw me in and make me feel that he sympathizes. Yet beneath the craft, I feel his curiosity.

"When I was ten," I begin, "my mother died. An accident, they said. But it wasn't."

"You're certain? Ten years old, you can misunderstand a lot."

"I'm certain. My father killed her."

Wister lets out a low whistle. "And you saw it?"

"I did."

There's a silence while he digests this. He's not as good at masking his thoughts as my father is. Finally, when it appears to be sorted into neat categories in his mind, he continues. "Old news. What else have you got?"

Nothing. Nothing but suspicions. "I can't tell you. Not yet."

"You're in no position to bargain right now, Mister." Wister is losing patience with me. "I'm through playing games. You're under arrest."

I waggle the knife at him. "I don't have time to be under arrest right now."

Wister sighs. "This is all bullshit, Dalt. Get the hell out of my car." It's tough to play good cop/bad cop when you're alone, but he's taking a shot at it.

"Look, I'll surrender next week. I've got something I've got to do first."

"A week?"

"Five days," I amended. If I can't find Naps and stop him before them, it won't matter anyway.

"This got to do with Sarini?" Wister asks.

"Some of it does."

He smirks. I almost punch him. He thinks I'm sleeping with her, that I don't want to give that up. Fine, let him think that.

93

"Three days, that's all. Come on, you know it would take that long to work out an immunity deal with the US Attorney if I decided to surrender."

"I'm not agreeing to this. Not at all."

"One more thing—that bit about Sarini and the drugs. Clear it up. Put out a retraction just like you put the story out in the first place."

"What story?"

We both know it's a pro forma objection. "When I see the retraction, I'll know we've got a deal."

"So this is all about vengeance, then? You're getting back at him for your mother's death?"

"You could say that. It sounds reasonable, doesn't it?"

He nods. "It will to a jury. Especially if we don't have to charge you with the homicide at Sarini's house."

"Okay, we have a deal."

"Not a deal," Wister says. "Since you're not surrendering."

"Three days, that's all." It's actually five days but three will be enough to get me out of the country and beyond his easy reach.

I have Wister drive down a side street and let me out. I run across traffic and before he can make a U-turn and follow, I'm gone.

Smooth, so smooth. The set-up, the escape, the entire story I fed him. I review the encounter and decide that it was possibly the best operation I've ever pulled off. No flaws that I can detect.

I am ashamed. And proud.

Muralis Island is always with me. I can't move beyond it, no matter how hard I try. A better priest would be able to cope with what happened there, would understand that he is forgiven, would put it behind him as God has and move on with his ministry.

I cannot.

No. I am a priest, damn it! A priest.

And a killer. During my days in the Navy, and most recently, the man at the man at Sarini's house. Their blood is on my hands, the stain is on my soul.

Intellectually, I understand that God has forgiven these sins, especially the ones that were committed during my Navy days. The killing at Sarini's house is a closer call, but not by much. If I hadn't intervened, he would've killed Sarini. He had already demonstrated his willingness to inflict serious bodily harm, and I had no doubt he would have taken it as far as necessary. I think even the court of law would find the innocent of that one, on the grounds of defense of others.

Still, there had been other options. I could have disabled him—yes, I could have. I know those techniques just as well is the ones I used to kill him. I could have disabled him, secured him, and called the police.

So why hadn't I?

Because I had acted according to my character and according to my training. And I killed him.

On another level, I harbor serious doubts that the stains from my days as a SEAL were truly wiped out. As far as the east is from the west, the scripture says. I knew that was so, I did—yet I did not believe it. I could feel the scars still, and my conduct in Sarini's house proved who I really was.

Again, the stunning lack of faith, such a fatal flaw in a priest. If I could not believe that I been forgiven, and that was not sufficient, that who was I to lead others? Who am I even to administer any of the rites that I was ordained to do, especially that of reconciliation.

For the last three years, I've trudged through the days, saying the daily offices and celebrating Eucharist, visiting men and women and talking about a just and loving God. But how close to God can I be when I can't even acknowledge my own forgiveness?

Even worse, at the very first opportunity, I killed again. What evidence of repentance is that? Am I no better than Caermon, bargaining with men's lives for the words he wanted me to say?

The hardest part of it all is that I have no regrets. Faced with the situation at Sarini's house again, I would do exactly the same thing. Cleaning the gene pool, we used to say in the SEALs. Kill a commie for your mommy. All those flip remarks we use to make light of taking a human life, to trivialize it and put it in a context we can deal with. Killing versus murder. Pretending there's a difference.

I cannot believe I've been forgiven for those killings or for abandoning my men on Muralis Island. I can't be—I haven't truly repented, not for all of it. I'm certain of that.

Because if I had known who Caermon was, what he had done, I would not have waited for the sniper.

Eleven

Five days left. Wister will either do what I want him to or he won't. I have planted the seed—if it does not come to fruition, my father will find me. Find me, and stop me.

I need two things: information and a weapon. While I'm convinced that Caermon was telling the truth, good planning requires that I confirm what he's told me.

Sarini—she's in a funk. Things have changed too rapidly for her, and, even worse, she has no control over anything. She is oddly unresponsive, her emotions and affect flattened. She is coping as best she can, but for now, she is more of a liability than an asset. If it were safe for her to return, I'd let her go.

But it's not safe to let her just go back to her life as though nothing happened. Like it or not, she's my responsibility and I know from Muralis Island how impossible it is to live with shirking those.

The church and the hospital can't help me now. The best I can expect of law enforcement, especially Wister, is that they'll stay out of my way and keep my father busy.

I have kept track of my shipmates in the SEALs from a distance through routine message correspondence, promotion list announcements, and unclassified information that makes its way into the *Navy Times* and the local papers. I don't stay in touch with any of them individually, though. Not any more. I tried that once when I first returned to San Diego, out of desperate loneliness. But there were three gulfs to cross: time, resigning from the

Teams, and ordination. In the end, I quit trying to talk to them and simply kept track of them.

The pressures on a new priest are different from those I experienced at any other time at my life. In the SEALS, and in the Navy in general, no matter where you are, you immediately belong. What's on your collar and shoulder tells you who you are, what you do and how you're expected to act and react in any situation.

This is especially true in close-knit units like the SEALS. You belong, you have to, because no matter how you may feel about each other personally, at some point your lives will depend on each other. There is an instant taking of each other's measure, and a bonding that takes place because of what you will face. It is cemented over time with experience and alcohol, but it exists from the very first moment you cross the Quarterdeck to check in.

Not so for priests. By our calling, we are set aside from the rest of the world. Our very appearance keeps people at a distance. People feel a vague sense of uneasiness around us, as though we know their secrets. It is the same problem I face with Sarini.

I came to chastity late in life, and have not found it easy. I want very much to get close Sarini, to know her as a person, to touch that skin and see if it's really as smooth under my fingertips as it looks, to see her eyes half-close, the need in them, and later—.

No. As I said, chastity has not been easy.

How much of what Caermon told me should I believe? Was Napier really going back to Muralis Island?

I know who will know. Bill Jenkins, my old swim buddy, now a chief petty officer and still in the SEALs. Jenkins is originally from New Hampshire, the kind of quiet, taciturn Yankee you expect from a remote area of the state. He doesn't talk much but manages to communicate a great deal in his short, clipped phrases and his expressions. He is as strong as any man I've ever met, not spare ounce of fat on him.

Every junior officer needs someone like Jenkins, an experienced noncommissioned officer who'll keep you from looking stupid. Jenkins was that to me—my sea daddy, in Navy lingo. He kept me out of trouble, at least until Muralis Island. Nothing could have saved me then.

Jenkins bought land decades ago in Crest, a small community to the south of El Cajon, back when land was still affordable. Twenty-five acres, much of it too steep to be usable, but with a large, flat ten-acre spot in the middle accessible only by a dirt road. He moved his family there and they lived in a trailer while he built their house, timber by timber. It took three years. I suspect it was the relative isolation that attracted him the most. The area is accessible only by the one road, an access easily controlled. I'm fairly sure he still lives there.

Jenkins is now operations chief for SEAL Group One. If anyone will know the down and dirty, he will.

Will he talk to me? I don't know. What I need to know is undoubtedly classified, as all operational details are. Even though I still have a Top Secret Compartmented clearance, I have no official need to know.

Getting complete sentences out of Jenkins isn't easy. It will be even more difficult with ten years in prison and a ten thousand dollar fine hanging over his head.

But even if I can't get information for Jenkins, I know what he will give me—what I couldn't retrieve from my own house.

Sarini is still asleep on the bed. Her face is peaceful. She believes herself to be safe with me, even alone under conditions that would raise suspicions otherwise. Unfortunately, she is right.

I sit on the small bed next her and touch her shoulder. She comes instantly awake and knows where she is.

"Good morning," I say. "Ready for something to eat?"

She yawns, then stretches like a cat under the thin blanket. She's used to working the night shifts, not to keeping these hours. In addition to everything else, the change in her schedule has her disoriented.

She crawls out of bed, stretches again, then runs her fingers through her hair. "Just a minute," she says. She disappears into the bathroom. I hear the toilet flush them and water running. Three minutes later, she emerges, looking completely awake.

"There's somewhere we need to go," I say. "A drive-through window breakfast okay?"

She nods. "Where?"

"I thought McDonald's."

She shakes her head. "No, I mean where are we going after that?"

I knew what she meant, but just for a moment I wanted desperately to pretend that everything was normal. "An old friend," I say. "I need information, and he may be willing to help."

"Navy?"

"Yes. SEALs." How much does she know about my past? She's probably heard the rumors around hospital, maybe even some of the classified stories. She may even know as much about me as I know about her.

I fill her in on part of the story on the way to Jenkins': that'd I'd been a SEAL, that a mission had gone wrong. I don't tell her everything, just enough so she'll understand.

"And then you decided to go to seminary," she says when I quit talking.

"No. I knew I was going to be a priest. Seminary was just a prerequisite."

She is silent for a moment then asks, "Why? You had some sort of religious experience or something?"

"Or something," I say. Someday, maybe I'll tell her what happened out on the rocks of Muralis Island.

Or maybe I won't. Even now, even though it is as real to me as though I was still there, I know that not everyone will understand. The few times I tried to discuss it in seminary, the reactions ranged from a detailed scientific explanation of life-threatening stress on the brain to an admonishment against pride. I have quit trying to explain it and content myself with the complete and utter certainty that God spoke personally to me.

I won't talk about it now. It's too much at odds with who I have to be to survive.

It's been six years since I made this drive, and the exits and surface roads in this part of El Cajon have changed. Finally, I find a dirt road—I missed it the first time, but find it as I come back. There's a line of mailboxes nearby, maybe sixteen of them. The setup looks ramshackle but I'm willing to bet it's far sturdier than it looks.

Jenkins' mailbox is somewhere in the middle, not standing out from anything else, not marking his driveway in particular. He would be careful like that, to give no indication that this was the road to his house. Nevertheless, I'm certain I remember it correctly.

The bushes next to the entrance are slightly overgrown, giving the driveway an untended look. This is intentional as well. I can see there's enough room for a car to pass through without scraping its sides if I make a slight jog to the left, and then one to the right. After that, the road opens up and is well-trimmed on either side.

The gravel road has a grated cattle crossing in the middle of it, and for a moment I wonder at that. The area around his house was fenced back then and I don't remember Jenkins raising cattle. But then I understand the purpose of it as we drive over—the distinctive rattling sound carries. I stop the car, get out, look around for a moment. It's around here somewhere, I suspect. It might even be equipment liberated from the SEALs, although not necessarily so. Technology is cheap. No need to steal what you can buy.

Then I spot it, high in the crook of a eucalyptus tree. A small black box, the lens aimed right at the road. The bushes are trimmed back to give it an excellent view.

I smile and wave. Jenkins will recognize me, but I'm not sure his wife will. No matter—by finding his surveillance camera, I have either put her on guard or let her know that I'm one of them. Or was at one time, at least.

I climb back in the car and pull away, going slowly. Sarini shoots me a curious look. "What was that all about?"

"Jenkins' a careful fellow. He values his privacy. I wasn't sure exactly where it would be, but I figured he would have a way of seeing who was coming and going."

She is slightly incredulou, but she had seen the camera. I think she may suspect that it was all show for her benefit. I'm fairly pleased myself that I managed to find it.

The road cuts back sharply once, twice, and curves around in front of the sprawling house. It's built of wood, the sides stained dark brown, and it blends well with the vegetation. It's richly landscaped, meticulously so, but with a sense of wildness and excellent use of native vegetation. A few chickens scatter when I pull up.

A large Rottweiler moves slowly out of the shadows, her back legs stiff, her tail held high. She stands by the car, not jumping up, just watching. The menace in their eyes is clear. I know that if I try to get out, I will regret it.

Sarini looks distinctly uneasy now. But she keeps quiet.

The Rottweiler betrays Jenkins by turning her head and wagging her tail. I glanced in the rear view mirror and see Jenkins approaching. He's carrying a shotgun at his side, and I have no doubt that it's loaded. He comes up on the side, at an awkward angle for anyone in the car to either see or draw down on.

"Hold your hands out and keep them in view," I say quietly to Sarini.

"This is a friend of yours?" she asks, but she complies. I make sure my own hands are visible from behind is well.

Then Jenkins is standing next to the window, looking in, as surprised as I've ever seen him. He turns to the dog and says, "Off." The Rottweiler immediately drops her menacing posture and ambles back to the shade. Then Jenkins turns back to me. He opens the door.

"Been a while," he says. "Something I can do for you?"

I nod, and feel myself starting to fall back into his rhythms. It's hard to be around him without feeling that you're entirely too talkative. "Maybe something I can do for you," I say.

He considers this for a moment, and grunts. I recognize it as a sound of agreement. He steps back from the door and I climb out slowly.

"Okay if she comes?" I say, motioning to Sarini.

He nods. "Hot out here." He glances overhead, and I wonder he's whether he's talking about more than the weather.

"Come on," I say to Sarini. She steps out then I sketched the introductions. We follow Jenkins into his house.

The inside hasn't changed much since the first time I saw it. There's a warm, comfortable air to it, somewhat at odds with how I perceive Jenkins himself, and nothing to indicate he's in the Navy. Perhaps I don't understand him as well as I thought, or perhaps it is his wife's influence. At any rate, the house feels immediately welcoming.

The house itself, aside from the relatively closed off front, is built as a gradual transition from outside the inside. The living room opens up onto a sunroom, with windows that slidee back and screens already in place. Past that there's a large porch covered with slats overhead allowing the sun in, open on the sides. There's a built-in barbecue grill and stove as well as countertops, sinks and running water. Just past that is a grassy area, with fruit trees and gardens. One can choose exactly the area of the house appropriate to the temperature that day.

I see something now that I missed on my earlier visits as well. Or maybe I didn't miss it but back then it was such a part of our lives that we took it for granted. But that tree house over there, positioned just so—Jenkins has this place set up as a fortress. He has firing positions, fields of fire well-defined, and I have no doubt that every member of his family has a specific assignment in event of an emergency. I wouldn't be surprised to find weapons cached outside within easy reach, just in case, protected from the environment by heavy plastic sheeting.

Jenkins sees my inspection and a wariness creeps into his eyes. I wasn't supposed to notice. I have no doubt that changes will be made after I leave.

"I'm in trouble, Jenkins," I say. I see a flicker of recognition in his eyes. The evening news reports. "I'm not a kidnapper, and he needed killing." I turned to Sarini. "Tell him what happened. I'm going to walk over there." I point over towards the chicken coop, well away from his defensive positions.

"Tell him yourself," she says.

I shake my head, my gaze locked on Jenkins'. "He wants to hear it from you, so he knows I don't have a hold on you. That you're here of your own free will. He's thinking that I may have a hostage somewhere, your kid or something. But I can tell you, if I did, the last person I'd want coming after me is Jenkins. So, tell him. I'll be back in a minute."

I turned, exposing my back to him and the shotgun. I head for the chicken coop, hearing Sarini's soft voice start behind me. I can't hear Jenkins say anything, but I know he's listening, searching her face for anything that she's not saying. He'll know if she's telling the truth or not, and that will affect his decision on whether or not to kill me.

I suppose I should be offended. After all, we're former teammates. Jenkins should simply believe my word over hers automatically.

But after what was on the news, I'm not going to ask that of him. So I let them talk, walking far enough away to not hear their voices.

It only takes a few moments, and Sarini says, "Come on back." I head back up the path to them. There's a look of approval in Jenkins' eyes.

"You got some troubles," he allows. "Looking for somewhere to hide out?"

I shake my head. "No. Just information and a weapon. A nine millimeter, if you have a spare one." My father's choice of weapons is not mine. Even if it was, I feel naked with only one weapon.

And of course Jenkins' got a spare one. Within the Teams, he was known for his love of weapons. He maybe a little bit reluctant to part with one, but I know he will, now that he believes I was justified in killing the man at Sarini's house.

"What do you want to know?" Jenkins waits.

"Where's Napier right now?" I ask.

"Out."

In the field, then. "Somewhere I've been?" I can't ask him if it's Muralis Island, but if he says yes, then at least I'll have a little confirmation of Caermon's story. But he's not going to answer, not the way he's looking and me. "I wouldn't ask if it weren't critical."

"Yes."

"Where?"

Another long silence. Finally, Jenkins speaks.

"Say there was an operation," he says. "A lot of planning going into it, a whole lot. Money, too. There's a couple of people who put their careers on the line about it, maybe. Security would be tight, tighter than anything you ever saw on the teams. Most people who would usually know things don't have a clue."

"So it's like that," I say. Jenkins nods. "How about a weapon at least? She told you what happened—I can't get to my own because they're watching my house. The next time, I might not be so lucky."

Jenkins' expression clears slightly. "I can do that."

I follow him into the back bedroom located on the north side of the house. He opens a gun safe, considers the possibilities, and then extracts a black nine millimeter. "This ought to be about what you're used to." He passes it to me, after checking to make sure it's unloaded, and opens the other cabinet to pull out some ammunition.

I take it, pull the slide back to check the chamber. I run my finger down the barrel, then, seeing Jenkins smile fade slightly, I rub it off on my shirt, removing the oils my fingers left on the barrel. "I'll take care of it," I promise. And I will, as much as I can under the circumstances.

He hands me two boxes in ammunition, two hundred rounds. "That enough?"

"If it's not, I'm in trouble."

I take the boxes and heft them, the weight so familiar. Yes, I made my choices, but the feel of the weapon, the smell, the bond between us as I reverently take what he has preserved—I revel in it, far beyond what I'd suspected.

God, how I miss this!

"I'll take care of it," I say again.

"Give me one, too," Sarini says unexpectedly.

Jenkins hesitates then turns to me. I nod. It's not fair to ask her to go unarmed when everyone else is.

He examines his arsenal. "Shotgun would be best. But I don't expect you'd want to be carrying one."

"Not a shotgun," Sarini says. "A small pistol."

Jenkins considers the issue a moment longer, then extracts a smaller handgun. It's a 38. Not the stopping power of my weapon, but probably easier to handle.

He reaches into the back of his safe and pulls out a smaller box of rounds. "Glaziers," he says.

With a Glazier round, Sarini won't have to be real accurate. All she'll have to do is hit her target somewhere. Touch him, and he's dead. Because the hollow-pointed nose on a Glazier breaks open on impact, and it acts like a small shotgun shell shredding everything in its path. Yes, it's got stopping power. More than enbugh.

He hands me the box. "Pricey little bastards, they are," he says. To Jenkins, anything he has to pay for is pricey. That's why he loads his own.

Sarini takes it, pops it open to make sure it's unloaded, and examines it. Jenkins nods his approval. She may not know it, but she's just passed a test.

"Grew up with them," she says. "You never know when you're going to run across a rattlesnake."

"Thought so. Country girl like that, you don't have to worry," he says.

How had he known that about her? With Jenkins, there always moments when he surprises you. He looks over at me, as though I've misled him. I haven't.

I hear footsteps. Suddenly a small, dark woman peers into the room. She speaks quietly to Jenkins, her accent so deep and hard I can barely understand her. Jenkins stares at me, his face ice. "Someone's coming."

Jenkins moves to the far corner of his bedroom, to a black and white monitor. It looks like an ordinary television, with an A/B switch on the table next to it. It's showing a grainy black and white picture, leaves obscuring one edge of it. Jenkins makes an impatient sound, then moves a joystick slightly. If you didn't know any better, you would think it was a video game set up.

The screen shows a car stopped at the cattle grate, motionless. I see two occupants. It's a nondescript sedan, black walled tires.

"Can you zoom in?" I ask.

Jenkins adjusts a small wheel on the side of the joystick stick, and the picture momentarily pulses, resolves, this time centered on the interior of the car.

I recognize both of them. The driver is the NCIS agent who'd taken down my name and address at the hospital, and passenger is Wister. They're both sitting, waiting for the gates open. Wister gets out and walks to the speaker box. He presses the button. A chime sounds in the house.

Jenkins looks over me. "Going to have to do something about this," he says. "This ain't Waco."

"How did he find me?" I ask. "Never mind, it doesn't matter now—we have to get out of here." Sarini is watching us with wide-eyed astonishment.

"You can't get out of here," Jenkins says. He points at the open window, and I can hear it clearly—the distinctive sound of a helicopter. "

"But why let me run?" I asked. "If we were under surveillance, they could have taken us any time."

Jenkins doesn't answer. He doesn't have to. We both know why. Wister wanted to see where I would go.

"Dark," Jenkins says, as though continuing conversation we were having. "That's the best plan."

Indeed it is, although it's not perfect. Even if we can make it to the tree line, if the helicopter is carrying infrared gear, he'll be able to track us. We'll have to wait until dark, when men on the ground will have a tougher time supporting the helicopter's locating data.

Jenkins goes to the large masonry fireplace in one corner of the room. It's almost five feet tall and clearly well-used. There's firewood stacked on the back porch. Jenkins reaches up the chimney, gropes around. Something goes clink, and he steps back out. He then kneels down, grabs a crack in the stone hearth, and yanks. After momentary resistance, a section of stone slides out of place and opens up onto blackness below.

"Down you go. Wait it out while I get rid of them."

Sarini is backing up, fear evident on her face. "This is where I quit."

"You said you were in."

"I know, but—"

"You asked for a weapon."

She falls silent at that. Yes, she did, and the time to object was when I handed it to her.

"There're candles down there," Jenkins says, not unkindly. "Won't be too long."

"How long is the drop?" I ask.

"About six feet."

I position myself over the opening, and support myself with my hands. I lower myself down, and let go, and drop to the ground. There's dirt under my feet, hard packed. From the light shining through the open opening, I locate the candles. Matches are nearby. He has thought of everything.

Sarini thumps down next to me. Her breathing is shallow and too fast.

"Claustrophobic?" I ask.

She nods, her face pale.

I hand her the candle. It may make her feels like she's got a little more control over things.

"Radio is one way only," Jenkins' voice says from speaker in the corner. "I'll shut it off if they get in so they won't hear the echo, but you can hear this first part." I suspect there's a way to turn the speaker on and off down here as well, but I don't say anything.

"Who is it?" we hear Jenkins' voice ask. There's an unintelligible response, then, "What do you want?" Another spate of noise, longer this time. Followed by, "Not without a warrant."

I wonder if that's a good move. Surely they can see a car that matches the description of my rental car in his yard, and they're going to know that we're here.

Then, "I want to see it first," Jenkins says, and I groan. Sarini puts her hand over my mouth, and I smell her fresh scent.

So they came with a warrant. They've got enough evidence, then, to convince some judge that I'm here. How long has the helo been watching us?

"Shutting down now. Keep quiet, I'll let you know when it's safe to come out." There's a small click and the faint background static from the speaker stops.

The compartment is roughly six by six feet, dirt walls, plywood overhead, and support beams along the walls. I suspect there's a layer of dirt between our ceiling and Jenkins' floor. He would not want any searcher to encounter a hollow spot as he walked across the floor. The compartment has that feeling of being underground, the quiet, sound-deadening quality to it.

I motion to Sarini, and draw her over against one wall. We sit down the floor and lean up against the wall. She's shivering, the candle flame flickering as she does. I gently take it and place it on the floor in front of us.

Time seems to stop. Under stress, without external input, it's impossible to tell how long something takes, and that can be a problem for SEALs. You swim forever, and then look at your watch to discover it's only been ten minutes. Or it's been five hours. That's why you look—you can't tell.

Sarini shivers, her breathing shallow and too fast. She tries to control it, to break the cycle of hyperventilating and panic, but she's not having much luck.

I move closer to her. Just a few inches, but close enough that I feel the blinding heat radiating off her body, her scent strong and overwhelming.

At first, she doesn't react, and then she moves closer to me. I slide an arm around her shoulder, pull her into the protective hollow next to me. She relaxes almost immediately, sagging against me as though to let my strength serve us both.

I've dream of this moment. My fingers move lightly where they touch her shoulder. Cotton under my fingertips, a thin veil separating my skin from hers. I slide my fingers down lower, touch the bare skin just below her sleeve. She turns her face to my chest, presses hard against me, and it is too natural to not draw her in close to me, put my arms around her and rest my chin on the top of her head.

Time is not the only thing that stops in the absence of light. So does rational thought. She is scared, frightened on a level that I understand. These are not the circumstances that would put me in that place, but I understand how it is when fear is your entire world, when it seems that at every second you are just one heartbeat away from dying. Under those circumstances, there is a blind compulsion to seek contact with another human, to feel another heart just to confirm that you're still alive.

My own breathing is out of control now, for different reasons. In the candlelight, reality is diffused and vague. There is nothing outside of this cave, outside of the two of us.

Her chest is pressed against mine, her body running the length of mine down to the waist. Below that, her right leg is pressed tightly against my left on, her body twisted at right angles to mine. It would take only the slightest pull to roll to my left and lay full length against her, intertwining legs, locking knees to draw her solidly against me, bring her mouth to the level of mine, cup the fragile back of her neck in one hand while exploring her with the other hand.

She would not resist. At this moment, she wants that as much as I do, although for different reasons. She is frightened beyond rational thought, desperate for the feel of another body, confirmation that she's alive.

It has been too long. I cannot resist this. I start to move, and her head slips across to the center of my chest. Her heads rests on a scar on my chest.

Are you fucking her? Somebody ought to. It would do her a world of good.

Shit.

I force myself to relax, to stop what seems inevitable. She is still shivering against me. I hold her and wait for it to pass. Eventually it does, and our breathing settles into a comfortable rhythm.

We will not talk about this. Not about what almost happened, not about whether or not it would. It is like that after moments like this, under extreme pressure, when souls are stripped bare in front of each other. We will leave here eventually, never speak of these moments again, and pretend that nothing ever happened.

For now, we wait.

Eventually, a shaft of light penetrates into the small compartment, blindingly intense after the darkness. We shield our eyes with our hands, opening our fingers gradually as our eyes adapt.

Sarini goes first, clearly grateful to be out of the dark. I follow, and when I emerge into the bedroom, her face is still pale and naked. There is a silent acknowledgement of what almost happened in the candlelight, embarrassment, and—am I imagining it?—the slightest trace of regret.

Jenkins doesn't see any of this. He is deeply disturbed by whatever happened while we were locked underground, shaken to his core.

I had not intended to draw him in like this, and he doesn't appreciate it. But he will say nothing, because they have now made it personal by invading his sanctuary.

Jenkins has been working on this safe haven for decades. It was prepared for just such an eventuality as this, although I don't know whether it was out of a deep Yankee suspicion for organized government or simply habit. Nevertheless, his cover is now blown. They know about his little retreat here, and they know about Jenkins. I wonder if he will move, start over somewhere else in the backcountry. I wouldn't be surprised.

"Sloppy," Jenkins says. "Didn't even suspect—they think you made it out into the woods somewhere, from what they were saying." I see grim satisfaction in his eyes.

"But I don't think they're completely convinced," Jenkins continues. "That Wister fellow—he's a smart one. The rest of 'em spent all their time talking to me, telling me why I ought to be cooperative, asking me about the car. But Wister didn't say much. He just kept looking at me. You know where he served?"

I shake my head. I don't know that Wister has ever been in the military, but it wouldn't surprise me if he had.

"We'll wait until dark," Jenkins says.

Twelve

While we wait, Jenkins goes out to survey his property. It is clear that they have seriously pissed him off, and this has gone far beyond helping out an old buddy. It's now personal.

Sarini and I stay inside, away from windows, not talking on the off chance there is a directional mike aimed at us. Jenkins suggests we retreat to the underground shelter again, but Sarini pales visibly at the idea. As a concession, he shows me how to operate the remote from a switch by the door.

When he comes back, he is grimly pleased. "They're on the main road. Right outside, and then further down. They think they've got us pretty well blocked off with that." The same things that make it hard to get in will make it hard to get out.

But Jenkins has a way out. Of course he does. Jenkins has not made all these preparations just to overlook an emergency egress route. I know that he knows that I know....

He studies me for a moment, and I can see his irritation growing. He doesn't want to use the last chance escape route, but there's really not any way around it.

The helicopter hangs around until dark then disappears. Another will take its place soon, probably with FLIR, the forward-looking infrared radar that turns night into shades of green, or some other form of night and low light surveillance equipment. I've been out too long. There's no telling how technology has progressed.

Jenkins monitors the local police channels on the scanner, but there's no traffic on it, at least nothing that sounds like it's about us. They're using whatever encrypted tactical frequencies they have to prevent us from listening.

"Skipper will be here before long," Jenkins says. If the Navy believes he is involved in hiding fugitives, his captain will not treat him as politely as Wister had. His captain won't wait for a warrant.

"I held you hostage," I suggest. That may save his ass, although it will certainly increase the danger for Sarini and me. Jenkins thinks about it for a minute then reluctantly nods.

We wait until it is dark—through civil, nautical and celestial twilight. The sun touches, bisects and disappears below the horizon.

Finally, it is as safe as it's going to get to move. We have not heard the helicopter return. The men barricading the road must have night vision goggles, but I'm pretty sure we won't be going out that way.

Jenkins pulls out a detailed topological chart of the Crest area. Immediately below us a cliff drops perhaps two thousand feet to the floor of the valley below.

"It's not as bad as it looks," he says by way of explanation. Then he talks me through the descent, pointing out the landmarks and hidden paths. And indeed, as he describes it, it isn't all that bad.

At least not for a SEAL. I look over Sarini, and wonder. Whoever came after her at her house and killed her neighbor will wonder if she's talked to Jenkins as well. Her life and career, now Jenkins'.

I warn Jenkins about that, and he just nods. "Already figured that."

But I'm beginning to think that Sarini will be safer here than attempting the climb down to the valley floor. I know I can do it, but I'm not so certain about her. Oh, physically, she's in shape. But it's the mental part that I wonder about.

She must see my concern, and in truth, she's not certain herself. We reach an unspoken agreement to defer the issue. But not for long.

"Low profile op," Jenkins says. He watches to see if I've got anything else to add.

I had not thought of it, but he's right. One helo, men waiting outside his entrance—not what you'd expect from a manhunt for a killer priest and kidnapper.

"All Feds," Jenkins continues. "No local cops, nothing. Even the helo—not marked."

I don't answer. I'm not sure he even expects one. Is it NCIS or my father's doing? Or both, perhaps, if my father offered me up in trade to Wister. Not that there's anything to trade, but that wouldn't stop him.

How had they found me here? Who knew I would be here? It's not likely that they'd have surveillance on every SEAL I'd ever worked with, and I doubt that anyone would have guessed that Jenkins would be my first choice. Even my father wouldn't have known about Jenkins.

Has Jenkins betrayed me? Called in the cops himself? Or his wife?

No. He's too annoyed that they're here, and I doubt his wife would have done it without his consent. So where does this circle begin?

"They followed us," I say slowly, speaking before I'd fully worked it out in my mind. "Somehow, they followed us."

Jenkins nods. "How?"

"I don't know. The rental car? But why didn't they take us before that?"

"Because they wanted to see where you would go," Jenkins suggests.

"Maybe. Or maybe—." I stop, and look at Sarini. "Did you bring a cell phone?"

"Yes."

"Let me see it."

She digs into a pocket and produces her cell phone and I see immediately the difference in pay between a Navy doctor and a Navy priest. Her phone's got all sorts of toys on it, Internet access, news service, everything. And it's on.

Jenkins swears quietly. Sarini looks puzzled.

"It's in constant contact with the cell phone network," I say. "It transmits a signal to check in with each cell. Not difficult to locate and triangulate on, once you know what you're looking for. It's got an FCC registration number."

She reaches for it, but I pull it away. "Turn it off then," she says.

"Not yet," I say. I glance over at Jenkins and see him nodding confirmation. "We turn it off, they know we know. There's at least a chance right now that they believe we won't think of it. And it may be our way out." I turn to Jenkins. "That path down the cliff—you thinking what I'm thinking?"

"Yeah. It blows the hostage story to hell, though."

"No. You go. Take one of the kids. I'm holding your wife and the others hostage here."

"That'd work. Okay, let me get ready."

Sarini is brighter than most. Even though special operations isn't her area, she picks up on what we're doing. "A decoy."

I nod. "They don't have all that many assets on us and they'll redeploy what they've got to intercept us at the bottom of the cliff. While they're covering the back way out, following your cell phone, we'll go out the front way.

"You think they'll leave the front unguarded?"

"They'll have to. They don't have enough people to do both." I'm not nearly as confident as I sound. Of course, there's a chance that they will, but it's much more likely that they'll leave one unit behind just in case. But one unit's a hell of a lot easier to cope with than what's out there now.

Sure, they could call in more people. But that poses a problem for them as well. Right now, the locals aren't involved. But if they start deploying multiple units, blanketing the entire area with men, cars and helos, sooner or later one of the locals is going to get worried.

Especially out here, in the backcountry. Publicity and alerting the local law enforcement folks, which would be the sheriff in this part of the country, is the last thing that either Wister or my father will want. If they weren't adverse to that, if there wasn't a need to keep it quiet, we'd have already seen flashing lights, hostage negotiators and a SWAT team.

Jenkins comes back dressed in black and has textured climbing shoes on his feet. He's got his oldest son with him, a boy about Sarini's size with a slender build. In the darkness, he'll pass.

"We're ready," Jenkins says. He holds out his hand, and I take it. His palm is rough and callused in my hand, the way mine used to feel. He shakes his head in wry regret. "You'd stuck around, you'd a been good."

"I couldn't. You know that."

He nods. He hesitates for a moment then says, "For what it's worth, I would have done the same thing."

"No, you wouldn't." He's not talking about now, not about current events. We're back on Muralis Island again.

"I would have. Better four alive than six dead."

"Not everybody saw it that way."

A look of disgust. "Better to be judged by three than carried by six." He looks at his boy. "Come on, let's get moving. You'll see what's going on soon enough. Ten minutes, I'd say."

Sarini surprises me by holding out her hand. "Thank you." He shakes it, then with one last look at me, heads out the back of the house. A few moments later, he's hidden from view by the tree line.

We wait, watching Wister and his people on the grainy display screen. They don't move for several minutes. Then one answers a shoulder radio call. There's a short conference, Wister in the center of it, his people agitated and Wister composed. The clot of people breaks apart, dashes for cars, and they withdraw.

"They bought it." Sarini is relieved.

"Yes." Maybe. I'd like to believe that Wister will pull everyone off the access road and reposition them to intercept Sarini's cell phone, now descending the cliff, but Wister strikes me as the sort of man who'll take precautions. The best we can hope for is better odds, but Sarini doesn't need to know that.

We wait three minutes then leave the cover of the house for the car. The Rottweiler watches us go.

From the end of the access road, I can turn either right or left. Right will take me toward Harbison Canyon and eventually to Interstate Eight in Alpine. Left will take us back the way we came. Six to ten minutes to the interstate. Either way, it's a two lane road, easy to block. I mentally flip a coin and turn right.

The road is deserted. Not unusual in this part of the county. The roads wind in and around the mountains, passing through overhanging trees and along the edges of cliffs.

How will they do it? Just pull a car across the road, probably. In many places, there's hardly any shoulder at all, just a straight drop down into a canyon.

"What's that?" Sarini asks, twisting in the seat to look behind us. "That noise."

"Helicopter." Night vision goggles, then. With enough experience, it's like flying in daylight.

Had Jenkins suspected that? Probably. He is in practice, accustomed to thinking about his opponents' capabilities and calculating probable courses of action. Yet he'd gone anyway.

I mash down on the accelerator. Sarini gasps as the car shoots forward and clamps her hands down on the door and the seat. She starts to object, but then stops. We're going too fast around the curves, but we'll need every bit of speed possible.

Just at the junction of Harbison Canyon Road, they're waiting. One car is stretched across the road, its bumper up against a vertical rise too steep for us to make, its front tires two feet from a sharp drop off. Wister's people are positioned part way up the slope, looking down on us.

"Hold this," I say.

Force equals speed times mass. Their car is a standard government-issue Taurus sedan. Mine is much heavier. At least they weren't stupid enough to stay in the car.

Sarini screams as she finally understands what I'm going to do. We slam into the Taurus, shoving it out of the way, throwing us both forward hard. The airbags inflate, blinding us.

My face smacks into the airbag. Between that and the seat belt digging into my gut, I'm temporarily breathless. But they'll be scrambling down off the hill any second now.

"The knife."

Sarini moans. She's in no condition to help. I fumble my pocket knife out, drop it and spend a few frantic moments scrambling for it, finally dredging it up from the crack between the seats. I stab my airbag, then hers, jamming the accelerator down at the same time and trying to keep the car pointed toward where I think the road is.

The airbag deflates. Not fast enough, but there's a thin strip of visibility across the top of the windshield now, growing larger every second. We're headed for a ditch, but I wrestle the car back onto the road at the last moment. One last swerve and we're around the curve and out of view, heading for Alpine.

"It will take them a few minutes to back up in place," I say. "That car's not going anywhere."

Sarini doesn't answer. Her eyes are open and a trickle of blood runs from her forehead down her cheek. Absentmindedly, she smears it away.

"You okay?"

"Yeah. Just shook up."

"Hit your head?"

"No." She did, but judging from the size of the cut and the fact that her pupils are equal and reactive, I doubt there's any serious damage.

"Roll down your window and listen for the helicopter." She does as I ask. I roll my own window down as well. There's no sound of it, but trees overhang the road and could easily mask the sound.

Gunfire, off in the distance. Sarini jumps then looks at me. "Jenkins?"

"We'll call him later," I say. "Make sure he's all right."

But he won't be. I know that already.

After this, the SEALs won't help me. Not even if Jenkins is still alive. Once again, I've betrayed a team mate, left him to die. No matter that it was Jenkins' choice, Jenkins' plan—it's still my fault.

First Bishop Oakes and the church. Now the SEALs. Everything I had built on my own, all the people and places and institutions I thought I could count on stripped away from me.

Perhaps I'd been wrong to trust them in the first place. Or perhaps it had never been as I thought. They'd never been able to rely on me. What kind of a priest refuses absolution to a dying man? What kind of a SEAL leaves men behind to die?

The kind of man who lives a lie.

There is one man who will understand what that means. One man who can help me, who will at least listen to me if only to find out what I know.

There's no loyalty, oath or honor left in anything I've built in my own life, but I have a hold over him. If he agrees to help me, I'll back up whatever story he chooses to tell Wister.

I haven't done too badly on my own, but I can't get to Muralis Island on my own. Not in time to stop what's happening there.

If he knew what was really happening, he might help me. Since I can't tell him, I'll have to rely on blackmail. After all, it's not as though he's a stranger to that. He'll understand that I have no choice.

My father's opinion still matters to me, even after all that has happened. I'm a little surprised to realize that.

Thirteen

I 've slipped far below the surface of life. The current is stronger now, drawing me away from sunlight and air. How many people understand what life is really about, the layers and layers that lie below the daily routine?

Jenkins understood. Most of his life was lived below the surface with only the trappings of his home and family protruding like a tip of an iceberg.

But had he ever been this deep before? I don't know. Certainly he had been on some operations—we all had. But there's normally a geographic separation between that life and real life, one that maintains the facade that the world sees. It's when the worlds start to converge that things get difficult.

The motel in Lakeside is no longer safe and I've kept our damaged rental car far too long. Another bit of the facade will have to be abandoned.

We've been so successful at losing our pursuers that I wonder whether or not it's just another of Wister's tactics. Am I that good or are they that inept?

More and more of the old life comes back to me every moment. I think I could still tell if we were being followed.

Sarini doesn't yet understand completely what's happening. Running the blockade has forced her to retreat from her earlier bravado at Jenkins' and has made the gun tucked into her pocket too real to her. She's reached that point at which you either decide to cope with the reality that you currently are in or you cannot, and flail away to the surface to try to deal with the random currents there.

Better to stick with a bottom current you know. They flow in unexpected directions, but they're strong, not as chaotic, and you have a better sense of which way you're going.

As the shock wears off, her hands begin to tremble. She finds her voice again, and the questions begin. I don't have good answers, but I try to tell her what I know.

"We need new wheels," I say. "After that, we're going to find somewhere to sit down and think."

"I haven't done anything," Sarini says. Her voice is soft and disbelieving. Things like this don't happen to doctors. They just don't.

I take Interstate 8 back into San Diego then turn south on Interstate 5 to the airport. A few minutes later, we're in the long-term parking area of Lindberg Field.

Sarini has figured out what I have in mind and she doesn't like it. But since the whole situation is so completely at odds with her reality, she has no positive suggestions, and her experience and training as a doctor keep her quiet. On some level, she understands it's as though she's had to call in a specialist. She's prepared to listen to what I have to say.

I pull into a parking slot, pocket the ticket and start looking for a replacement vehicle. It has to be an older one but in good shape. I don't have time to deal with alarm systems or risk security responding to one. I cruise the aisles, looking for an older car with a well-kept exterior. People who maintain their cars on the outside are more likely to keep it into shape mechanically as well.

Finally, I find it. It's an older Cadillac, one of the midsize ones. It's a dark blue, the sort of bland color that does not immediately attract the attention of every law enforcement officer on the road. Its registration is current and it looks like it's been painted within the last five years. It's waxed and there's not a scratch on it.

Now is the time to move quickly. There's undoubtedly some sort of surveillance in the lot. I spot cameras high on the poles, so it's essential that we not attract the attention of whoever is watching them. I don't

Wythe County Public Library
Wytheville, VA

think that will be difficult to do. The security at the airport seems to be staffed mostly by minimum wage workers tarted up in uniforms.

I approach the driver's door and fumble with the keys, checking to make sure there's no flashing light indicating an alarm system. I turn toward Sarini as I do. We are a happy couple returning from vacation, very casual, nothing suspicious about us.

Unless you notice the lack of luggage. Unless the camera can read the look on Sarini's face.

I turned to her. "Don't jump when I break the window." She nods.

I smash the butt of the gun into the window. Even knowing it's coming, she can't help flinching. I reach in, unlock the door, open it, slid in, and use the automatic door lock to unlock her side. At the same moment, I'm already leaning under the dashboard, finding the right wires, cutting them and cross-connecting them. The ignition lock—I forgot about that. I pop it off with the knife on my keychain, cross the right wires and the car starts.

Next to me, Sarini is buckling her seat belt. I rolled down my window, and hers as well so that the broken glass will not be immediately visible.

I brush the broken glass off the dashboard and seat, back out of the slot and head for the cashier's kiosk with the ticket in my hand. Between the two of us, we have enough to pay the parking charges.

We pay the charges and leave, and I head immediately downtown.   If someone saw us stealing the car, they have not moved quickly enough report it.

"Where are we going?" Sarini asks.

I'm not sure, but I can't let her know that. "Somewhere we can talk and try to figure out what we do next."

"We're in over our heads," she says. "We need to go to the police. Now. Or," she continues, seeing the look on my face, "at least to the Navy. David, we're throwing everything away, and we're not at fault. This is all out of control."

She's right about one thing. She's not at fault. At least I don't think she is. I still have some very serious questions about what Caermon told her, but those can wait.

I steer clear of the worst areas of downtown, on the theory that there will be fewer cops. I head down Sixth Avenue, going past the family courthouse and toward Balboa Park.

The diocese office is off to my left and for a moment I'm tempted to go in and throw myself on the bishop's mercy. But I know what he will want me to do—and I can't. Not yet.

Still, Bishop Oakes had given me an idea, and I drive into Balboa Park and park the car. "Let's go for a walk."

Sarini is still fixed on the idea that this can all be made right. She's clinging to it like a drowning person strapping herself to a log floating on the surface, hoping it will save her. She can't see that the log is waterlogged and will eventually pull her under. She has no idea what going to the police now would do.

I take her along the path that Bishop Oakes and I followed a few days ago. The deepening woods blocks out the noise of the city traffic. We head downhill, and the canopy shields us from the sun. It's markedly cooler now and will be cold at night when cold air pools in this valley.

I realize I have already decided we will spend the night.

A crosshatch of fallen trees can provide some cover should we need it. There's a large rock protruding from the ground and I sit down on it. It's warm and it will retain that heat well into the night.

Sarini sits down next me. She's already convinced herself that she will persuade me to come in from the cold.

"Now look," she says, her voice entirely calm and reasonable. "This can't continue. Surely you understand that."

I recognize the tone of voice from the emergency room. It's the one she uses on a patient who wants to refuse treatment, or on an intern who is heading straight down the wrong diagnostic path. It is her god voice, the all-knowing one, the one that admits no other possible viewpoint. It's not arrogant or pompous and is even more effective for that. It implies that she is the one authorized to make the decision and that decision has been made. If she had been either arrogant or pompous, the listener would be left with something to rail against, some fault to fix on in supporting rebellion. But when Sarini uses this particular god voice, there can be no argument because there is no issue. It is simply a statement of reality.

But it's her reality, not mine, and her reality is not based on the facts as they are but on the facts as she wishes they were.

"No."

She's expecting more of an argument and when it doesn't come, she's slightly at a loss. But she recovers quickly and then pushes herself up off the rock. She brushes leaves and dirt off her pants and puts her hands on her hips. "Very well. But I'm not going a step further with this."

"No."

That single word again. Sarini is not accustomed to having her decisions questioned, particularly not when a god decision has been made, a pronouncement from on high. "I'm going back."

"You can't."

"I most certainly can."

"Let me explain a few things to you," I say. I want to stay sitting on this rock, maybe even lie back on it and feel the heat soak into me. I am far colder than the weather would warrant. I have been avoiding this moment for the last day and a half. "If you go back now, you will be charged with murder. Perhaps espionage as well, depending on how creative they want to be. The murder charge, though, is a certainty."

"Nonsense. I didn't kill that man."

"Not him. Caermon."

"I was his *doctor*."

"You were the one who authorized taking him outside. Oh, sure, I'll certainly be charged with murder as well. But looking at it objectively, I can't see any way that you'll be able to fight the conspiracy charge. I mean, why else would you disobey the orders in his chart?"

"This is ridiculous." But she has stopped walking away and is standing, listening.

"No, it's not. I know these people. You don't."

"What people? You keep talking like this is cops and robbers, or cowboys and Indians. Like it's a game."

"It's not a game. At least," I amend, "not a kids' game. It's very, very real."

"Who are you?" she asks finally. "You're not really a priest, are you?"

I find this encouraging, the first step toward understanding about bottom currents. "Oh, I'm definitely a priest. Now.

"But I wasn't always. That's why I know this game better than you ever will." I sit back down on the rock and pat the spot next to me. I'm aware I'm using my version of her god voice on her. It has an impact, but she's not quite ready to admit that this isn't her world. And that it is mine.

"What are you going to do if I don't?" she asks. "Handcuff me to a tree?"

I shake my head. "I don't have any handcuffs." I don't tell her I can think of ten ways to restrain her just using my belt. "If you're going to the cops, it wouldn't make sense for me to tell you what I intend to do, would it? Just hear me out for a few minutes. Then if you still want to leave, I'll show you how to get out of here." I make that point as an afterthought, because it has not yet occurred to her that she doesn't know the way back to the car.

She comes back slowly, reluctance clear on her face. Instead of sitting next me, she stands in front of me, arms crossed across her chest. "Okay, talk." Another order, but I don't mind obeying this one.

I take a deep breath and start. "Have you ever done any scuba diving? Or any sort of open water swimming? Lakes, ocean, anything?"

"I got my PADI certification while I was in college."

"Then you know how warm and calm it can be on the surface. So perfect a day on top. But it's not that way all the way down to the bottom, is it? Once you get below the surface, the water is cold. And there are the currents. Huge currents, way out of your reach, far below the surface, that completely encircle the world. The Gulf Stream, for instance, goes all the way up the Atlantic coast, into the Arctic, and down along the coast of England and Ireland. It's still warm when it makes it all the way across, at least warmer than the surrounding water."

That look is back on her face, the smoothed over one she uses when she's dealing with families. The one she wore when she talked to Heidi Caermon.

I try again. "It's like a patient. Like with Caermon. You can tell there's something wrong with him, something you can't see. Most doctors have to wait for the lab results, but you don't. Not always."

"Are you leading up to a profound analogy of some sort? Because I have to tell you, you're not making much sense to me."

"Why did you run your hands over Caermon's belly?"

"I was palpating his abdominal cavity, looking for masses."

"No, you weren't. I've seen other doctors do that, I've seen you do it, and that's not what you were doing. It was something else, something you don't talk about. You get a feel for what's going on inside, don't you? One you can't really explain."

"You make it sound like voodoo."

"No. It's just a gift you have. A healing gift. One that tells you about your patients." She starts to interrupt but I keep going. "Call it instinct, call it intuition, call it experience. Whatever it is, you ending up knowing things you can't exactly quantify."

"Your point?"

"This is the same sort of thing. The water analogy, that's the way I explain it to myself. Right now, you don't know what kind of water we're in. You haven't, not since Caermon was killed. I didn't either, not right off, although I had my suspicions."

"And what kind of water is it? Go ahead, enlighten me."

I'm losing her. This was the wrong way to start. She deals and facts, in what she can observe and test. I've seen that in the emergency room as well, in how she treated me, in when she would let me talk to patients.

Almost every doctor will admit that there have been results he doesn't understand. If you use the word miracle, they get uncomfortable, shy away from the word as though admitting that God might be at work might somehow dilute their own powers. Admitting to results you don't understand is one thing, acknowledging that God intervened entirely another.

"I was a good SEAL. At least, up until my last mission."

Faintly, I heard the screaming. The shots around me. The cold.

I pulled back from Muralis Island and continued. "There are SEALs and then there are—well, there are specialists. It's the difference between the general practitioner and an oncologist."

She understands that. "What kind of specialists?"

"For sensitive operations," I say. "You have to understand, everything any SEAL squad does is classified top secret. Our training syllabus, our budget, everything. But even beyond that routine secrecy there's a black hole, one that no information ever gets out of." I shrug, try to manage a smile. "I'm risking twenty years in Leavenworth just telling you this much."

She nods and I continue with, "I don't want to go into details about what we did. Partly for reasons on security, but partly because I don't want to think about them. I put all that behind me when I went to seminary. At least, I thought I did. Until Caermon showed up."

"You knew Caermon?"

"No. But he knew who I was. When I went into see him, he recognized my last name. Well, not exactly mine— my father's. Admiral Dalt. He seemed to be under the impression my father sent me to see him."

"Did he?"

"No. My father and I don't talk."

"Caermon wasn't making any sense by then," Sarini said briskly. "If you're basing all this on the drug-induced fantasies of a dying man, then that's—."

"He called me by my code name," I said quietly. Fear flashes through me again, the fear that I'm exposed, that everything I have will be ripped away from me. "It was a classified code name. We all had them. Unless he was intimately connected with certain special operations, he wouldn't have access to that information."

"So what? Maybe he was cleared for it once."

"But he made the connection immediately," I say. "And I've been out of the SEALs for five years now. That tells me that he was worried about something connected with us, something he didn't want anyone to know. And since my father immediately came to mind as well, it had to do with him as well."

"And then he was killed," she says slowly, processing now, her analytical line mind driving her to the same conclusion I reached the moment the first shot at Caermon had been fired. "The order that he wasn't to leave his room. This whole special operations thing."

I can't say anything more. Any further explanation, and I'm treading on the dark line drawn around those days and that last mission.

"That's what this is all about? Whatever Caermon told you before he died?"

"I think so. Or at least what someone *thinks* he might have told me."

"What did he—." She stops, a look of frustration on her face. She already knows I can't tell her what he said. "So what is all this about currents?"

"It's just the way I think of things." It sounds lame, but I don't know how else to explain it to her. "Not everything is what it seems to be. There's a whole surface layer of reality that most of the time we all agree on. But it's not really what's going on. There are always layers under everything. Nothing is entirely what it seems."

"If I were a psychiatrist, I would wonder about paranoia," she says carefully, as though to avoid setting me off.

"I'm not talking about everyone being out to get me," I say. "I *am* talking about things not always being exactly what they appear to be. Let's take you, for instance."

"Let's not."

"I think we have to. For a couple of reasons, and primarily because you're not sure about what you've done so far. You asked Jenkins for a weapon, but now you want out. You saw the story they're putting out on you, but you still want to believe you can simply go to the cops and they'll straighten everything out."

"I don't want to talk about it."

I press on. "You've had plenty of chances to run, but you haven't. Part of that I can chalk off to shock, particularly after what happened at your house. But shock doesn't last that long. You could have left at the motel. You could have run away at the airport. There were any number of times when you could have done what you keep threatening to do, go to the cops."

"You seemed to know what you're doing," and now it's her turn to sound lame.

"That's not it. There's this huge mismatch between who you are and what you're doing." I hold up my hand to forestall comment. "I'm not accusing you of anything. I'm making an observation. And the second thing is, you're lying to me about Caermon."

"No, I'm not."

"You are. And up until now, I didn't think it was critical to know why. Or what. But he said something to you when he recognized my name in the ER and I need to know what he said."

"Oh, I see. Your priest-penitent confidence has to be kept but not my doctor-patient one, is that it?"

"There's no doctor-patient privilege in the military."

"He was retired, not on active duty."

"So what? Even if it applied originally, it doesn't now. He's dead. The privilege doesn't survive the patient's death."

"You haven't demonstrated any real need to know, have you?"

There are other exceptions to the doctor-patient privilege and one of them applies here. The privilege does not apply to furthering or covering up a criminal act and Caermon's treason was undoubtedly that. However, I can't tell her that he committed treason. There's no similar exception to the priest-penitent privilege.

"Besides that, you've got a little latitude that I don't have," I say, reaching back into my limited knowledge of the law. "Tarasof—you've got a duty to warn if there's a danger to others."

She shook her head. "Like you said, he's dead. What danger could he be to you now?"

"There might be other people in danger." She doesn't answer. It's like dancing with the devil, trying to find a way through this morass of privileges.

Indecision wars on her face. She may not have told me what I wanted to know but she's taken the first step toward understanding the bottom currents. Nor has she denied that she may not be exactly who she appears to be.

"This is ridiculous." She turns to leave.

"You don't understand what's going on here. Not yet. Neither do I, for that matter, at least not completely.

131

And until we know what kind of current we're in, it makes no sense to head for the surface. Best that we find a current going in the direction that we want to move before we surface.

"If I can strain the analogy, what we have to do right now is find the right oceanographer. Somebody who understands this part of the ocean better than I do. I've got a general sense of what's going on—or at least, what I think is going on. But that's not enough."

"And I suppose you have someone in mind for the role of star oceanographer?"

"Unfortunately, I do. My father."

Sarini is not at all pleased with the idea of spending the night in the park. I had not expected her to be squeamish about the possibility of snakes and bugs, but she is. Even when we curl up in the lee of our large, warm rock, she's not reassured. I pointed out to her the practical difficulties and danger associated with sleeping in the car. It may have been reported stolen by now. In fact, we can't risk going back to it at all.

"So we steal another car tomorrow?" She yawns, unable to fight off the exhaustion overcoming her. As the attending physician in the emergency room, she's used to long shifts and she knows how to survive the grueling hours: coffee, short naps, sometimes even sleeping standing up.

But this isn't the sort of stress she's trained for. She's not used to being assaulted, chased, or even much physical exertion aside from trying to stay awake and alert. Most importantly, she's not used to someone trying to kill her.

Eventually she dozes off. I piled some leaves and branches over her for warmth and she's too tired to resist. I do the same for myself then concentrate on getting my mind to shut down.

I suspect that my father will get a great deal of pleasure out of the fact that I have to ask for his help, especially since I rejected it at the hospital. He would never be so obvious as to gloat but that's exactly what he'll be doing.

It won't matter that Wister's asking questions about Mother's death, if it's to that point yet. He'll be amused.

Still, it can't be helped. If there is a key to understanding this, he holds it.

More than understanding it—preventing what will certainly happen without his help. I have to get to Muralis Island and I can't think of a way of accomplishing that without his assistance.

There's not even any assurance that he will agree to help me at all. If I'm stomping across sacred ground, intruding on some operation he currently has in play, he may well write me off as another casualty.

Certainly he was quite ready to do that with my mother. Why should I be any different?

Finally, I forced myself to doze. I keep the nine millimeter in my hand, the safety on and my fingers outside of the trigger guard. I dream of deep water.

We are up at first light the next morning. Sarini looks somewhat rested and I'm impressed by her ability to sleep under strange conditions. Granted, she is not in a pleasant mood and her eyes are puffy, but she's oriented within moments of waking up and does not immediately began a litany of complaints.

While we're brushing leaves and dirt off, I explained what I have in mind. We will find a pay phone, call my father's office, and see what happens.

"Will he help us?" Sarini asks. There's no mention now of simply going to the police. Our discussion yesterday must have been mulling around in her head overnight and she's come to the conclusion that things are not as they seem to be.

"I think so," I say. I'm not nearly as confident as I sound.

It takes us twenty minutes to get back to the main park area, and I quickly locate a telephone near the zoo. I dial my father's office. His Chief of Staff, Captain Gallagher recognizes my voice and puts me through to him.

On some level, my father must have known I'd call him. But when he answers the phone, his voice reveals nothing.

"You're recording this, aren't you?" I say. "Tracing it?"

"Whatever happened to hello?" my father asks.

"We're a bit past that, don't you think? I'm giving you one last chance. Meet me where I learned to swim. I know you remember where that was." I hang up.

Sarini's staring at me. "Not close, are you?"

I shrug. "There are issues." *Issues.*

"Will he be there?" she asks.

I don't answer. I don't know myself.

Fourteen

We rent a small boat from the pier in Pacific Beach, paying cash. It's a cabin cruiser, twenty feet long, barely adequate in these waters, particularly not if the ocean is any rougher. We promise to stay inside the bay. We don't.

Outside the breakwaters and jetties, the sea is rougher, the swells long and hard. Somewhere in the last four years, I've lost my sea legs and the pitch and roll of the boat bothers me.

Ashore, clusters of sunbathers, surfers and fishermen dot the sand. I find the spot easily enough. I wonder if my father will still know it.

Then I see him. He's in civilian clothes, tan shorts, a blue shirt, white court shoes and white socks. I cut hard toward land and the boat rocks precariously. I'm not going ashore—surely he realizes that.

"Go below," I tell Sarini. "Don't let him know you're here." She starts to protest, then does what I ask.

My father bends over and pulls off his shoes and socks. He walks to the edge of the water, wades as far as he can, and then begins swimming with that hard, economical stroke I remember. His shoes are still on the shore.

Have I engineered this, on some level, to try to humiliate him? If so, it was a mistake. It would take more than an unplanned swim to shake him.

I cut the engine and put the boarding ladder over the side. The boat heels over as he comes aboard. As soon as I'm sure he's onboard, I gun the engine and head for deeper water. He stands without holding on to anything, balancing himself against the roll of the waves. I used to be able to do that, too.

Everything I've planned to say to him can wait for a moment. We stand side by side, both in another time, feeling the boat take the waves and the wind cool against our faces. He must be cold, in wet clothes in this breeze, but he says nothing. If he'd been driving instead of me, it could have been twenty years ago.

I pull into a cove that will shield us from the waves, and slow to bare steerageway. I turn to face him. "You came."

My father nods. "We could have talked at the hospital."

"Things have happened since then. What did Wister tell you?"

"Just what happened at the hospital." My father shrugs. By now he knows everything NCIS does and probably a bit more. It's the nature of who and what he is in the Navy. "Wister said he needs to talk to you again. After what I saw on the news last night, he'll have more in mind that just talking."

He doesn't ask me if it's true. He doesn't ask me why I left, why this obscure meeting place. It's not because he believes implicitly in my innocence, that I've got a good reason for doing this all. In his world, it's better not to know certain things, and that has always carried over into his dealings with his family.

I don't ask him if he was sure he wasn't followed. There's no need to insult him, not after making him swim out to the boat. I wonder if his shoes will still be there when we return.

"You did see the news last night?" he asks.

"Yes. None of it's true, at least not the way they tell it. But I need your help."

136

My father stares at me, his face impassive. "I thought you could take care of yourself."

"I can. But it's getting out of hand. And I'm not the only one at risk right now."

"That doctor?" he asks.

"Among others."

"The others being—."

"Being what I can't tell you about."

He sighs. "Then it makes it difficult for me to do anything about it, doesn't it?"

"It makes it impossible for you—but not for me."

My father could confirm where Napier was going. He could get me there in time to stop Napier, to prevent him from walking into a trap.

I start to ask him to arrange it then stop. Cold settles into my stomach.

There's a helicopter off on the horizon. It's just a black speck, hovering. Not uncommon around here, not with this much naval and marine aviation, not to mention the Coast Guard.

No reason to think it's there because of me, to wonder if there's a directional mike trained on us taking in every word. No reason at all.

"You said you need my help," my father says.

What absurd childhood reflex convinced me that all would be well if I could just find my father? "Never mind." I turn away, pretend to concentrate on the helm. "You wouldn't do it anyway."

I had been harboring fantasies of a dramatic reunion. Some shred of childhood awe still remained, the conviction that daddy could make everything all right.

"How do you know if you don't ask?"

"I just know." I take a deep breath, watch the helicopter for a moment. Is it coming closer? "Look, this was a mistake. I didn't think it through. I'll take you back." I turn the boat back toward shore.

My father grabs me by the shoulder and spins me around. For a moment, he looks like he's going to hit me. "That's it? I haven't seen you in a year, then all at once I have NCIS bulling their way into my office, see your face plastered on the evening news—and you won't tell me why?"

"It was a mistake."

My father is irritated. And something else—fear, perhaps? I'm not certain, because I can never recall seeing that particular expression on his face. It's gone before I have time to study it. "You can't play games with Arcadia."

So he does know. I understand the need for organizations such as Arcadia and the one my father heads up. The other side never plays fair—never. Too many men and women die if you play by the rules.

I counter with, "How well did you know Caermon?"

For a moment, I think he won't answer. Then he surprises me. "Well enough. And for a long time. Some of our responsibilities overlap. He's good at what he does, but he enjoys it too much. He is—was—depraved, I would say. He had his own agenda and had the freedom to do what he wanted within the scope of his powers. He liked to add twists to things, twists that only he knew about or enjoyed. Arcadia is the sort of place that allows that." I hear the disapproval in his voice and almost laugh. If anyone enjoyed constructing labyrinths, it would be my father.

"Did you kill Caermon?" I ask.

It was his father's turn to laugh. "Isn't it a little late for that?"

"Just answer me."

"No," my father says. "I had nothing to do with it. None of my people did. My turn now—that fellow at your girlfriend's house. Did you kill him?"

"She's not my girlfriend. But, yes. Guilty with an explanation."

My father's not surprised. He even looks a bit impressed. "Her story will back you up?" Again, not the concern about the truth, just that the stories will overlap, the truth as he chooses to create it will be seamless.

"Yes."

"It can be straightened out, then."

"I keep hearing that, and I keep telling people that it won't work."

"People?" My father's tone is sharp. "What people? Who else knows about this, David?"

"You worried someone will talk if you have me killed?" I regret the words as soon as I say them.

"Do you really think I would do that?"

"Did you forget who you're talking to? Yes, I think you would. I *know* you would. Under the right circumstances."

My father stands, for the first time holding on to the gunwale to maintain his balance. "What do you want? Tell me or take me back."

Stick with the plan. You can't act on impulse around him. "I need to get to Europe. Quietly. With the right documents. No Interpol, no Customs."

He regards me with a closed expression. "You have a great deal of confidence in my abilities."

"Not unjustified, though."

He nods. "Perhaps."

"What would make you want to?"

"Convince me that it's important."

I shook my head. "I can't tell you what he said. You know that."

My father looks off in the distance, calculating. He's matching up this request with what he knows of the world and what's going on in it, sorting through the possible reasons I need to get to Europe. He's already tumbled to the Arcadia involvement and I have no idea how or why. Sarini was right when she called him a star oceanographer. I'm as much of an amateur as Wister is, compared to my father.

"When?" he asks.

"Immediately. Today."

"Not impossible. But tricky."

I can't stop him from following me once we get there. Even if I manage to lose him once we're on the ground, he'll arrange things to suit himself. Customs won't stop me at any border—his documents are too good for that—but they'll tell him where I'm going. Eventually, he'll find me. If things work out right, by the time he knows where I am, it will be too late.

"Are you going to tell me why?" he asks.

"I can't."

"Nonsense. You *won't*."

"No. *Can't*. Not and remain who I am."

"You wouldn't be who you are without me. You wouldn't be *here*." He laughs, bitter now.

He never says anything without a purpose. I pause now to consider what it might be, and can't quite get a grip on it. He's telling me something, something I should be able to figure out for myself, and he's watching to see if I can figure it out.

Caermon. It started with Caermon's confession. And I heard that because Bill McCallister was out sick. Out sick with the crud that McCallister said was contagious.

I see Haynes face staring at me over his gutted computer, his eyes assessing me before he hands me McCallister's SI patient list.

McCallister said he was ....

McCallister said he was ....

No. The *doctor* said he was highly contagious. That's what Haynes said. The doctor.

Had Haynes talked to McCallister at all? Suddenly I doubted it. A doctor had called in, told him McCallister was sick and contagious. Not McCallister himself.

"You couldn't know that he'd give me McCallister's patients," I said, and I saw a flash of satisfaction on his face. "You couldn't. There are three other chaplains, four if you count Haynes. The odds were—."

"A Baptist, a Methodist, and a rabbi. Haynes is a Southern Baptist, too. Who's he going to give a Catholic priest's patients to? A Buddhist? You don't have to be a priest to predict that one."

You can wear your collar. The gentle fraud of denominations.

"Did Captain Haynes know?"

"He's not a player." Dismissal.

"Where is McCallister?"

He waves off the question. Irrelevant. McCallister could be dead for all I know. Would be, if it suited my father's plan. "What did he tell you, David? You wouldn't have heard it at all without my intervention, so doesn't that give me some sort of rights?"

It's my boat. I'm supposed to be in control. But the balance of power has shifted and we both know it. It was a mistake to let him know I needed him. It has always been a mistake to admit weakness in front of him.

"McCallister," I say.

"He's fine. At home." He sees the look on my face and sighs. "Call him. He's okay."

"I will."

"Okay. So. Caermon."

"Passports. Two. One for me, one for Sarini. Transportation to Europe and ten grand in cash." I make my tone as resolute as I can manage.

My faith has always been mine alone. It was one thing in which my father had no hand. Even after I came back on active duty as a chaplain, as far as I could tell, he'd never interfered with my career. If he did manage me from afar, it was from the shadows.

Come to think of it, I wasn't absolutely sure he was really still on active duty. The things he does go so far into black programs that the lines of responsibility and command blur into dark forces rather than organizational charts.

"If you don't help me, I'll tell them what I know. Everything. All of it. You can't afford to have that come out, can you? No. You can't." I'm pleased that my voice sounds calm and reasonable, at least to my ears.

Evidently my father hears the same thing, because for the first time, he looks worried. "You're bluffing."

"Willing to take that chance?"

He does not speak. It's another of his tactics—I know it all too well. It's intended to make me uneasy, to make me speak first. It's like forcing a seller to state a price first, knowing that he'll be high, but not so high as to queer the deal. The one to define the playing field and the fields of fire wins.

His eyes scour me, but I stand firm. I *am* bluffing, but he can't know that.

That's the danger in any truly secret operation. Secrecy breeds paranoia. Anyone on the inside of an op knows a thousand ways it can be compromised, a million things that can go wrong. It's not surprising when something leaks—it's surprising when it doesn't. There are scores of counter-espionage types that spend careers reviewing credit card slips, random phone conversations, even utility meters, ferreting out the deployment patterns of special forces personnel.

My father knows that. And so do I.

"You don't know anything. If you did, you wouldn't pull this bullshit."

"Tell me what I don't know, then."

"Ha. Right." He goes still for a moment and I suddenly wonder if I've overlooked something. I scan the horizon for the helicopter and can't find it.

Boats? Is someone on the way right now to intercept us?

Then I recognize his stillness for what it is. He's not waiting for something to happen, not at all. It's that ability he has to completely block out the world—or his family—when he has to make critical decisions. He's gathered all the information he needs and is processing it, focusing solely on what he knows to the exclusion of anything happening around him. It's a cold, analytical process, all variables and numbers.

No room for grace. No room for the divine.

He reached into his pocket, extracts a sealed plastic bag and hands it to me. Two passports, blue covers, not the brown used on military ones. I open them—one for me, one for Sarini. They looked slightly used, a few marks on the back pages. All the data on mine, including the picture, is accurate. Hers will be, too.

"I have a Gulfstream IV standing by," he says quietly. "I have a place for us to stay tonight. We'll leave tomorrow morning."

Of course he'd anticipated what I needed. Why else would I be calling him unless I needed to leave the country?

"Don't you think it's time I met her?" he asks.

I win. It should feel better. Instead, I'm so frightened I would be hard pressed to spit.

Have I really won? Or am I doing exactly what he wanted all along?

We take his car to a cabin east of San Diego located in a national forest. It's stocked with canned food and water and a generator provides power. Better than sleeping in the park again. I don't ask him how he arranged it and he doesn't volunteer any information.

I heat up canned spaghetti while my father makes some calls on his cell phone. He joins us at the table when he's done and tells us what we're going to do.

Sarini isn't pleased. Understatement. She's furious. If she were the type to throw plates, I would be wearing spaghetti right now.

"Absolutely not," she says.

"You have to go with us. Come on, Sarah. You're not safe here, you know that."

She shakes her head, both in refusal and denial. "No. This stops now, David. It stops now. My life is in shambles and I'm not going to stand for it anymore. Tomorrow morning, I go to the Director and surrender myself. I don't know what he'll do. Captain's Mast, certainly. Maybe a court martial."

"You can't. Not yet." I reach out to take her hand, but she pulls it back. "It's never going to be finished unless I finish it. They came for you once—they'll come again. And keep coming, until they know what Caermon told you."

"He didn't tell me anything!" She mutters an oath. "I keep telling you that, and you still think that—."

"You're lying. That's why. And we both know it."

"Why would I lie about it?"

I shrug. "I don't know. I'm a priest, not a clairvoyant. But you *are* lying—I saw it that day at your house. And you're lying now. The only way to keep you safe is to take you with me."

"I'm going to the cops."

"They can't protect you. Not against this. And they're even better at smelling lies than I am. They'll know the second you start talking and they'll hold you there until they figure out why." I'm not nearly as certain that the local cops are quite that prescient, but I won't tell Sarini that. She has to go with us, she has to. She will die otherwise.

"I wish to Christ I'd never met you," she spits out.

The blasphemy rolls right past me. Right now, tired, hurting, and pretty much without hope, I'm not so sure Christ wouldn't have felt the same way.

Fifteen

The next twenty-two hours pass in a blur of aircraft and foreign cars. Logistical support again, this time far beyond tuition and fraternity dues. I have no control over what is happening, nor do I have any desire to take it in hand. This is my father's business, and he knows all too well how to do it.

He shouldn't be here, watching me, waiting for my face to betray secrets, moving people into place for whatever abstruse purposes constitute his *raison d'etre*. But he had pointed out that the possibility of compromise increased with every additional agency involved, and making sure there were no Customs problems in either country would mean involving others. In the end, I conceded that it would be far better to simply arrive in a government aircraft, bypass the normal embarkation exams and be on our way.

The Gulfstream IV is handsomely equipped and has an un-refueled transatlantic range. We're headed for Germany and I've resisted all my father's questions about whether I'd prefer somewhere else.

If Sarini is God in the emergency room, then that's what my father is here. I ask some questions—where we're landing, how long until we get there—just as I would on a real SEAL mission supported by an outside command. I chaff a little at some of the decisions he makes but far less than Sarini did at mine. At least I've had practiced at *not* being God, and far more recently than either of them.

I wonder what He thinks of this all. The real God, the one I am supposedly ordained to serve. I have not had a sense that He hears me since I spoke with Bishop Oakes in the park. A result of the letter of prohibition? Has the bishop put a fix in on my communication with God? It's surprising and a bit embarrassing how little this bothers me.

And, if I'm honest, I'm angry at the divine silence. After all, I'm in this predicament because I followed the rules. Shouldn't I be granted some sort of solace, just a brief flash of some sort of reassurance?

It will all have to be sorted out when we return, but not before then. There's no time.

Sarini is not helping matters any. She has sunken into a sullen silence. She will respond to direct questions, but does not offer any opinion on anything. At first I think she's just in shock at the speed at which things are moving. This is so far out of her experience. But then I realize it's more than that. Her authority has been challenged too many times in the past few days, and she's not equipped to deal with that. To be wrong, to make a mistake—yes, she can deal with that, but not this complete lack of control over anything that happens. She has set up a wall to protect herself, pretending that she really doesn't care where we're going or why.

Or maybe it's a reaction to my father. He's normally quite aloof, and his disapproval voiced primarily through a palpably cold voice. But with Sarini, he goes out of his way to try to provoke her. His constant references to her as my girlfriend grate on my nerves as well. Whenever faults Sarini may have, she doesn't deserve this.

With me, he is cold as well, but in a way I understand. I finally abandon my Christian duty and quit trying to play peacemaker. Churlish, perhaps, but I tell myself it's my way of staying focused on the mission at hand.

Most of the time, I try to sleep. The lull of the aircraft's engines, the lack of sleep, all conspire against me.

An hour out of Germany, my father wakes me. Sarini has dozed off in a couple of seats to the rear of the aircraft and is still asleep.

"We need to talk about her," he says, glancing back at Sarini. "She can stay in Germany for a while. I know people. She would be safe."

'Know people'. I just bet you do. "Could, but I'd rather not."

"Depends on what she wants, doesn't it?" he asks.

"No." Until I know who shot Caermon, I'm not letting her out of my sight.

He is silent, thinking, but not debating the point. Sarini isn't a player. Either one of us could manipulate her with the utmost ease. It's not a question of whether he could turn her against me. It's whether it's worth it enough to him to force the matter now.

"Where are we?" Sarini asks, now pulling herself up into a sitting position. Her face is still clouded with sleep.

"An hour out of Germany," I say.

She nods and proceeds to the restroom. I hear water running.

We finally touch down on a private airfield just north of Berlin. It appears to be well-maintained and efficient. The aircraft are parked in precise lines, each tied down with no slack in the lines, the noses lined up evenly.

We taxi to the refueling facility and shut down. The truck comes around. After a brief discussion with the pilot, refueling begins, two men handling the hose and a third standing by with a fire extinguisher.

"Let's go." My father unfolds himself from his seat and leads the way forward. We follow. The boarding ladder is already folded down.

A wood and cinderblock building surrounded by a chain link fence sits inside the airfield fencing. It has been recently whitewashed. The antennas are mounted in an orderly fashion.

Flight Ops has a predictable feel to it, no matter what country you're in, just the way a church does. Half of this building is devoted to flight services, the ancillary functions that can be found at any airfield. There are always fuel bills to pay, flight plans to file, perhaps an outpost of Customs.

The other half of the building is a small commissary and exudes the distinctive smell of German food mixed with airfield sliders. More fat, more pickling, deeper aromas than you'd have in the States but that's the only difference. Outside, the tables are filled with groups of men and women eating, talking, reenacting their last flights by flying their hands through the air.

A few moments of dislocation, then German makes sense again. The babbling turns into words and I start hearing snippets of conversations. All at once, the faces and dress look normal to me and I start slipping into the current of this world.

My father is scanning the crowd just as I am, reflex as much as anything, looking for anything out of place or anyone showing too much interest in us. Faces turn toward us, curious, noting the American clothing and bearing. I hear a few comments—some are certain we can't speak their language and their comments about Sarini are blunt. Others have evidently learned not to underestimate all foreigners.

One table of men is not looking at us. No sin in that, except that everyone else is. There is something about them that sounds an alarm with me on a level I can't identify.

Then it hits me. Sarini—they're not looking at *her*. They're the only men in the place who aren't.

My father notices it, too, but he's slower to pick up the import in it. They're priests, probably Jesuits, from an order accustomed to deflecting their gazes away from women, automatically warding off temptation for those who have chosen celibacy. Their faces are intelligent, pale, and they are clearly old friends.

They're looking for me.

For a moment, the revelation stuns me. I could understand if a local Anglican priest had been dispatched to have a look around a local airfield. It would have been an unusual request but he would have complied. The Episcopal church doesn't have an enforcement arm, no ecclesiastical police to try to track down a priest on the run. Neither do our new brothers, the Lutherans, who have a much larger presence in Germany than we do.

But the Roman Catholics, ah—now that's a different story, or at least rumor has it so. If any order within any church would be tasked with watching for a renegade American priest, it would be the Jesuits.

No, this is insane. They may be Jesuits, but they're not looking for me. Perhaps they own one of the aircraft we passed on the flight line or perhaps they're taking a private plane to Rome. There are hundreds of reasons for three priests to be sitting outside Flight Ops.

Then they stand. There's no hesitation in their movements, no final conversations. One moves off quickly to circle back behind us, the other two walk toward us. I can't see their hands.

"Run," my father snaps. He shoves Sarini toward me and darts forward, distracting the two coming toward us.

Sarini yelps and clutches my arm. I grab her hand and break away, intending on running a pattern around the remaining priest.

But she balks, jerking me back. I drag her along for another step then turn loose of her hand.

The third priest knows what's happened. He's crouched slightly, waiting for me. He slips his hand inside his jacket.

I move as fast as I've ever moved. I'm on him before he has the weapon clear of his holster, slamming him to the ground then flipping him over to pull his right arm up behind him. I relieve him of his weapon, crack him over the head with the butt and then I'm moving again. It takes no longer than a few seconds, but there are shouts of alarm and the sound of hard-soled feet pounding against pavement behind me. I run.

Around on the other side of the building, the front side, a man is just getting out of his Mercedes. I shout an apology, grab the keys from his hand, and slam into the car. It starts immediately—no anti-theft devices to deal with, thank god. The tires screech as I pull out of the parking lot and onto a feeder street. Signs just ahead direct me onto the Autobahn.

I have a general idea of where we are in Germany and I'd noted familiar landmarks during the approach. But it's been six years, maybe seven, since I've been here. Will the roads I memorized before have changed?

Not that it matters. Not yet. For now, all I have to do is lose my pursuers.

I've gotten enough of a lead that they can't spot me immediately. I make it to the autobahn, head north, and start checking my rear view mirror. If they've had the foresight to take two cars, they will split up. If not, I've got a fifty-fifty chance of being right.

I accelerate to an ungodly speed in kilometers per hours, watching for pursuit. But it's hard to tell who's following me when everyone is driving like a maniac. I exit, pull over, and watch. No one follows me. I wait for fifteen minutes then head into the nearest town. Fuel and a map—then I'll decide what to do.

My plan has more holes in it than I would like. If I were still in the SEALs, I would not be allowed to deploy until I filled in the blank spots.

But I am not in the SEALs and there is so little time left. Twenty-eight hours—if I can't make it to Muralis Island by then, there will be no point in going at all.

Muralis Island is fifty miles northwest of the northern part of Norway. Not a difficult trip, not if you have cash. Hard currency, particularly American dollars, overcomes any number of logistical problems.

Travel within the European Economic Union is simple and one rarely even has to show a passport. The route in should be fairly clear. I will fly into Switzerland then head into Norway on a local train, on the theory that it will be less likely to be watched at border crossings.

Theoretically, getting into Norway ought to be a bit tougher, but in practice it's not.

Once across the border, I'll hire a private aircraft to take me north. From there, it will be fairly easy to make the arrangements for the last part of the trip.

That evening, I cross the border into Norway, heading for an airfield I remember, one where the pilots aren't likely to ask any questions. If it's not still there, I imagine I'll be able to find its replacement. As long as there are opportunities for profits, there will be men who will take advantage of them.

Arranging the flight north is surprisingly simple. All parties speak English and the transaction proceeds smoothly as soon as I produce American dollars. I'm not overly worried about treachery, although it is a possibility. As odd as it may seem, businesses such as this rely on their reputations. If I get rolled, relieved of my wallet or killed, word will get out.

Honor among thieves? No. Just good business practices.

The pilot is a congenial although careful to not ask any questions. It's not a matter of politeness. He doesn't want to know, in case anyone comes asking later. We leave an hour later and he produces two large flasks of hot sweet tea, a flask of vodka to fortify it, and sandwiches. The aircraft's cockpit is heated, but not very effectively. The hot tea is welcome. I passed on the vodka, but accept a sandwich.

Once we are airborne, we spend a few minutes in desultory conversation and then lapse into silence. The flight north takes six hours. When we land, it is still light, since daylight extends far into the nights this far north at this time of year.

I debate whether to ask the pilot to wait here or to send him back to his point of origin. It would be convenient to have him here for the return trip. Enough people down south know where we were headed that it's not a matter of operational security. When he volunteers that he has family in the area and wouldn't mind a few days visiting them, I make it worth his while.

I leave him to chock and chain the aircraft and make arrangements for refueling. A taxi takes me down to the waterfront.

Norway is a nation of mariners. It runs deep in their veins in a way that is hard to understand. Every family has some connection with the sea, whether working in a business that that supports the Marine industry, working on the boats or simply benefiting from the activity. Everything revolves around sea—everything.

The commercial pier looks well-maintained. The condition of the boats degenerates as you move out along the pier. Past the last boat tied up, a number of boats are anchored out, and these are on par with the ones closest to shore. But their business is different, of a nature that they would prefer to have a little warning before someone comes aboard.

Nothing has changed, nothing. There is every chance that I can pull this off, at least this part of it. Once I'm on Muralis Island, I'm not so sure.

If I'd asked my pilot, I'm sure he could have given me an introduction to someone in the same line of business. But I didn't want to leave a trail, so I'd struck out on my own.

The boats anchored out have dinghies tied up to the end of pier. The men lounging around know what I'm after. Most of them speak some English, enough to understand what I'm asking. Yes, they're available immediately.

Just as I am about to toss my bags into one of the dinghies, there is a murmur among my new friends. I turn back to look.

It is my father, striding down the pier as though he does this every day. And just to his right, slightly behind him, is Sarini.

Sixteen

The night my mother died, I learned about the layers of the ocean. I was in the sea, treading water, being pushed away from the boat by the current. The water was chilly on the very top, warm just a few inches below the surface. Then, down around my toes, perhaps four feet below the surface, a thread of cold water ran. It wasn't a constant layer. As I treaded water, I would occasionally dip into it, feel its bite on my toes.

My father was shouting at first then screaming her name, angry then distraught. He made far more noise in the ocean that I did and much more than my mother.

There was a moment when everything stopped. Time, the flow of water, the stars, everything froze into one whole, complete and exquisite in every detail. I held my breath, the waters layered against my skin, not wanting it to ever change.

For a moment, I thought it was forever. Then a wavelet smacked me in the face and I breathed water. The momentary panic was enough to break the spell.

I cried out and I heard my father shout my name. No longer the confident swimmer I'd been just seconds before, I flailed toward him. Within seconds, he was next to me, effortlessly shoving my hands away as I tried to climb on top of him. He flipped me over on my back, tucked my head onto his shoulder and towed me back to the boat.

It seemed to take a long time to get back to the boat. I tried to talk, to ask him where my mother was, but every time I opened my mouth, the protective spell shivered and shattered and water came flooding in. Finally I quit trying.

He shoved me over the gunwales and then heaved himself over, flopping down with a peculiar lack of coordination. I lay where I'd fallen, on my back, staring up at stars reeling from the motion of the boat.

Mysticism is the art of union with Reality, at least according to Evelyn Underhill, a noted modern mystic. That's Reality with a capital R, the one that Plato was on about all the time, not the reality with a small r that we all experience every day.

Reality is that which really is, in an existential sort of sense. Transcendent and beyond, the subject of infinite debates about what is, object permanence, perception and just about anything else you can think of. It's not something you spend a whole lot of time thinking about in the military.

Or is it? Duty, honor, courage, a higher calling—all that's the stuff mystics wallow in. The military just isn't too big into the transcendent emotional aspects of it all.

That's me—just another mystic warrior priest.

"You've made the arrangements, then?" my father asks.

Blind berserk fear, no more than a flash before rage replaces it. It is as it has always been, my father stepping in and ruining my plans. I bite back the questions. I won't ask him how he knew where to find me. I never do. It gives him too much satisfaction.

"I've made *my* arrangements," I say, relatively pleased with my tone of voice. It gives nothing away, concedes no hit. "Just go away. You've done your part and there's nothing you can do here."

My father tosses his bag into the boat. "To the contrary. You need current intelligence, and I've got it. And equipment. If you're serious about doing this—and I think you are—then you ought to welcome my help."

"You don't know what I'm doing."

"Ah." My father fixes me with that mocking gaze I know too well.

"You *couldn't* know."

"Call it an educated guess."

"Let her go."

His smile broadens slightly. "Evidently you're operating under some mistaken assumptions." He turns slightly to Sarini. "I didn't force you to come, did I?"

Sarini regards him, distaste evident on her face.

"You can't stop me," I say.

Sarini plants her hand on her hips. "You've got to listen to him. *None of this* makes sense. Come back to States. We'll straighten everything out. There's got to be a way. This, all this—it's insane."

My father raises one eyebrow. "Ah. I can see my son isn't the only one who's slightly off the mark. Did you really think I was going to stop him, my dear?"

Sarini is stunned. "But you said—. "

My father waves aside her objections. "No, of course I'm not going to stop him." He turns to me, his smile cold. "I'm going with him. And so are you."

I shake my head. "Out of the question. I'll take the information you have, but you're not going."

"That's my price. I won't go ashore, but I will be on the boat waiting for you." Suddenly, he seems to lose his temper. There's no telling whether it's an act or not. "Damn it, David, I understand the position you're in. But surely, with the responsibilities I have, you don't expect me to just ignore this, do you? There are questions of national security, of operational security—this is my field, not yours. Not any more."

He's right about that, but something is ringing a false note. The facts rattled through my brain, clearly stated and arranged in a logical order. I match those up against what I know and come to a rather surprising conclusion.

If he's so convinced this is his business rather than mine, why doesn't he have an entire team here? And what

155

is he doing out in the field? That's not what he does, not at all.

It's ironic. He has the same problem Wister did. I squash the impulse to snicker. "You haven't told anybody, have you? That you're here, that I'm involved with this. This isn't your business at all, not the way you're trying to make it sound. It's personal, or you wouldn't be here yourself."

"It's not what you think."

"You were after Caermon yourself, weren't you? The only reason Wister was there was because he knew what was happening. But as to *how* you know, ah, that's the problem. You're not supposed to know—or at least, you don't want people to know that you know. That's why you can't use any of your people, because this is a private deal. What was it, intell of some sort?"

"I don't have time to explain." He tosses another bag aboard. "Are we going to do this or not?"

"You bastard," Sarini says quietly. "You're just as bad as he is, aren't you? You lied to me."

"I didn't lie to you."

"Your whole life is a lie. Like father, like son."

So now I've got another reason to keep her by my side. If there is any hope of keeping this quiet, she'll have to go with us. Everything she owns, including her money and her passport, is on the boat, but that won't stop her. She'll try to stop us, and I can't run the risk. Not when we're so close.

My father is watching me and nods as he sees me come to a conclusion. "Let's go, then." He places one hand on Sarini's shoulder. She jerks back, and suddenly he has her arm wrapped behind her.

The men around us are impassive. These things happen routinely in their world, although usually not on the pier. "If you don't come with us, they will kill you," my father says, nodding at the men. "You know who they are."

All of the resistance drains out of her. She quits fighting and climbs into the boat, not looking at either of us. The men carrying the crates follow.

156

The ship is underway, and the sea is beginning to take her. The gentle rocking deepens into long, slow swells, and I eye the sky, trying to decide what sort of weather I can expect. I could ask the master. He speaks English and he's intimately familiar with these waters. But some part of me wants to work it out on my own. "How long?" I ask my father.

"Eight hours," my father says. "This is the working fishing boat, and it's best to follow the routine. To make a straight run in wouldn't do at all."

"Still too early," I say, checking my watch. It's new, the latest in underwater timepieces. Courtesy of my father, along with all the other gear in the crates stowed on the stern.

"It won't start getting dark until around midnight," my father answers, "and you won't have much time at all. You best get some sleep. We'll be there in time."

He turns to leave, and then he turns back to me, a gleam in his eyes. "Since this was short notice, the captain has had to leave three of his own people ashore. You're on the manifest as part of the crew. If we're approached, you and the girl will have to play your parts."

"And how is she manifested?" I asked.

"There wasn't a line for whore, so we put her down as a cook." Before I can express my outrage, he's gone.

Sarini is above decks, on the opposite side of the ship from us. I fill her in, then suggest she go below and get some sleep. There's only one compartment for the crew, and captain hasn't been gracious enough to offer his own compartment for her privacy. All three of us are bunked in with the crew.

Sarini vaults easily into a top bunk, crawls under the sheets and blanket, then pulls one end of the sheet around her head and over, covering her exposed ear and eyes and leaving her mouth and nose free. It's a well-practiced procedure. One hand settles in to keep the blanket in place. Within minutes, her breathing changes and becomes slow and regular.

I take longer to drop off. I keep remembering the last time I did this.

Seventeen

Ritual aligns one's thoughts in an order that allows one to perceive what is greater than oneself. With repetition, the words of any liturgy sink into the soul, passing conscious levels, and begin shaping our actions and thoughts. It is so with any focused activity, and special operations is no exception.

In my own squad, there were group rituals as well as individual ones. We assembled, came together as a congregation of fighting men, each bringing our own sacraments to those moments. Our weapons, protective gear, each individual item carefully prepared—even worshipped. We examined ourselves for flaws and then examined each other.

We gathered together, having each completed our individual preparations for this final rite. In the presence of each other, we don our gear, apply cammie paint to our faces unless we were swimming ashore. We shunned outsiders. They would not understand the careless chatter that took place, the rude, often profane or cruel things we said to each other. But they were the same things we said every time, reminders of whom we were to each other and what we were doing.

The last thing I always did was wind five feet of duct tape around a hard cardboard spindle. I never needed it, but somehow I felt that if I didn't take it, I would need it. The fact that I had it made me feel secure.

I had no indication that night that it would be the last time I suited up, the last time that I ran my finger along the edge of my knife to feel its edge to make sure it was still sharp.

I remember in seminary, having a feeling of *deja vu* as we donned vestments and practiced the special wraps and knots the kept the surplice in place. It was not until later that I realized the feeling in the room as we studied each other, corrected our dress, rearranged the folds of the vestments, reminded the of the last moments before a mission.

And here I am, back where I swore I would never be. It is so familiar, so—comforting in a way, to be a priest no longer. Because this I can do, have already done many times before. It is a simple, direct, immediate connection with the physical world where right and wrong are clearly spelled out. Action, reaction, consequences. All far more easily defined categories than they are in the more esoteric spiritual regions.

That's the problem with God, isn't it? You pray but you don't get the burning bush to tell you what's true and what's not. And if things don't work out the way you asked for them to, you just tell yourself there's a higher purpose at work, that it's all somehow part of God's great plan, which by definition ought to be a *good* plan.

But what if that's not true? What if none of it's true? As one theologian said: if God is God, he's not good. And if he's good, he's not God.

All this time, I've tried to get back to that state when the stars and the sea and the waves merged into one. I've gotten close a few times—once in seminary, a few times praying with patients in ICU. It's a state of being that's as impossible to forget as it is to describe. Begin by imagining that time and space no longer exist. It's then that the interrelatedness and irrelevancy of every aspect of life start to emerge. It's an exercise in will and faith and intellect that takes a lifetime to practice.

As entranced as I've been with the mystic, things are far simpler at the moment. Point, squeeze, dead. Call it instant gratification.

160

The last time I went to Muralis Island, everything had gone smoothly in the beginning. We inserted via submarine, lockout, and went ashore with swimmer delivery vehicles. It was a two-hour transit, but the wet suits kept us warm, the equipment operated well, and the only real challenge we faced was fighting off the boredom.

There were six of us: Jim Napier, Bill Jenkins, Sean Maltierre, Ron Thomas, and me. And Jeremy Forsythe.

Forsythe was a pain in the ass. He was on his second enlistment, a corpsman by training, and probably the worst shot in our entire team. Bear in mind that a bad shot in the SEALs is an expert marksman anywhere else. But in such elite company, a small tendency towards average is a fatal flaw.

Nevertheless, he always managed to squeak by on the yearly qualifications and we kept him because he was the best swimmer in our unit and had an uncanny sense of direction. With him along, we were rarely confused about where we were. His endurance extended to the land is well and he ran marathons almost at will without any training. He wasn't fast on short distances, but the slow twitch muscle fibers in his legs must have outnumbered his brain cells.

In most ways, he was a fairly adequate SEAL. But there was something about his manner that I never entirely trusted, a slacker in him that was just below the surface. I always had a tendency to double check his work, make sure he turned in reports, asked him if he verified expiration dates on his medical gear. I never caught him gundecking anything but I always thought that I might.

The two-hour swim through black water went according to plan, as did the transition from sea to shore.

The compound we were headed for was exactly where it was supposed to be, the security around it exactly as we'd been briefed. The minutes of the mission slipped by smoothly, everything going exactly according to plan.

That should've been a warning to me, I suppose. Rarely do things go that smoothly and when they do, it is usually a short-lived illusion. But I had no sense at that moment that it was all about to go to shit. I was in the groove, moving, in complete mission-mode.

Unless you've been there, actually done it, it's hard to understand mission-mode. It's exactly like the mystic experiences I've had.

You're completely focused, so in tune with and as one with your environment that you feel invisible. You move silently through underbrush, not disturbing it because you're part of the brush. The adrenaline pumps and you're invincible, even if some part of your mind observes that you're not. But you don't care, you don't listen—you remain focused on your objective as if that's all that will ever matter in your life.

That's how it was that night, rolling ashore at the rocky point, concealed in black rocks wet from the surf, timing the change of the guards, moving in silently, avoiding the motion and pressure sensors.

As briefed, the compound itself was not fenced. Perhaps the Russians felt that the pressure and motion sensors were sufficient safeguards, but that was a mistake. There's always somebody an insider, someone who's willing to help you out. Tonight, it was the man monitoring the sensors. All the alarms would be turned off, I was told, and given the lack of reaction to our egress, it appeared that it happened.

Our objective was fairly mundane—a set of trucks located at the southeast corner of the compound. Satellite intelligence showed an odd configuration on the truck beds, and there was some concern that they were long-range missile launchers. We were to go in, verify the function of the trucks, take a quick look around to see if there was any evidence of missile launchers or other preparations, and get out.

As soon as we were ashore, we broke into three groups of two, each with their own assignment. Forsythe went with Thomas, a man I would have trusted with my very soul, and his job was to make sure that Forsythe stayed out of trouble.

Napier and Jenkins were to circle around to the south side of the compound and take a look at a fuel farm that photo-intelligence was interested in. Thomas and Forsythe headed for a windowless building that we suspected held the weapons. Maltierre and I were to take a quick look at the truck farm itself, the closest objective, then fall back to provide covering fire if needed to the other two patrols, since they had further to travel than we did.

The truck farm covered two acres and was lit with overhead floods, though half of them were burnt out. Sentries patrolled solo at regular intervals. Our biggest worry was the possibility of guard dogs. Intell said there were none, but that didn't mean there weren't.

We spent thirty minutes examining each truck, looking under tarps for launch assemblies and checking out a collection of spare parts to make sure they really weren't launcher parts. Evading the patrols wasn't difficult.

Exactly on time, we were out and on our way back. So far, no evidence of launchers.

Napier came back next, arriving a few minutes before Jenkins did. I could tell from the expressions on their faces that they were pissed—some disagreement over how to execute the search and I'd bet Napier had pulled rank on Jenkins. For my money, I'd have trusted Jenkins' judgment before Napier's. A quick, whispered debrief revealed they had nothing interesting to report.

Thomas and Forsythe were due back in a couple of minutes and I could already feel the adrenaline starting to fade. We'd regroup, take a routine swim back out to the sub, and then we'd be out of there, bitching about whether or not the whole thing had been a useless waste of time. They tell me that negative intelligence can be just as valuable as confirmation of suspicions, but it's not nearly as satisfying for the guy on the ground.

We were just loosening up for the swim, griping about Thomas being slow, when all hell broke loose. Dogs barking, people shouting, lights coming on around the compound.

Thomas came staggering out of the dark. His face was twisted, desperate. "Forsythe never came out," Thomas said. "I saw him go in, I waited by the door, and he never came out. I heard the first sound, I went in to pull him out, but he wasn't there."

"What do you mean, he wasn't there?" I grabbed him by the shoulder to study him. "What do you mean?"

"He wasn't there. I figured he ran out the back door, that he'd head back on his own. When I didn't see him here, I went back to check."

Gunfire. The first burst hit Maltierre. He screamed, spun around and then slammed into the rocks. Broken. Dead or dying. You didn't have to be a corpsman to know he was gone.

We sought cover behind the rocks, spread out over the jetty. They were watching, waiting, even the two I couldn't see.

"Go!" I pointed at the water. "Now! Go!"

No one moved.

They had to know what I was thinking, they had to. I was the least-experienced man on the squad but I was the officer in charge. They knew that if we didn't leave then, we'd all die. Every second that passed made it more certain.

Jenkins grabbed me by the shoulders and held me at arm's length for a moment. He stared deep into my eyes and started to speak. "Chief, get them in the water. Now."

And still no one moved. Thomas was behind the rock next to mine and looked like he was ready to cry. "We have to go back, we have to get him, we have to—." He started back toward the compound and two men grabbed him. He struggled, but not with his full strength behind it. We dragged him to the water. The gunfire started again. The sea was safety.

By then, Thomas was crying openly. I turned him toward the water and shoved him hard. He stumbled toward the water. "Chief. In the water. Now."

Jenkins hesitated a moment longer then said, "You heard the Ensign." He started for the water.

The others followed. Within moments, we were gone, nothing more than a ripple that the waves quickly destroyed.

Underwater, we paired up again, putting Thomas alone in the middle. The trip back to the submarine seemed to take less time than coming ashore did, although I knew that wasn't true. There was no way to talk, no way to discuss what had just happened. We were each alone with our thoughts, an almost a sensory deprivation state, a world defined by the sound of our own breathing, the beat of our hearts. Only the necessity for watching for black shadows in the water around us reminded us that we were not truly alone.

My stomach churned, my soul turned dark. There was no other option, I told myself, knowing that it was true. What would be the point of everyone dying? No point.

I told myself that Forsythe would not have wanted us to die trying to get him out. He was a SEAL, even if he wasn't a particularly good one. He would have understood.

No. He wouldn't have understood. He wouldn't have expected his team to leave without him. Because that's not something that ever happens. You always brought everyone back, always. Always.

Was he still alive? If he was, he probably believed we were on our way back. He would be holding on, clinging to that thought, and enduring every torture or mistreatment he was given, knowing that we would not have left him.

That I would not have left him.

And yet I did.

At that moment, I knew my career in the SEALs was over. Because for all that the others might slap me on the back and tell me it was a bad break, assure me privately that I did the right thing, I knew that no SEAL would ever trust me again. I'd left two SEALs behind.

Maltierre, dead on the black rocks, might be explainable, if not forgivable. The only thing that holds the team together is the utter, unshakable conviction that you will not be left behind. The cold solace for your widow will be to have your body in custody, and buried with the honor you deserve.

Forsythe was another matter entirely, treason and betrayal so foul it could not even be explained. I'd left a live SEAL behind. No SEAL would ever serve with me again, not knowing that I might leave him behind.

Finally, we reached the submarine. We waited for the lockout chamber to empty, for the green light, and then the crew below opened the hatch. They crowded around the ladder, waiting for us, their faces clean, rested, smooth, eager to hear what happened. The submarine was already turning away and heading out of area, and the captain was dividing his attention between his officer of the deck, the navigator, and us.

Four of us came down the ladder. I heard a muffled exclamation. An officer stepped in behind us and looked up the trunk, a puzzled expression on his face. He turned back to us, his lips moving as he counted, as if somehow he had made a mistake in either recording the number that left or the number that came back.

The captain knew immediately what had happened. He had delivered SEALs on so many of these missions, had spent enough time with us to know what the absolutes were in our world. As much as anyone can, he knew perhaps even more than I did what I'd done.

We stripped down, started moving our gear out of the area and forward to a compartment in the bow that's ours. A mess cook followed us, six cups of hot coffee on a plate, six sandwiches ready to go. Without a word, he offered them to us.

No one wanted to take either coffee or a sandwich, because no one wanted to see the ones left on the tray. Finally, I took the extras off the trays, set them aside, and passed the four remaining rations around.

We slumped down on the deck, utterly exhausted. The man with the coffee and sandwiches left, taking away Maltierre's and Forsythe's share.

The captain stood at the hatch, waiting. I didn't know what to say to him—did not want to say the words that would make what had happened any more real than it already was. He seemed to understand that, but both of us had duties that we couldn't ignore for very long.

He could have ordered me to come to his stateroom, to debrief him privately. Instead, he crossed over the hatch and squatted down beside me. I saw the deepest sympathy burning in his face. "Killed or missing?"

"Both missing." I glanced around at the rest of the men to see if there was any disagreement. There wasn't, of course. We all knew that the MIA label would keep their pay coming for their families.

The captain nodded and said, "I'll have my XO draft the message for your signature. When you're ready."

I stood. There really wasn't any time to waste. Maltierre was dead. If Forsythe had been captured, the Russians would parade him down their streets, the outward and visible sign of our inward treachery invading their shores. There would be calls for congressional inquiries, Inspectors General would be appointed, and the Maltierre and Forsythe families' agonies would be forgotten when the public circus started.

"I'll draft it, sir."

He made a motion with his head toward the hatch. Time for a private conference now, to discuss those things only discussed between officers in his world. But it wasn't like that in the Seal Teams—everyone knew what happened.

We went to his stateroom and he slid the plastic door shut. He pointed at his rack, now made up into the couch, and took the hard-backed chair pushed into his desk. "I'll help you with the wording."

I appreciated his offer, because every syllable would be picked over later. The message would be admitted into evidence, analyzed in public hearings, and probably offered up as a training example to future classes of officers. It was important that I got it right.

The captain poured me another cup of hot coffee from a flask on his desk and we went to work.

Twenty minutes later, we were done. He'd made several suggestions quietly, not insisting, but I knew what he intended. He paraphrased my language to account for the later possibility of a court-martial, slanted some phrases that might slightly lessen my culpability. He emphasized the danger we were in, the probability that the rest of the squad would have died.

Although it might have made a difference if I'd been court-martialed, it only deepened my disgrace within the SEAL community. They saw the legal obfuscation as an attempt to escape responsibility, to justify what could not be justified. In truth, I think my skipper wished that I had died there.

I went back to my men. The color was returning to their faces, and they were moving now, stretching to keep their muscles from freezing up after two hard swims. There was a desultory sort of chatter going on, typical post-mission stuff.

They fell silent when I walked in.

I handed Chief Thomas my copy of the message. He read it then passed it around. After everyone had read it, it ended up back in my hands.

There were no words to justify or explain, so I didn't try. Instead, we returned to the routine tasks that comforted us, rechecking gear, fixing what was broken, cleaning and repacking it for storage. When we were done, we all sat down to prepare the formal after action report. That's normally when we tell bad jokes, start the new legends that form around every squad, and brag. Eventually, I would boil the bluster down into the bare facts, leaving in a little bragging but only the sort that other SEALs would catch.

This time, it was different. No jokes, no bragging— just facts. Yes, we accomplished the mission. The trucks were not long-range missile launchers, the fuel farm was only partially operable, and there were no weapons found.

I printed out the after action report and took it to the captain for release. He released it without change.

Three days later, we were back in port. We straggled out to be met by my Team commander and the Commodore. My commander handed me a board of inquiry convening order.

Eighteen

The image on the radar screen is familiar after all these years. Muralis Island covers almost five square miles, longer from north to south than east to west. It's as though someone took a low mountain range and pinched it in the middle. The southern and northern ends are jagged cliffs plunging down the water. Along the east and west sides, narrow strips of approachable shoreline almost meet in the middle, separated by a few high spires of rock.

According to the briefing packet my father provided, Muralis Island is ringed with defensive and security measures, including infrared and acoustic detection devices.

From the updated reports my father has, the Russians have been busy in the years since I've been here. The original compound is surrounded by clusters of additional buildings, although the written analysis notes that some of them have deteriorated and not been repaired in the last two years, more evidence of Russia's failing financial infrastructure.

My father. He has accepted the fact that I am not speaking to him and we pretend that it is normal. It is, for us, but this time we have the excuse of the present rather than the past. He has taken to spending time with Sarini, which surprises me. They play gin rummy, whiling away the hours in conversations about the hands. He cheats and either she does not notice or she chooses not to.

I sleep, eat, and study the new charts and reports and check the gear my father brought aboard. He's brought two sets of everything. My father has included instruction manuals.

For the last twelve hours, the crew has been engaging in normal behavior for a fishing boat while we steadily work our way north. We trudge ahead, slow to deploy the nets, then move ahead slowly, paying out the line behind us. The crew is quiet, either from boredom or anticipation, I can't read their faces well enough to know.

It goes on for hours. As the drag on the boat from the full nets reaches some magical point, the captain shouts out the order and the winches are powered up. The deafening howl prevents conversation for another hour as the lines are wound in, the stern dipping down as the nets come alongside. The crew becomes animated, shouting warnings and orders as the heavy nets filled with fish are drawn up to just below the surface of the water. There is a final, shuddering effort by the winches and the nets are over the gunwales. Masses of fishes clog the nets, heads and tails poking out at odd angles, the whole thing twisting and wriggling as the fishes choke on the air. The nets are pulled over to the cargo hold and the fish dumped into it. The boat settles lower in the water.

The waters here are rich with tuna, and the boat is already riding more steadily in the water as her catch fills the hull. Even without what I've paid the master, this would be a profitable trip for him and his crew. I watch them, the rhythm of the sea creeping back into my bones.

Finally, the island is just ahead. Fog signals sound at regular intervals, low, haunting sounds somehow different from their American counterparts. A single occulting red light atop the mast must be an antenna, the light a warning to low-flying aircraft to stay clear.

We approach the island from the west. The eastern side is patrolled, although not as often as it was during my first trip. There is still the occasional patrol boat, but the captain knows each one of them and has evidently paid his dues to be allowed fishing rights here. They approach just close enough to hail us and verify his identity then we're allowed to pass on.

We slow to a crawl and the crew swings the nets out over the side again. The master will approach no closer than two miles and evidently even that is straining the arrangement he has with the Russians. Money has changed hands in exchange for a blind eye and access to the relatively warm, shallow waters that are teaming with schools of fish. It is part of the regular arrangement, and I have no doubt that my father contributes to it. But two miles should be sufficient.

It would have been an easy swim when I was in shape. It'll be a bit tougher now but I'm confident I can manage it. The water is cold but the wetsuit has a small battery pack heater.

Just as I'm finishing getting ready, a shout from the upper deck interrupts me. The Norwegian phrases are completely incomprehensible, but the alarm in their voices is plain. The master barks out something that sounds like an argument.

My father enters the crew compartment. "The patrol boat is coming back," he says. "We'll have to get you out ahead of schedule. They're approaching from astern. No time to put you in fisherman's clothes and try to sort this out and still get you in the water on time."

It had been a risky plan at best. All it would take was asking a few questions in either Russian or Norwegian, and my cover would be blown. I had not believed it would work from the beginning.

"I'll handle the girl," my father says.

We never should have made her come with us. It was a tactically smart but morally a disaster. At heart, she is fundamentally too much a part of the power structure to understand about the bottom currents and the world my father and I know.

I can hear the noise from the other boat now as it approaches. Its engines have a smooth deep growl that tell me there's no point in trying to run.

Our boat swings hard to port. My father grabs my shoulder. "He's got them bow on. Go! " I head astern to the exit to the fantail.

Gunfire. Heavy rounds smash into the bow of the ship, devastating it. The bow immediately drops lower as cold water floods in. Panic on the deck above.

Sarini is just coming up from the crew compartment. She freezes at the gunfire. I grab the extra wetsuit in one hand, her wrist with the other and drag her after me toward the stern.

How long could she survive the water without a wet suit? I don't know. But whatever is happening here is certainly not survivable. At least she has a chance ashore.

"No." My father grabs and tries to pull her away.

For all that he stays physically fit, my father is still twenty-five years my senior. While I may not be in the shape that I was when I was in the Teams, I have far more experience at hand-to-hand combat than he does. A few quick moves and I take him down. The deck cants deeply forward now and it's difficult to keep our balance.

"Come on." I drag Sarini out to the stern. I shove the wetsuit at her. "Put it on." She's done this enough times that she wriggles into it automatically, hopping first one one leg and then another as I drag her toward the stern. The suit's a bit large for her, which makes it easier to get on. The down side is that it'll make it less effective in the water at keeping her warm.

She's still struggling with one shoulder when we get to the stern but the boat is heeling hard to the side now. It's far more dangerous to make an uncontrolled entry into the water than go in half-dressed. I grab Sarini around the waist and vault over the low railing.

The water is too cold to be painful. For just a second, every nerve ending seems to go numb, paralyzing me. I am temporarily confused, overwhelmed by the sheer pain of the cold water.

Sarini is struggling in my arms, fighting her way to the surface for air. I go with her and let her take a few deep breathes before I grab her by the shoulders.

"Listen to me. You remember how to buddy breath?" I hold the mouthpiece out to her. She nods, her gaze now riveted on my face.

"Show me." I watch as she slips it into her mouth and breathes, then passes it back to me. "All right. That's how we'll do it. We're heading in. You'll feel better once we get moving."

I have done this before, swimming through water this cold, and it is excruciatingly painful. It's not something I'd attempt unless I were in top condition.

I pass Sarini the regulator for a breath. She grabs it greedily. Fear and adrenaline are making her breath far too fast. I wonder how long the air is going to last.

We swim, heading for the shore, staying shallow, no more than five feet below the surface of the troughs, just deep enough to keep underwater and out of sight. They won't suspect this. They can't. Not unless—.

Not unless they know why we're here. Not unless they know there are Americans onboard and that I intend to go ashore.

Sound travels well underwater. I hear an explosion behind us as a pressure wave as much as a sound. The fishing boat—it has to be. Gunfire would not make this deep, resonating bass sound.

I should not do this, but I have to know. Besides, I rationalize, it will help preserve our air supply.

I surface, drawing Sarini along with me. As soon as we break the surface, it's obvious. The blackness is broken by an ugly red scar on the water, orange and red flames twisting. The Russian patrol boat has backed off to a safe distance and is watching it burn. There is not even a pretense of trying to rescue any survivors. While I watch, their lights shift, they come about and speed off to the north.

I feel nothing. I tell myself it's because I am too completely focused on the mission, that I must be in order to survive, but I'm not certain that's true. Even under the calmest of circumstances, would I feel any regret at my father's death?

I will when this is over, I promise myself, although I am not sure why it matters at all. But perhaps there is some biological bond that will invoke grief and override my real emotions. I don't know and I don't have time to worry about it now.

Sarini twitches under me, and I know she's seen the flames. She's breathing greedily, although an occasional wave splashes in her face. I stuff the mouthpiece in her mouth, take a deep, cleansing breath myself, and head back underwater.

It'll take more than five minutes to reach ashore, but Sarini has no way of knowing that. She may be counting off the seconds even now, but I doubt it. Her world has narrowed down to simple survival, the imperative of getting air, not freezing to death, and waiting. Sometimes that's all there is to life.

Even through the wetsuit, I'm conscious of her body near mine. The travel underwater quickly becomes boring, even under these circumstances. The water is featureless, increasingly murky as we approach ashore, and visibility is less than four feet.

Once we're ashore, it's going to be worse. I am equipped for one person, not two.

But she's doing well under the circumstances. I wonder how I would do if our situations were reversed. I have a sneaky suspicion not as well at all.

Nineteen

By the time we reach the island, my legs are burning. I cannot imagine how Sarini has endured it.

A natural jetty of rocks juts out from the eastern shore. It's where we went in before and, judging from the charts my father brought, still the best ingress point. The noise of waves pounding against rocks increases the ambient noise level and the jagged profile of the rocks will mask our noise and our movements.

The trick to approaching rocks in the water, particularly jetties, is to keep moving fast enough to maintain control but not so fast that you can't avoid contact. It's best to approach at an obtuse angle. That way, if you hit it, it's a glancing blow rather than a more damaging collision. It helps if you've got strong legs so you can push off from the rocks when you miscalculate.

I time the wave motion and shove Sarini up onto the rocks, then follow her up. I pull out an insulated thin waterproof blanket from a pouch and wrap it around us both. We lie there panting, waiting for our breath to slow.

"Stay here," I say when my breathing is regular again. If they're already ashore, they'll have come in this way.

My swim boots are corrugated on the bottom, providing traction on the rocks. The jetty is not long, a little over fifty feet. Near the end of the jetty, black lines snake down into the water, mooring lines leading to the swimmer delivery vehicles.

Sarini is shivering and trying to stay out of the wind, nestling in the cleft of the rocks. She's not used to this sort of exhaustion, the physical and mental, but she knows how to force herself to concentrate when exhausted.

"So what now?" she asks.

"I have to go. You wait here until I get back."

"The boat. Is there a chance?"

I shake my head. Nothing survived that fireball.

"What went wrong?"

"I don't know."

"Your father. I'm sorry."

"The Russians may have taken the crew off," I lie. "He might be a hostage." I don't believe it, but there's no time to wonder about that now.

I shelter my watch with my hand and punch the button to light it up. Napier and his men are in position, fighting off muscle cramps and boredom, waiting for exactly the right time.

"Half an hour," I say.

"And if you don't come back?" She stirs under the blanket, then peels it back and begins folding it up. "No. I'm going with you." Her hands tremble.

"No. It's too dangerous." Even as I say it, it sounds ridiculous. "You'd slow me down."

She stands, a bit shaky, the blanket wrapped tightly around her. "I'll follow you. You don't have time to argue with me, do you?"

If I wait any longer, my muscles will begin stiffening up. "All right, then. Stay close."

We head toward the line of trees growing between the hills and the shore, taking advantage of what cover there is. The base is west and north, facing on the ocean. A pass between the rocks to its south provides the best means of access, or at least so we'd determined during the last mission. The SEALs won't take that way, not after what happened six years ago, but any other approach requires considerably more gear than we have. There is no choice. We will approach from the south.

There was a time when the terrain would have spoken to me. I would have known where they were, have seen the choices they made and their reasoning. Now there is not even an echo of their presence. I have no idea where they are.

But I know where they're going.

Sarini moves doggedly behind me. How she manages to keep up is beyond me. The cold from the ocean sapped her energy, but keep up she does. Perhaps the movement is curing the cold.

I push forward faster than I should. Time is running out. It should take us an hour to execute this approach if we do it the right way, but there's no time for that. Twenty minutes, that's all we've got. Less if they've moved their plans up.

Somewhere out there, six men are moving slowly toward the same objective, taking their time. I can almost feel them, know what they're thinking. Undoubtedly they are remembering what happened last time SEALs were here. The squad will be thinking of the men who died here, and Napier will be thinking of me. Whatever happens, he won't repeat my mistakes. But he will be thinking of the last time we saw each other.

It had been outside the Naval Legal Services Office, on the day that the charges against me were dismissed. I had already handed in the letter of resignation and it was making its way up the chain of command with unprecedented speed. The Navy was ignoring the normal six months waiting period and had indicated that I would be transferred to the inactive reserves within the month.

Technically, I wasn't resigning. I couldn't. My original contract with the Navy required me to spend four years on active duty and four years in the Reserves. Although I'd offered to resign completely, the Navy hadn't been all that eager to turn loose of me completely.

What I had done was not a criminal offense under the Uniform Code of Military Justice. The law allowed—even required—me to pull back and leave those men behind. Legally, I was not guilty.

But the reality of it was far worse than any court of law could adjudicate. I had betrayed my men, the brotherhood, everything we stood for. If they could have killed me for it, they would have, and I was almost surprised that no one tried.

But this is a more civilized military than in earlier days, at least when units are in the States. There would have been an investigation, inquiries, and too much chance that they would be caught, and the trail would have eventually led back to Muralis Island. If there's anything the Special Forces hates, it's having to air dirty linen in public. The security classification problems alone in taking me to trial would have been significant. But as long as I was in the Reserves, the Navy, should it decide to proceed against me, wouldn't have to recall me to active duty to do it.

Napier met me outside the courthouse. I saw him coming, moving in that peculiarly deceptively slow manner of his. There was a looseness to his joints, an awkwardness that could explode into speed.

He had been in the field when we'd returned from Muralis Island and had just returned two days ago. Whether because he was under orders or as a matter of personal preference, he had not spoken to me. He had gone out of his way to avoid the SEAL compound, taking advantage of the stand down time allowed after any mission.

He stood in the middle of the sidewalk, barring my way. My attorney, a sharp lieutenant commander, was a step behind me, and touched my arm to pull me back. He must have sensed that there was danger.

If I'd been in my right mind, I would have run. But it had all gone too fast, the mission, the consequences, the court martial, and I was hardly coping with reality.

Naps waited until I was five paces from him, then let me catch a glimpse of the knife in his hand. It was a Kabar. The sun flashed on it so quickly that my lawyer did not notice it. But, just as Naps had intended, I did.

I stopped within arms reach of him, inside his killing zone. It took a few tries, but finally I said, "I'm sorry."

Naps' face was cold, so cold. Not since BUDS had I seen his face so devoid of expression, a blank slate, reduced to sheer reflex. I think, in that moment, he might have killed me if my lawyer had not tried to step between us, unable to understand just how close Naps was to killing both of us.

To this day, I have never been sure what stopped him. I'm not sure I want to know.

But whatever it was, Naps lashed out, slapped me open-handed across the face, then turned and walked away. My lawyer started shouting, even started to go after him. I recovered enough to grab him.

"What was that all about?" he said when I finally turned him loose. His dignity and uniform were ruffled. "Come on, I want to get Base Security—."

"No," I said. "That was Napier."

"Let go of me." The lawyer kept trying to get away but I barely even felt him struggling. "That's a battery. You've done nothing wrong. He's got no right to commit battery."

"He's got every right."

And he did. I lost two of the men he'd entrusted to me, two of *his*, and no amount of apologies would ever make up for that. By entrusting them to me, he'd failed them.

Would he kill me now, years later, when he'd let me live before? I didn't know but he was the first one who came to mind.

Napier was a year younger than I was. He was a fierce man, a throwback to some other time. He believed in the SEALs with the faith of the saved. From what I knew of his background, that wasn't far from the truth.

Brilliant, driven Napier. If I had had just an ounce of his character, I would be dead on Muralis Island.

Nominally, we had much in common. We were both from middle class backgrounds, with military fathers. While my father was moving up the officer ranks, Napier's father was moving up the enlisted side of the house. We had both knocked around a fair part of the world in our parents' transfers.

The differences, though, were significant. Napier came from a loud, chaotic family. He was the second-born of seven children, the first son. I had visited his family, which reminded me of a school of fish, moving as one but with so many parts that it was impossible to watch any one individual.

Napier's father ruled with a congenially brutal hand, even his adult children. There were rules, and the punishment for breaking them severe, but there weren't that many. There was no doubt he was fiercely proud of his son, the first officer in the family, a SEAL at that.

After we'd finished BUDS, Napier had invited me home with him for the holidays. By that time, my father was already disappearing on mysterious missions for weeks on end. I was expected to understand that duty came first, but this particular winter, just fresh from BUDS, I had a strange nostalgia for people who had families during the holidays.

I relished the chaos at the Napier household. To an only child raised in my circumstances, the noise and chaos was virtually incomprehensible. There was no corner of the house that didn't have noise in it. Napier bitched about it, but it was clear that he missed it. No wonder he'd had such an easier time than I had adapting to the confines of the training barracks. At least there he had his own locker.

Maltierre's face is the one I see in my nightmares. I wonder if Napier does, too.

The terrain turns downhill, and the trees are sparser, but still denser than they were the last time I was here. "Quietly," I tell Sarini, warning her although I'm not sure there's anything she can do differently.

According to my father's charts, the motion detectors start just at the perimeter of the trees. The closer we get to them, the more danger that they'll notice us, although the trees will block us somewhat. Still, it's not a chance I'm willing to take if I don't have to.

Another twenty feet, and I motion to Sarini to stay behind. There's no need for her to go any further, but if I leave her too far behind I may have trouble finding her when it's time to get out.

This is the only part of the entire plan I've had figured out from the beginning. Simple problem, simple solution, and one that I hope will get us both out of here alive.

It won't take much to trip this trap. A few rounds fired into the compound, no matter if I hit anything or not, and they'll be on full alert within minutes. Lights, guns, dogs, everything. The reverberations may confuse the direction enough to give us some time. If we can get back to the jetty, we can hitch a ride home with the SEALs.

The flaw in the plan, of course, is twofold. First, getting back to the jetty in time. Second, I'm getting entirely too close to breaking the seal of the confessional. Not that that matters to Sarini or Napier. I've already verged too close to the line by accepting help from my father, and while I may grab a ride with the SEALs, I'm not answering any questions about it.

God knows how I'll explain it to Napier. Assuming that he lets me live long enough to say anything.

I've gone far enough. Any closer and I'll worry about tripping the motion detectors. That would perhaps do as a method of tripping the trap, but it will assuredly rob us of the slight advantage that might help us escape.

The nearest guard tower is centered in my sights. One shot there, that's all. They'll be on alert anyway, since they know we're coming, but they'll be expecting something besides rounds fired from the tree line.

Take a deep breath, hold it, squeeze—I'm just slipping my finger inside the trigger guard when Sarini screams.

Twenty

An arm snakes around my neck. Somebody kicks my feet out from under me and I hit the ground. Cold steel lays flat against my neck, requiring only the slightest pressure to turn and slice into my throat.

"Who are you?" a quiet voice asks. "You're not them—that's the wrong pattern of cammie."

"Dalt. The mission is compromised. Call it off."

Silence. The sounds of the forest seemed loud.

"If they want us to abort, they've got ways of getting in touch."

I start to shake my head, and feel the pressure of the knife increase slightly. "It's all compromised—all of it. They're waiting for you. It's a trap.

"Why should I believe you?"

"Where's Naps? He knows me."

I wait. They're discussing this over the whispernet, their field communications headsets. I hear movement.

Another voice, one that I recognize. It's Napier. "Dalt? David Dalt?"

"Yes."

"Aw, shit." Small sounds as people move around me, then a red light flashes in my face. "It's him. Let him up."

The knife against my throat doesn't move. "Maybe he is who he says he is, but that doesn't explain anything else."

"*That* Dalt?" someone asks. Another long silence, and just as suddenly as it had found my neck, the cold steel is gone. Now free to move, I prop myself up on one elbow. Three men crouch on the ground around me, their faces camouflaged painted, their expressions grave. Sarini is sitting up now, a man standing behind her.

Napier is just as I remember him, lean and dark, the hungry look in his eyes. "Just stay on the deck until we get this sorted out. I'm going to call back for guidance."

"Don't do that," I say. "It's all compromised—all blown. The Russians have your frequencies, the gear to frequency skip, the crypto—everything they need. You check in now, they know exactly where you are, and know that it's been blown."

Napier doesn't believe me, but he doesn't key the gear, either. "How do you know that?"

Sarini speaks up for the first time. "He can't tell you."

"And who the hell are you?"

"Sarah Sarini. I'm a doctor at Balboa."

"Oh, a doctor. Then of course I should believe you." Napier turns back to me with an ugly expression on his face. "Good move, asshole. Compromise the entire mission and bring a chick along for company. I got to admire your style."

"Nappy, you know I'm a priest now, right? There are things I can't tell you. But don't go in. Please, Nappy, you can't."

Napier grunts. "I'm not aborting on your word alone. And if what you say is true, there's no way to verify what you're saying. Pretty convenient, isn't it?"

"At least change the plan," I say. "I swear to God, they're waiting for you. They know exactly how you're coming in. How do you think I found you?"

"Suppose I do change the plan? How do I know that's not a trap?"

Napier has a reason not to believe what I'm telling him, but the last thing I expected was to have a problem convincing him that he was in danger. But from the sound of it, he will go ahead anyway. I wonder what he has been told about it.

"Naps, what if we came in from the south?" a new voice asks. "If what this guy is saying is the truth, it would still work, but they wouldn't be expecting it."

Napier shifts his gaze to the man who'd spoken, a flat challenge. But he's too good at what he does not to recognize the possibility that I'm right and allow for it. "Comments?"

"It would work," another voice says.

"Sure."

Napier considers it for a moment, then nodded. "Okay."

Relief. Not as good as having them abort, but better than walking into an ambush. "OK, then. We'll meet you back at the SDVs—yeah, I found them," I say.

Napier shakes his head. His expression is difficult to read with the cammie paint and in the night, but I can see he's not convinced. "Oh, no. That's not how it works." He stabs his finger at me. "You're coming with me. And your playmate goes with Carter." A wolfish grin appears on his face. "Just like old times, huh, Boomer?"

Napier steps up until his face was just inches from mine. I can see the strain and determination around his eyes. "If you're setting us up, Dalt, I'll kill you myself."

Twenty-one

The approach from the south takes us through low hills covered with stunted trees and brush. Sarini is ahead of me with a man they call Shorty. More formal introductions have not been tendered, but by the bulk and shape of his gear, I know he is a corpsman.

Sarini does well, from what I can see. Noisier than we are, but not so much as to cause danger. That reassures me—I am not so sure that Napier would tolerate much more. He has always been rigid, adverse to change, but the ease with which he has agreed to alter the approach impresses me.

Finally, we are at the nearest point of approach. The compound is as I remember it with the new buildings far less obvious than they had appeared from the briefing photos I'd studied. The six men speak briefly into their whisperphones, short phrases coordinating other last minute alterations in the plan. No one wants to take Sarini—it's decided that she will wait here alone. I wonder if she will go along with that then realize that she will have little choice in the matter.

One man touches Napier's shoulder then flashes a hand signal I recognize: *quiet—someone's coming*. Napier gives me the hand signal for *follow me*, and waits to see if I recognize it. I nod, and follow him. Sarini follows my lead.

Now I hear what spooked the kid. Someone is moving through the sparse underbrush, trying to be careful but without the skill to pull it off. Even Sarini had more woodcraft.

Napier loops around behind a small grove, one with a clutter of dead branches beneath it. He points, then signals: *wait here.* Sarini and I crouch down in the hollow. Almost as an afterthought, Napier pulls a 9mm pistol out of a leg pocket and gives it to me, along with an extra clip. I don't have to check to see if a round is chambered. No weapon in a SEAL's pocket on a mission is ever unloaded.

The brush rustles, then silence. No cries, no alarms raised. It's repeated moments later as the second man is taken down.

Napier reappears. The team converges on him, a bit noisier than before since they're carrying two bodies. They dump them unceremoniously—but quietly—on the ground next to me, and began piling branches and leaves over them.

I say an abbreviated version of extreme unction, make the sign of the cross over the bodies. The SEALS ignore me. Sarini is still the cold, expressionless person she's been since the jetty.

"Only two, routine patrol." The explanation is for my benefit, and I nod. "Alpha point—ten minutes." Napier signs for me to follow him.

We creep around the compound, moving slowly at first, then faster when Napier realizes Sarini and I can keep up with him. My leg muscles scream in protest, threaten to buckle under me. If I have to swim back out, I'm done for. I don't have that much strength left.

That's not how you survive something like this. You focus on the second right in front of you, then the minute. You stick to the plan. You don't think about the pain, about how you're going to get out, about anything at all except the one instant you're living at that moment.

I lose track of the other men, and barely keep up with Napier. We move through the darkness forever, but the longer I walk, the more old habits and skills come back to me. By the time Napier signals a halt, it is though I have never left the teams.

It is so familiar, the exhaustion waiting just behind the edge of adrenaline, the fear, the sense of not being alone as long as you know that the rest of your team is with you.

Alpha point—the thought strikes me suddenly. They had planned for this—they had to. You always had contingencies upon contingencies, just on the off chance that everything went to shit at the last moment. Why had I ever tried to tell them what they ought to do—I should have known better.

Hope flashes through me. The reason I hadn't thought of it was that I wasn't a SEAL anymore. Not really. Despite how familiar things seemed, no matter that I still recognize the hand signals, equipment and practices of the team, I no longer belong.

There's no sense of loss, rather one of moving past and beyond, from printing capital letters to cursive writing. As a SEAL, the first thing that would have gone through my mind upon seeing the bodies of the guards was relief. As a priest, it was a prayer. With a sigh of relief, I turn loose of that past.

The SEALs knew I was past it, too. They have since the moment with the cross. They're double-checking my moves, keeping me close, making sure I don't screw up or betray them.

Napier raises his hand. I stop. We're at the edge of the woods, at the point that is the closest approach to the compound. Seeing it from a different angle now, it's not as easily accessible, but it's doable. There were advantages to make up for the shortcomings, this closer approach to the compound itself.

From here, it is simply a matter of making our way to the power facility on the east side of the compound, planting the explosives and getting out. We have thirty minutes, no more. More than enough time if everything goes well, far too little if things don't.

Something had been bothering me the entire time, something I couldn't put my finger on. But now, as I watch for shadows shifting and moving, almost invisible across the open space, low and barely moving, I know what it was.

Caermon set this up and sold the team out. Wister, maybe my father, maybe other entities, suspected that Caermon was dirty. And yet, seeing as I do now my own ineptness in my old craft, I wonder how I had managed to evade both Wister and my father the entire time.

At the time, I hadn't questioned it. But now, evaluating it in light of my own demonstrated inadequacies, I see how ludicrous it is.

The first escape from the hospital, okay: I had the element of surprise on my side. But after that, when I went to Sarini's house and later contacted my father and Wister and when Wister had followed me to Crest—just exactly how was I able to pull it all off?

At the time, I'd thought it was because the need for secrecy limited their resources. Too many agents, too many helicopters and road blocks and somebody would start asking questions.

But that wasn't reasonable, was it?

No. It wasn't.

There were too many times that they should have had me, should've stopped it all. And they didn't. Why not? How did they know where I was, get so close, and still let me slip through their fingers. What is the common thread?

My father. The realization sank in as cold that cut through to my heart. In every instance, my father was involved, had known what was happening, or had been the instigator.

And he had died on the fishing boat.

Or did he?

Oh, doubting Thomas who must see the wounds. Is that who I am?

Yes. There are plenty of Pauls in the world, plenty of Johns and Simons. But as for Thomases, those who had to see reality, touch it with their own hands, feel the blood—well, that had been my role in the teams, and that is my role now.

I had not seen my father's body. I heard the shot, heard my father cry out. And I made the logical assumption. Just as I was supposed to.

But why?

I am so cold. Colder than I'd been since the last time I was here.

Why have I made it to this point? How?

Because this is supposed to fail. Because someone wants the SEAL team driven this way, wanted them off their original task. And that someone is my father.

I move forward to touch Napier's arm, then remember my communications set. I start to speak, trying to arrange the words in a logical sequence.

Too late.

Lights around the compound flare to life, shattering light against the fog. Friendly shadows disappeared, and the edges of the woods are well lit.

For a moment, I'm blinded. There's a confused mutter of voices over my headset, barely words, more curses. A shadow in the open field breaks into a run, zigging and zagging across the landscape.

"Come on!" I hear the voice simultaneously in my headset and from the dark figure in front of me. Napier grabs my arm and pulls me along with him, stealth and craft giving way to the sheer necessity of covering distance. I run, trying to avoid the branches but concentrating on driving my feet and my legs into the ground like pile drivers, letting them propel me through the forest as fast as was possible.

I crash along six feet behind Napier, close enough to follow him yet just far enough away to give me a chance of surviving if he hits a booby trap. Sarini is with Shorty. He grabbed her by the arm as soon as the noise started.

I know what Shorty must be thinking. Sarini isn't a member of the team. She is, at this point, simply a liability. For all the self-serving noise we make about protecting civilians, in the field our only duty is to each other. It is not their fault I brought her into this—it is mine. And it's my responsibility to make sure she gets out if we do.

I drop back a bit from Napier, and then head off in the direction I saw Shorty and Sarini headed. They're not hard to follow—we're making no effort at concealment, not now. Distance is safety.

They're not difficult to catch. Sarini, despite being in good shape and full of adrenaline, is slowing him down. She's just slammed into a tree and is staggering. Shorty is dragging her along, swearing, and I know he's almost done with her.

"Dalt! Where the hell are you?" It's Napier, just realizing that I'm not behind him. My status here is questionable, but, as a former member of the team, higher than Sarini's. They may make an effort to get me out alive.

"Shorty, just behind you," I say in response. It would be of little help to Sarini to have Shorty kill me. "Coming up now." I crash through a last stand of saplings and I'm on them.

Shorty is breathing hard, his eyes narrowed and cold. He drops Sarini's elbow. "Take her." He takes off immediately, leaving me to deal with her. Sarini crumples to the ground. I pulled her up. "Come on. This isn't safe place. We have to get out of here."

She nods, but I can see she doesn't understand. There's no time to explain, no time to repair a drowning psyche. I simply grab her arms, pull her up and begin dragging her through the underbrush. "Come on, come on."

Perhaps because I set the pace, she begins responding. Soon she's doing her best to keep up with me.

It's not good enough. I can hear them behind us, the men and the dogs getting closer every second. I don't know if even the SEALs can get to a place of safety. But I know where they are headed. I know where there SDVs are, and that will be their first choice for escape.

I angle us toward the beach, intending to intercept the rest of the team who will have regrouped and will be arcing to the beach. If we can cut across their arc we may

194

have a chance to get to our SDV and follow them to the sub. Undoubtedly Napier is leading his pursuers into some sort of diversion or trap to give the team time to escape. Now if they will just all follow the team instead of us, we may be able to get there in time.

"Dalt. How did they know?" Napier's voice is coming in short gasps now, but still quiet.

"I told you it was blown," I told him. I've got too much to do keeping Sarini on her feet and moving and watching for obstacles to get into an argument with him. If he doesn't believe me now, we are done for. Our delivery vehicle is moored next to theirs. "I tried to tell you." Even if we make it, I'm not convinced that Napier won't kill me himself.

The light changes, as do the sounds. We're nearing the edge of the trees, almost to the beach. I stop, pulling Sarini close me, and whisper in her ear. "Very quietly now. Just for a little longer. If nobody is there, we'll be back in the water in just a few minutes." I don't tell her that I have no idea where the submarine is or even whether the SEALs will allow us to follow them.

Sarini is beyond answering, completely focused on what she's doing, hanging on to my every word as though I have divine revelations. I don't, but it will not help things to tell her that.

We moved slowly and quietly to the edge of the trees. I can see the beach now, rough and strewn with rocks. In the distance, the jetty. The sounds of pursuit behind us have faded away for the moment. I allow myself to hope.

"Shorty—point." Napier is assigning Sarini's former guard to check out the area. A single click acknowledges his command.

I don't know where they are, but they must be near, within running range of the jetty and the delivery vehicles. In a matter of seconds we will know.

Suddenly, a star explodes overhead and slashes a hard circle of light on the beach. No, not a star—a helicopter that has moved in quietly, now playing its light over the sand looking for us.

Sarini draws in a deep breath, and I know she's about to scream. I put my hand over her mouth and pull her close, holding on as she shakes and twists away from me. "Now, now," I whisper in her ear. "It's okay, it's okay."

But it is far from okay. If the helicopter is there, so are the men. Even if there are no ground troops, the helicopter can mow us down as easily as anything.

A sharp crack, and a hard ping. Someone from the squad is firing at the helicopter, but to no effect. Evidently it's a ground action helicopter, hardened underneath for just this occasion. They'll shift their aim point now to the cockpit, I know. But I doubt that they're carrying high enough caliber weapons to make much of a dent.

"Naps. You have to believe me." I say quietly, urgently. "I'm in the tree line—if I was behind this, would I be trying to get out? And would I bring a girl along?" I have to convince him. They have an alternative egress route, but I have no idea where it is. If they decide to head for it without taking us along, we're trapped.

"Proceed north," Napier says finally. There are no other directions.

"Swim?" I asked. A single click acknowledges the question. I shut my eyes, cold creeping through my gut. Sarini can't be up to this, not after what she's been through already. A free swim out to the submarine is within the capabilities of any SEAL.

Any SEAL with the right gear. With the right training. Sarini may be a strong swimmer, but she's light years out of their league.

"Come on," I say, and pull her after me. "There's a boat coming in for us."

It's not, but I have no intention of telling her what's ahead. She'll just have to face it when we get there.

We head back the way we came, crossing almost under the helicopter, moving quickly and silently now. She's trying, but it's not working. I know how Shorty must have felt, the adrenaline surging through him, moving quietly and trying to stay alive while saddled with Sarini.

No. I am not that man. I will not leave her here as Shorty would have. It is my fault she's here, and we will either leave or die together. But something in my flesh keeps insisting that no one will ever know, that it will look like an unavoidable accident. Even the rest of the team would not know exactly how it happened, although they might suspect the worst of me. God knows I've given them reason to. But no one would betray me. This is very different from what happened with Forsythe.

"Dalt. You there?" I click once. "About two miles. There's a stretch of trees, almost to the water. You know it?" The image from the chart springs into my mind. I click.

"We won't wait. If you bring her, she's your responsibility."

"I know," I say.

"We're not waiting for you, either. Fifteen minutes, Dalt. Then we go."

Fifteen minutes. I suspect he's leaving some leeway because seven minute miles would be require a superhuman effort in this terrain. Still, I can't afford to count on it. "We have to hurry," I say to Sarini. "They're not going to wait long for us." Not at all, but that falls into that category again of things she doesn't need to know.

I set a grueling pace, one that is tough even on me. I hear her breathing hard, out of control, sobbing at times until she realizes it's a waste of energy. Her breathing is harsh and ragged, but I can't slow the pace. She's got to keep up. This is the only chance we have.

"Stop," Napier says. "You're too loud."

I stop, wondering what he intends. Will he let us approach at all? Or will he simply order us to remain where we are while he leads the rest of the team off the island? I'm very cold and urgently need to pee.

There is a short burst of gunfire. It sounds almost innocuous. Napier swears quietly over the whispernet.

Then the helicopter is back, the light blasting down on the sand.

"Damn you, Dalt. I'll see you in hell." There is no doubt in Napier's voice.

"No. It wasn't me."

There is no answer.

Is there a third egress? I imagine so. A primary and two alternates, three possibly. That is the standard we used to plan to. Where would I have made it? I can think of a number of possibilities, but all of them involve communicating with the submarine, letting it know that there's a change in the plans. If I lose them now, we will never get off.

"I told you. The entire operation is compromised," I say, moving away from the edge and deeper into the woods. "The mission, the egress points—everything. And it wasn't me. I came here to make you abort."

Still no answer. I am beyond the pale, a non-entity. If Napier or the others see me, they will put a bullet in my head without question. Sarini, too.

"If you leave me here, then you're no better than I was," I say finally. It is my last shot. There can be no man out here who has not heard about me and what I did. "Look, if you have a third egress point in your plans, it's compromised. They know everything, Naps. Everything."

I am so rusty, so out of practice. I doubt I could evade capture on my own, even without Sarini to slow me down, for more than half an hour. I am clumsy, too loud, too slow. What was I thinking, to bring her here?

Better to let her drowned on the boat? And your father would not have left her back, either. If you had not agreed to bring her and she had not agreed to come, he would not have gotten you here.

Why? Why had he agreed at all? This still puzzles me, but there's something else behind that worry that's demanding to be heard, some other idea that I can't ignore.

I'm old, rusty, and it has been years since I've been here. I'm out of date. I am—.

Not compromised. In a blinding flash, I see the old map before me, the one we briefed on before heading in last time. Now I know why something looked odd to me. There were things missing. An updated chart, my father said. Not the terrain itself but the infrastructure. If I can just remember—.

I do. "Napier," I say, barely able to control my voice. "Your third point—they'll be there, too. I told you, it's all compromised. I've seen your charts. But it isn't the same chart we used when we were here last time. There's a drainage system, Naps. It's not on your chart. But it was on mine back then. If it's still there, it's a way out. It dumps into deep water."

More silence but I'm certain he's listening. Napier is not dumb. He knows that everything that has happened so far is also consistent with my explanation and warning. He's wondering whether he's doing the right thing or not.

The safest thing for Naps to do is to abandon us. But as I pointed out to him, he would be no better than I was. That is going to hit hard, and he won't be able to resist denying it. He'll have to consider the possibility that I might telling the truth, particularly if the third egress point is compromised.

"I'm heading for the cliffs," I say, certain now that it's the only way out. "If you try the third route, come back and meet me there." I pull out my ground chart and read off a set of coordinates, hoping my memory's right. "It might be a few hundred feet off either way. I remember where it was, inset between two spires. There's a tunnel there that reaches back into the drainage system. And an access hatch—that's what it's there for, to clear blockages. It was one of our alternates, Naps. We can get there, signal the submarine and get away from shore without having to cross the beach."

More silence. Sarini is trying to control her breathing and listen to what I'm saying, but my voice is barely audible. She pulls back suddenly, jerking me to halt. "What's happening?"

"I know how we can get out of here. But I'm not sure he believes me. He thinks I'm leading them to him, and he's thinking about it."

"If we can get there, at least we can get out. " She seizes on this straightforward concept, but it's not that simple.

"We need them," I say gently. "I don't know what frequency the submarine is on and we have no way of contacting it on our own. We need their air, too."

"How wide is it?" she asks, and I see the shadow of claustrophobia in her eyes again.

"It's pretty big," I say. "Look, let's go. We can worry about that when we get there, okay? One thing at a time."

That reassures her. There's a plan and someone is in control, even if isn't her.

It's about three miles from where we are right now, but this time we have the dubious luxury of being able to move more slowly. The sooner we can get there, the better. They'll be expecting us to head to the third egress point, and they will be waiting there for Napier. At least he'll go slowly and try to lose them in the forest.

It takes forty-five minutes to reach the to the other edge of the trees, moving carefully. Twice I hear sounds of a patrol, and I bring us to a halt. We wait, barely breathing, as the sounds fade away in the distance. Whoever these guys are, they're not nearly as careful about making noise as we are.

The rocks that formed this island are volcanic, the remnants of an undersea volcano long dead. The rubble and scree at the base of the spires tends to be boulders rather than sliding shale, much easier to manage.

We stop at the edge of the wood line and I point out the features to her. If something happens to me, at least she'll have a chance.

I hope Napier is not waiting too long. In another forty-five minutes, the sun will be coming up.

It doesn't look exactly as I remembered, but close enough. The tunnel should be right behind the first of spires, set slightly back from it and not visible from here.

At one time, there was a path that wound around to the right and through a gap. Although I can see the general shapes of the rocks, I can't make out enough detail to see the path.

I study the terrain until I'm as certain as I can be that I know where we are. Then, I tap Sarini lightly on the shoulder. "Just follow me. We're going to climb."

"Shouldn't we wait for them?"

"Now." Better that she not think about it, but Napier and his men, if they are walking into another trap, are an excellent diversion. And we need all the help we can get.

I lead the way, moving slowly, picking my way through the boulders until I find what might be the start of a path. I follow it for twenty feet until it cuts back into a dead end. Frustrated, I backtrack, then began searching at the base of the cliffs again.

"Over there," Sarini says. The night is perceptively lighter, just enough so that details are beginning to emerge. I squint, not seeing what she's pointing out, and then I have it. "Let's go."

We start up again, still moving carefully but increasingly aware of the time. There's no doubt now—it is getting lighter, and every second increases our danger.

The path leads up then cuts back just as I remember. The entrance is set into the north side of one of the spires and I'm fairly sure I know where it is. I hurry for it, not risking using my flashlight just yet, then stop suddenly.

Yes, this is where the tunnel is. Or, was. It looks like part of a spire has broken off, leaving a rough semi circle of the first part of it exposed. What was a solid floor is now a one-foot ledge sticking out from the side of a sheer rock wall. Below that is a three hundred foot drop down to the forest. I move up to the edge, getting as close as I can, wondering if the rock under my feet is going to crumble.

Now I know why this egress point was not on Napier's map.

Twenty feet in, the tunnel is still intact. I think I can see a dark door set into the rock at the end of it, but I'm not sure. There's barely enough light to see, even now that our eyes have recovered from the helicopter's blinding light.

I strip off my gear and pile it on the ground. I take out my length of rope, tie it under my arms and belay it off a boulder. There's no way Sarini alone can support my weight, but I could climb back up on my own if I fall.

"Be careful," Sarini says. She has not asked any questions. It's fairly obvious what I'm doing.

Before I try it, I remember to brief Napier. If anything happens to me, they may have a chance. "Naps, one side of the tunnel is down. There's a ledge about a foot wide that leads to where the tunnel picks up again. Going to try to traverse it and see if it'll take my weight. I'm leaving the girl here with my stuff."

More silence. Then, finally, barely audible, a single click of acknowledgment. Relief courses through me.

I edge out onto the ledge, my face pressed against the rock. So far it seems stable. Inch by inch, I work my way across the bare cliff face, heading for the tunnel. I try to remember to breathe.

The rock is cold, sucking the warmth out of my fingers. I grasp for handholds on the face of the cliff, knowing that if the rock crumbles under me I'll not have the strength to hold on, but determined to give it a shot if I can.

It's definitely lighter now. If we're going to do this, we have to hurry.

Finally, I'm there. I step onto the solid rock, kneel down just a moment to catch my breath. The shakes hit me, but only for a moment, then I'm fine again. I look up and see Sarini staring at me wide-eyed.

Reluctantly, I unfastened the rope around my waist. It would not do me any good now if the tunnel collapsed, since the falling rock would surely crush me. Nevertheless, it has felt like a lifeline and I hate giving it up. I toss the rope out into gloom. "Your turn. A square

202

knot around the waist, then do just as I did. It's very solid, with plenty of room for your feet. Don't look down and go slowly."

"I—." Sarini starts to protest, as some part of her mind tries to convince her she still has a choice.

"The others will be here soon. You have to move now!"

Sarini fastens the rope around her waist, then, with a deep breath, forces herself out onto the ledge. At least she has the advantage of having seen it done and has some reason to believe it will not crumble under her feet.

She takes no longer than I did and she collapses on the floor. I look back and groan. Our gear is still on the cliff, along with my remaining air tank. I will have to go back and retrieve it.

Just then, the whispernet clicks. "Dalt. We're at the base."

No time for discussion of what happened. I give them directions to the path up and wait, watching. As they round the corner, and I see there are only three of them. Shorty and who else—I tried to remember the missing man's name, but can't. Sarini unties the rope and starts to toss it back to them. I have a better idea, and loop our end around a rock on this end. It will form a sort of a railing. Not that I think they need it. Not nearly as much as I did. Napier divides up my gear between them, and they begin crossing. The extra weight makes them dangerously unbalanced, but they're more capable of handling it than I was.

The SEALs move quickly across the ledge into our sanctuary, and once again I am reminded of how little I have kept from those days. Napier hands me my air tank and checks the gauge. He looks at me, his face impassive. "Not much. How long is the tunnel?"

"Not long," I say. One of the other men groans.

Napier cut him off. "We'll manage." His gaze switches to Sarini.

"Buddy breath," I say. "She's good at it. PADI certification."

Napier nods. More than he had hoped for, but that's not saying much.

He checks all the gear and the gauges and divides up the remaining air. There's a good chance we'll all be breathing off one or two bottles by the time we make it to open water.

Meanwhile, one of the other men is speaking quietly into a miniature satellite transponder. The green bars indicating signal strength are not maxing out, but it's the best he can do. I see him glance over at Napier, and hear the unspoken conversation. He would get better reception if he climbed to higher ground, but Napier is not willing to risk it. The man nods agreement, and transmits his message. The submarine will be monitoring that satellite frequency every two hours and receive the recorded message.

"Let's do it." Napier double-checks everyone's fittings, and submits to an examination himself. He leads the way to the end of the tunnel where a steel hatch is set into the rock. There's a chain lock holding it shut, but that poses no difficulty. Napier starts to open it, and stops. He turns to me. "How often is it in use?"

"Back then, not often. It could be bone dry right now."

The man standing next to Napier swayed slightly. Then he reaches out one hand to steady himself against the wall. One of the other SEALs is at his side immediately, taking his gear.

"Where?" Napier demands.

"Ribs. I think it just grazed me." Sarini moves to his side, a new light in her eyes. This is something she knows how to deal with, a situation she understands. For the first time in three days, she is again God.

"I'm a doctor. Let me see it," she says briskly.

Napier shoots me a glance. I nodded confirmation. "Go ahead."

He undoes his wet suit and pulls up his T-shirt. Someone hands Sarini a bandage from the medical pack. She dabs the blood off and examines the wound. The

SEAL's face is still as she pokes and prods, just as she did with Caermon, reading his illness through her fingertips.

"It's more than a graze," she says. "The good news is it missed the lungs. The bad news is I think you've cracked three ribs. And the bleeding, the exit wound especially."

Napier grunted. "How are you doing?" he asked the man. It wasn't a question about his medical condition, it was aimed at his state of mind. There is only one appropriate response.

"I'm fine." Translation: I can make it.

That was the primary lesson learned in BUDS, the basic underwater demolition course we all went through: the power of the mind over the body, the ability of the man to keep going under all circumstances as long as he believes he is capable of doing it. I have seen men run on broken bones, swim as their core temperature plummeted far below safe levels, hold their breath longer than humanly possible. All that, and survive.

Besides, there really is no other option. He has no choice but to be fine. If we could call in a medical evacuation flight, we wouldn't be standing in this partially-collapsed tunnel.

Sarini's hands are still busy, taping, packing, strapping. Without asking, she plunges a hypodermic into his arm, emptying part of it. "Morphine. Just enough to get you out of here."

Napier lets Sarini deal with his injured team member and moves over to hatch. He tests the dogging wheel then lays his face against it, pressing his ear against the cold metal. He puts his hand over his other ear so as not to be distracted. He shuts his eyes.

A few moments later, he says, a faint trace of relief in his expression, "No water. At least not now."

That at least was good news.

Sarini has finished. Her patient pulls his wetsuit back on and reaches for his gear. Another SEAL hands him his air tanks, and he shrugs into his pack, buckling slightly under the weight.

Napier returns to the group. With a small, almost imperceptible hand movement and a nod, he talks to his pack. The squad is so tightly integrated that they understand immediately what he's ordered them to do. The injured SEAL's gear has to go out so that there's no trace that they've been here, but the injured SEAL isn't going to carry it.

Napier surveys his merry little band, his face cold and calculating, then with an economy of motion and words spoken only to deal with Sarini and me, he pairs us all up, taking the injured SEAL as his own partner. "Let's go. We got a ride home waiting."

His new swim buddy says something quietly to Napier. Surprise, followed by impatience flash across Napier's face. Then he turned to me. "Deal with it." He stalks away, and begins opening the hatch.

The SEAL draws me aside, away from the others as though not to contaminate them. I can see it in his face now, the hunger for reassurance. He looks to be about twenty-two years old, long enough to have some experience in what can go wrong in SEAL egress operations and young enough for this to be the first time he considers it happening to him. "I'm going to make it, you know," he says.

He's a soul in need of his God right now, if ever there was one. This is why priests exist. Not to build sanctuaries or hold prayer breakfasts or bingo. Past all the ritual, liturgy and corporate structure of the church today, it boils down to this: the sacraments that bind man to God.

Am I a priest? Yes, just as Bishop Oakes said, nothing can remove me from the apostolic succession. I am, however, under a letter of prohibition, ordered by my bishop to abstain from exercising those priestly powers.

This young SEAL needs me now. No, not me. He needs reassurance that God is with him. The unworthiness of the priest does not invalidate the sacrament.

Standing here, confronted with the need in his eyes, my calling rings as true as it did the first time I heard it. I am called to be a priest and nothing can change that.

"What's your name, son?" I ask.

"Harold. Harold Duke."

I lay my hands on his head. "Harold, are you truly sorry for all the sins you have committed in your life?"

"Yes."

"Do you repent and turn again to Christ?"

"Yes."

I remove my right hand and make the sign of the cross on his forehead. "Rejoice, for that which was lost has been found again. Go in peace, and know that your sins are forgiven."

He closes his eyes for a moment then nods. "Thank you." Harold sticks out his hand and shakes mine. "See you on the boat." He joins the rest of them and I follow.

I start to ask if anyone else wants absolution, but then decide not to. As much as they studiously ignored us, they all knew what I was doing. If they want it, they have to ask for it. Even Caermon himself had known that.

Napier assigns us to our deployment order, and pats the first team on their backs as they slide into the pipe. He gives the first one a thirty second head start, then taps his partner on the shoulder. The noise from their transit down echoes up through the pipe like peas rattling in a pod. Napier sticks his head into the pipe, listens, then gives us a thumbs up. "You okay?" he shouts down the pipe.

The reply came back faintly. "Dry all way down to the water level. The pipe's pretty rough in spots. Lots of floating debris in the water, down for about three feet, but you can get through it."

"Okay, go."

Sarini and I are next. He holds us back for forty-five seconds, giving the first team time to clear the way. He checks my air and regulator one last time then thumps me on the back. I grab the top of the hatch, swing my legs in, and sit on the edge for a second. I look back at Sarini.

She is backing away, her face pale and panicked. The claustrophobia again. "Come on, it will be fine." I try to reassure her, but she's not hearing anything. I look at Napier, but his face is unreadable. "Go. She'll be right behind you." Two SEALs grab her and she screams. I start to climb out of the pipe. Napier puts one hand in the middle of my back and shoves hard.

I hit the opposite side of the pipe, bounce off it, and end up on my stomach, feet first, sliding down. It's a steep angle, but no worse than I've seen at water parks. Even as I pick up speed, I manage to roll over on my back.

If I tilt my head back, I can see a faint patch of light far above me, as the dawn shines through the open hatch. Then that's blocked out for a moment and a high-pitched scream fills the enclosed area, echoing up and down. It continues on and on and on, grating on my nerves, and I feel that sudden surge of identification with Shorty again. Why the hell can't she just shut up? Does she think any of us like this? But there's no choice, none at all, and she might as well just deal with it and concentrate on staying alive.

We slide down the pipe like that for two, perhaps three minutes, Sarini thirty seconds above me but linked to me by her vocal cords.

I hit the water. The shock rattles my legs as if I'd landed after a parachute drop. Then I am under, cold water on my face. Something slams into my face, and something else knocks me on the side of my head. I hold my hand over the mouthpiece and breath deeply, waiting for my motion to stop. No point in surfacing now, not when Sarini should be hitting the water shortly. If she lands on me without the water to slow her down, it could be fatal. I count off the seconds.

She hits the water twenty-two seconds after I do. I can only imagine her panic, and she didn't even have fresh air rushing into her mouth to reassure her. Her leg touches me then she kicks and heads for the surface. I wait a second then follow her up.

She is in a dead panic, flailing, not even trying to tread water. She keeps going under and surfaces choking. As soon she sees me, she grabs and tries to climb up me, not even thinking rationally enough to go for my mouthpiece. I grab her, spin her around, try to pin her arms to her side, but fear gives her strength. She jabs back with an elbow, smashing my cheekbone, and tries to climb up on top of me again.

I move out her way and let her sink. The fastest way to get her under control is to let her verge on unconsciousness from oxygen deprivation. There's no time to waste trying to reassure or reason with her, not with the next team heading down the tube shortly. Thirty seconds pass. I duck back under, grab her and shove the mouthpiece into her mouth. I switch on my flashlight, and hold it under my face.

She sucks greedily on the air, not entirely conscious yet. As she revives, the panic returns. I head for the surface, holding her against my chest and shielding her from the junk floating. As soon as we break through, I start talking to her, my mouth hard against her ear so she hears nothing except the sound of my voice. The words matter less than the tone of voice. "It's okay, it's okay, it'll be over soon," again and again, battering down the fear.

With a supreme effort of will, she regains control. I can hear Napier shouting down at us. We're running out of time. "We have to go. The next two are coming."

Sarini's flailing is slowing down. She's backed off from terror to simple panic but even in her agitated state, she knows there's no other choice. She can't find her voice but she nods, her eyes wide and unblinking.

I hold my voice level and calm. "Let's go, then. The air in here is probably toxic anyway." She nods again. "Here we go."

I slow down treading water, sinking lower in the water. She fights me for a moment then, with a tremendous effort of will, clamps her hands on my shoulders and follows me down.

As with so many other things, the dread was far worse than the actual experience. Below the surface, sounds go dead. They travel further but they take on a peculiar quality you only find underwater. Hollow, as though they're imposed on a far more fundamental reality. You get a sense of the transient nature of life, of how fragile the shifting sounds and shapes and emotions of the surface are contrasted to the timelessness of the sea.

It's not an easy trip. The pipeline angles down every so slightly and the pressure increases. Debris drifts in the water, some of it floating and some so waterlogged it hangs motionless in the water until I push it aside. Our passage stirs up ancient silt.

Sarini has a death grip on the penlight. We settle into the rhythm of the swim and the circle of light bobs against the edges of the pipeline. It's slightly larger than the shaft was, the surface dark and rough.

My arms and legs burn so I try to disassociate myself from my body. I focus on the last rites I'd administered to the injured SEAL. What was his name? Harold. Harold Duke. Will it matter to him that he's my very last parishioner?

Another odd connection occurs to me. In the Episcopal Church, confession is known as reconciliation. If you shorten that to recon, how different is it from what any SEAL team does as it enters strange territory? Had all the times I'd taken point prepared me later to be ordained? My left thigh cramps hard.

Perhaps Muralis Island drove me to the seminary instead of the cemetery. If it hadn't been for that, I would have stayed in the Navy as a SEAL and probably done well at it. I had liked the life, enjoyed it even.

Reconciliation or recon? Seminary or cemetery? Were those my only choices?

The water seems colder and rougher. It seems like I've been swimming for hours but it can't have been that long. At most, it's half a mile to open sea, if I remember the old charts correctly.

I'm dimly aware that I'm flailing in the water, sucking on an empty tank and that it won't be much longer before the cold and the pain rob me of the ability to resist trying to breath water. Peace envelopes me, as powerful as it is unexpected. I still fight, yes, even knowing that it is useless. Because that is the compulsion of the flesh, the will to live even when the mind knows the soul is immortal and that to die would be to be reunited with God and to know transcendence.

I will die in the water around Muralis Island. Will die now where I should have died before rather than leave Forsythe and Maltierre behind. As Napier would have died to get me out, as the crew of the fishing boat died to get me here, as anyone else would have done.

The water around me is warmer. Hot, almost. Pain surges through my hands and feet at the circulation returns and the warmth radiates up my limbs, driving the cold back before it. Sweet cool air fills my lungs—not air, not exactly. It's too thick, too hard to breath, but it floods my mouth and lungs when I inhale. I take deep, satisfying gulps of it, swallowing down a sense of peace at the same time. Everything is going to be all right. It has *always* been all right. I have just been too foolish to open my eyes to it.

"So. You're back." The voice is friendly, cheerful, and familiar although I have not heard it precisely like this since my first time on Muralis Island. "What is it with you and air tanks, huh?"

I open my eyes and see Him again. He's sitting on a rock just like the one I remember but the waves are much calmer. It's warmer, too. Overhead the sky is a flawless blue.

"Hi," I say. I should be on my knees, reciting formal prayers in Latin, something more appropriate, but He doesn't seem to mind. "Am I dead?" Not that I'm really worried about it. It's impossible to worry about much when you're around Him, as I learned the last time. The last time—the beginning of the last four years.

"You worry too much," he says. "What did I tell you last time?"

"You said, 'Look at me.' I have been. I'm a priest now."

"I know." Of course He knows. This is the odd part—how does one even attempt to have a casual conversation with Jesus? Yet that's what he seems to want, this gentle one-on-one banter. "But are you a priest right now?" He asks. "At this very moment?"

"I'm always a priest," I say. "That's what they told me."

"And do you believe that?"

"I believe in You. The rest of it, I don't know. I guess I do."

"Ah. And this whole swimming bit, the deal with the air tanks—that's something priests do, right?" Gentle humor, but with a point.

"I didn't know what else to do. Should I have told them about Caermon's confession?"

"No, of course not. You did the right thing. But here you are again, aren't you? Think about that. Back right where we were last time. You've never really left Muralis Island. Not the way I wanted you to."

"If I were a better priest, I would have. Post traumatic stress, all that—I *know* about it, I can deal with it."

"And yet here you are again. Still in the thick of it. You always come back to the sea, don't you? Why do you think that is?"

"I like the water."

"Do you? Really and truly? Are you sure?" He smiles at me, and the radiance is almost unbearable. "Something to think about."

My vision blurs. I no longer see island, water, sky and Jesus. It is one vast kaleidoscope of color encompassing everything in the world. His voice chimes at the very edge of my perception. "Go back, David. And watch those air tanks from now on, okay?"

Consciousness fades. I float.

Twenty-two

The pain brings me back, striking deep into tortured calve and thigh muscles. It radiates up into my gut, twisting my stomach inside out. I vomit and am oddly surprised when I don't breath water.

I flail, trying to connect with whoever is holding me away from the water. I won't die on land—I won't.

"Feisty bastard, isn't he?" a voice says. American—not Russian.

I open my eyes and find I'm in a small compartment, a medical sick bay by the looks of it. Three men in blue jumpsuits look down at me. One on either side holds my wrist down.

"It's okay. You're safe," one man says. "You're onboard USS *Centurion*, a submarine, in sick bay. They pulled you in half-drowned."

I try to speak. All I can do is produce deep, hacking coughs. One man holds out a glass of water and helps me sip from it. "Salt water is rough as hell on vocal cords. Just take small sips. I'd rather not start you puking again." My world narrows down to the paper cup that I can touch but I can't hold.

"Slide one arm around his back," the man ordered the other. "Hold him steady so we can get some of this down him." A strong arm is suddenly behind my back, helping me sit.

I concentrate on the water, and count it as a victory when I can support more of the weight of the cup myself. Finally, when I've choked down half of it, the man says,

"That's enough for now. Okay, now don't try to talk. Just nod your head if you can. Can you do that?"

I try to speak then nod.

"Good, good. Do you know your name? Just nod."

Nod.

"And do you know what day it is?"

This one throws me a bit. Standard orientation questions—am I oriented times three, person, place and time—but I've lost track of time.

"Probably not," the other man said. "They lose track of time out there, and god knows how long he'd been traveling to get there."

"And do you know where you are?"

Nod. *Yes. You just told me. On a submarine.*

But how? The last thing I remember is suddenly feeling warmer in the water as I lost all feeling in my legs. I was swimming, trying to catch up with Napier, but it was so cold and they were so far ahead of me, so far—what had happened?

"The other SEALs pulled you into the airlock. They did mouth-to-mouth and buddy breathing while we brought them in. You weren't breathing when they dumped you on me, but you seem to have gotten the trick of that back fairly easily." The man smiles. "I'm Doctor Denarius, Pete Denarius, the medical officer. This is Commander Arnholt, the skipper, and I guess you know this fellow." He pointed at the third man.

It's Napier. Showered, shaved, probably fed, but with deep line of exhaustion still around his eyes. I recognize the pain—it has been in my eyes, too, the last time we were at Muralis Island.

"You pulled me out." It hurts to talk.

"Yeah, partly. You were already on your way."

"All?" I croak, hoping Napier understands what I'm asking.

He does. "Everyone's here."

"Alive?"

He shakes his head. "Shorty didn't make it. We were almost here when he died. I was buddy breathing with Sarah the last stretch, then put her on his tank. We were worried about blood in the water on the way out—the sharks, you know—but they weren't much of a problem. Couple of them had their eyes on you, though."

All bodies accounted for. A profound sense of relief sweeps through me, followed immediately by bone-deep weariness.

"I saw Jesus," I say. Denarius and Arnholt exchange a concerned look. "Really. Like last time."

"Sleep now. You guys can talk later." Denarius pushes a syringe into the IV line running into my arm.

"No. I have to tell you about my father." The worlds don't sound intelligible even to me, as my vocal cords give out. I have to tell them who betrayed us, why it went so wrong—the darkness claims me before I can even finish forming the thought.

Denarius keeps me out for another twelve hours. I wake ravenous. Food appears almost as soon as I can ask for it, and for the first few minutes I simply gorge myself. Denarius won't let me have seconds, though.

Somehow during the time I was out, I have made a decision. I will not tell anyone yet what I suspect about my father. Not yet.

I force myself to spend the remainder of my time sleeping and resting up and thinking about my latest—I'm not really sure what to call it. A vision? Near death experience? An encounter with the transcendent divinity or the last gasp of consciousness giving way to hypoxia? There are arguments for both, but I know one thing to be true—He was right. On some level, I am still on Muralis Island and I will have to deal with that to avoid returning in one way or another.

That first mission, I now know, was compromised by Caermon. And by my father. We were sent there as a signal, left to die on the beach.

I consider simply killing him. The plan has the advantage of simplicity. But there are two drawbacks.

First, I do not relish the possibility that I would spend the rest of my days in prison for patricide.

Oh, perhaps it would be a chance to develop an exciting new ministry. I could hold Bible studies, win men for Christ, spend days in studies, deepening spiritually in the harsh conditions.

Shit, no.

Second, I find myself completely incapable of contemplating it. The revulsion overcomes me. Perhaps it is innate and the reason we do not see scriptural stories about sons killing fathers, some deep biological constraints on killing the source of our genes.

No. Murder versus killing. I have killed. I won't murder.

Then what? Do nothing?

No. I cannot return to who I was unless I set this straight.

Would my father have left me to die on Muralis Island the first time I was there? Did he even know that I was involved? I try to tell myself that it would have made a difference to him, but I'm not convinced.

And it doesn't matter. What he did to my brothers, he did to me. Hurt one of us, all react. I am a priest, yes, and I believe that with all my heart. But I am also Scorpion, and will remain Scorpion until what was wrong is set right.

Caermon.

MccCallister's illness.

I was set up to hear what Caermon had to say. Oh, my father knows me too well, far better than I ever suspected. And he knew Caermon as well.

And he thought I would tell him whether Caermon named him. Thought that at least he would be able to read it on my face, tell immediately whether Caermon had implicated him.

And then I disappeared. Or tried to. With all of the assets at his command, my father must have been able to locate me immediately. He let me run, even kept Wister off of me. Why?

216

He must have been relieved the day I called him and asked him to meet me. He would have believed that if Caermon had told me anything, I would not ask to meet him.

In the long run, a few lives more or less make no difference to his plans. What matters is that he himself is not exposed.

Twenty-three

I have performed six marriages since my ordination. Six couples, participating in a sacramental rite, standing before the congregation, their friends, and in the presence of God swearing their undying commitment. I studied their faces afterwards, looking for a sign that they have experienced instant bonding, the immutable melding of souls that Scripture says occurs. If it happens, it's not detectable to mortal eyes right then. You can see it later, if the marriage survives, but not immediately.

Not so with combat. If you live through it, there is a deep and immediate change. Men who stood with you are your brothers. You may not like them, you may even hate them, but the bond runs far deeper than one forged anywhere else.

So I endure the congratulations, the slaps on my aching shoulder and punches in the biceps with good grace. Nothing has changed. It is as it was last time. What we have done together binds us in a way that no other experience can mimic.

The *Centurion* takes two days to clear the area, and then is within range of the aircraft carrier *USS United States*. A helo is dispatched and we are hoisted up from the sail and transported to the carrier. A medical team meets us on the flight deck and those of us with the slightest injury are slapped onto stretchers and transported to Sick Bay for evaluation.

They keep me in sick bay for full a twenty-four hours, along with the others. There is no need—I have done this before, and I know the sounds my body makes when it is seriously injured and when it is not. But they don't take my word for it and make their decisions based on their tests. I stay on the ward, sleeping, eating, and thinking—far too much thinking.

The others are jubilant. Of course they are—it is that soaring spirit when you should be dead, when by all rights you should be a rotting corpse on foreign soil, and yet despite the odds, you find yourself still alive. It's not a conscious thing. The physical body has its own imperatives, whether or not the conscious mind is in agreement, and staying alive is right at the top of the corporal list. But for me, there is a lingering regret that I'm back in this world and not on the beach with Him.

The doctors do serve one useful purpose. Their orders are not opened for debate. I'm restricted to the ward, to have no visitors other than those operationally necessary, and those must be screened in advance. This is their way of allowing the admiral to come down to congratulate us first, ask after our well-being and shake my hand. He is not happy that I cannot muster that enthusiasm that he expects me to show. And since I'm in a hospital gown instead of my uniform, there's no cross on my collar to remind him of how wrong it would be.

"I have another visitor for you," the admiral says, still forcing the smile on his face despite my lack of enthusiasm. "And this ought to cheer you up." He walks to the door and beckons. I feel a cold chill. I already know who it is.

My father. He's never looked this old.

When I was young, just growing up, I had the sense that he was completely invincible. In the early days, he still wore his uniform, and over the years added stripes, the gold increasing every year as did the fruit salad on his chest. Some time in my early teens, he changed what he was doing, and from then on wore civilian clothes. The uniform came out occasionally for special events, but less often over the years.

He was dressed casually now, another recent change. The IBM business suits had given way to khakis, then to even more casual garb. A blue pullover knit shirt, white pants—nautical without being a uniform. I wonder if he'd even brought one with him and if anyone other than me knew exactly who he was.

"Two minutes," the doctor warns him, and he stands by the door to make sure his order is obeyed.

You did well," he says. "I was worried, you know."

I do not speak. We both know he if he had had his way, I would not be here now. But since I am, the inevitable reshaping of history will begin, with those who stood sufficiently on the sideline stepping forward now to take credit and proclaiming their past support.

"There was a dinghy," my father says. "I got off the boat just in time with an emergency radio. The carrier picked up the distress signal and sent a helo out for me. Just in case you were interested." There's a sharp edge now to his voice, not necessarily out of concern but an effort to prod me into reacting. He wants to know what I know, what I suspect, and he can't tell that until I talk.

I don't believe him.

"I guess you still have it in you," my father says. He's aware that doctor is watching us, and even at this moment is crafting more of his personal legend.

A sacrament is an outward sign of an inward and spiritual grace, the church teaches. What does it mean that my thoughts don't show on my face? Is it a sign that there's no inward or spiritual grace? Maybe. Or maybe I'm not making any sense.

"They say you'll be fine," he says. My father raises his voice now so the doctor can hear him. "Probably let you out of here tomorrow."

"I'm going to tell them," I say. I keep my voice low so that only he can hear me. "Tell them everything."

My father turns to look at the doctor. "I wonder if we could have some privacy? There are some operational details to discuss."

"Of course." The doctor withdraws and shuts the door behind him.

My father waits until he hears footsteps going away and then says, "You think you know something, is that it?"

I nod.

"Ah." He pauses as though considering that, and I am aware of the deep sense of manipulation again. "Don't you think you owe me the courtesy of an explanation?"

"I don't owe you anything. If I do, it's not this."

"I see. 'I didn't ask to be born,' instead of 'Honor thy mother and father'?"

"Don't quote Scripture at me."

"Don't try to practice intelligence work with me." For the first time, there's an undercurrent of anger in his voice. My father covets information above all else, and I know something that he doesn't.

"No one else knew where I was going," I say, speaking slowly. There's a moment coming that I don't want to face, yet there seems to be no way around it.

He makes an impatient gesture. "You muddy the waters wherever you go. I covered your tracks as best I could."

"Covering your tracks. Is that why you had the crew of the fishing boat killed? There was no dinghy, or at least there wasn't one you escaped in. You were on the Russian patrol boat."

"Believe what you will. You always have."

"They'll charge you with espionage. Treason, whatever the right words are. And for murder."

"The fishing boat? Come on, David, think about that. Even if there were any evidence—which there isn't—who's the more likely suspect? A fugitive or his grieving father?"

"I'm not talking about the fishing boat. Mother. She wasn't depressed and didn't go overboard by herself. You killed her."

He hadn't seen that coming and it stops him for a moment. But not for long. He's had a lifetime to fashion this particular legend, and he's very practiced with it.

"You were young. You couldn't possibly have known how she felt."

Ah, but I had. He was gone so much, so much. Mother and I drew together to create our own world and he had occupied a space of mythic proportions in it. He was to me who she said he was. Until that last night.

"I knew her better than you did, " I say.

"Death by misadventure," he says. "That was the coroner's finding." He starts to say something else then stops. "Although you caused a good deal of trouble, talking to Wister about it. More than you can know."

"There's no statute of limitations," I say. "If there's a way, he'll prosecute you."

"Then you'll be there as a codefendant," he says, his voice gone cold. "You think you know what happened that night—you don't. You know what I told you. And what I told you was in your best interests."

"Right."

"You were always a willful child," he says. "You had to go swimming that night—you had to. Even if she'd been awake, it wouldn't have made a difference. By then she was drinking so heavily that she had no judgment whatsoever. Whatever you wanted, you got. I was the only stabilizing influence in your life."

"If you call brutality stabilizing."

He ignored me. "That night, you waited until you thought we were both asleep. Fortunately, I was still awake. I heard the splash and got up to see what it was. I think I knew right then what you'd done.

"Your mother heard me get up—she had passed out about two hours earlier, long enough for some of the booze to metabolize. That part of it that she hadn't puked up. She was just like you, you know, sneaky and willful. She evidently heard me get up but she waited until I was on the deck before she followed me up."

"I didn't jump in first. Mother did."

"You *did*. The current had already caught you and was dragging you off. I tried throwing the life preserver, but you couldn't get to it. I think your mother realized how serious it was then. She jumped in after you, screaming and crying. She wasn't much of a swimmer, even weaker

223

than you were. And not an ounce of common sense in her, not a bit."

"That's not what happened. That's not!"

"Oh, but it is. That's exactly what happened. I had both of you in the water and I was throwing life preservers at both of you. I went in—and I went to you. I pulled you up, strapped the life preserver on you, and turned around to look for her. She was already gone."

"No." *Yes.* At some level, I knew what he was telling me was true. "What you told everyone...."

"I didn't want you to go through life knowing you'd been responsible for your mother's death."

Theology is replete with stories of father's sacrificing sons in service of their gods. Abraham on the mount. Christ hanging on the cross.

Why are there no stories in Christian scripture about sons sacrificing fathers?

In the ancient Greek and Roman worlds, sons routinely challenged their fathers for control of the heavens, and that is reflected in mortal literature is well. Oedipus killing his father, sleeping with his mother. And every single time it is an act of heresy, of sacrilege. The duty that runs from father to son is not the same as the one from son to father.

Scorpion made promises, too. I walked away from them, thought I could begin again, that the rite of ordination would supersede all other obligations, both Scorpion's and those I owed my father.

But duties don't work like that. They don't simply replace each other. Instead, they are layered, intertwined, until so many layers accrete and the burden becomes a gridlocked immovable mass.

If I am ever to break free, there is only one way. I have to go back to the beginning, to the first broken vow. I have been Scorpion, and now am no more. I must now be a son.

"Turn yourself in. Confess," I say.

He laughs. "Right. You sanctimonious prick, you're the one responsible. You keep secrets, I keep secrets.

Whatever you think you know, you'll keep to yourself, you understand?"

"No."

My father steps closer and examines my face carefully. There's an unhealthy smell about him, as though he hasn't bathed in days. Perhaps just the result of eating Russian food on the patrol boat.

He sighs and steps back. "You won't, will you? I should have known. Even after all I've done for you—kept your secret your entire life. I could have told people, you know. What happened that night. But I wanted more for you—you were all I had left. I thought."

"When did you realize you hated me?" I ask.

He sighs. "At the funeral. You were sitting next to me at the memorial, and the priest was talking about eternity. All I could think of was that I was separated from her *now*. And you were crying, like you had anything to cry about. It was all your fault."

"I was a child."

"I could have had other children."

"I was a child!"

"You destroyed my life. Just like you're trying to do now."

He's across the room and at my side in an instant. Dull black metal flickers in his right hand. He thrusts hard, aiming for my gut, the knife already starting an upward twisting motion.

I managed to get my free hand in front of it and knock it down. The blade skims my side instead. He jerks back, but I throw myself out of the bed, pivoting on the restrained arm, and pin his arm while forcing him to the ground. If I am rusty and out of shape, he is even more so.

He sprawls below me, the knife still in his hand. Before he can move, I have my heel resting on his throat, pushing down, while I fumble with the restraining band on my right wrist.

He grabs my foot and tries to slide out from under, but I shift my weight and increase the pressure. I feel tissue give way and he tries to suck in a breath but can

225

only produce a thin sound. My heel has closed his airway, and there is no more panic-inducing feeling than trying to breath and not being able to.

"I could kill you now," I say softly. "You know I could." I let a bit more weight fall on that leg, and wonder if it's already too late. There's panic in his eyes now, true fear for the first time I can remember.

"Stop it!" a voice shouts. Doctors and corpsmen pour into the room and overpower me. I'm pulled back onto the bed, and restraining straps reaffixed, this time in ways I can't get to. No matter—I have exhausted the little energy I have left and couldn't resist even if I want to.

Sarini appears in the doorway then, in uniform. She comes to the side of the bed and touches me lightly on the arm. "You'll be okay," she says softly. "It's all okay." She turns back to the rest of them. "Aftereffects of the hypoxia, don't you think?'

"No." I recognize the voice even though I can't see him. "No." I heard footsteps and then Wister is standing by the bed.

The doctors have pulled my father to his feet and are checking his throat. There's an angry swath of red where my heel rest on his throat.

"Any permanent damage?" Wister asks.

The doctor shakes his head. "He was lucky. He could have crushed his throat."

"Not so lucky." Wister pulls out a small laminated card from his wallet. He clears his throat, then says, "You have the right to consult an attorney...." and continues on through a recitation of the Miranda rights.

"Wired," I say when he's finished. "You did it again."

Wister nods. "Yeah. But this time, it worked."

Twenty-four

I walk away from the final hearing, after hearing my father sentenced to what will amount to a life term. He will not survive long in prison. Whether it will be the hardships of prison life that take him or the actions of some other inmate, I don't know. I suspect he will not wait for either. He has always liked to time his own life, and he will take control of this as well.

My father's attorney, a round, chubby man in a rumpled uniform, catches up with me, panting. How my father must despise him! I wonder why he chose him to start with.

He holds out an envelope. "Your father wanted you to have this."

I don't even stop walking or look at him. Why would I care what my father had to say to me?

"He said to tell you it's the last answer," the attorney says. "Come on, Dalt. Don't be an ass. The man's going away for very long time—the least you can do is read it."

His time in prison will not be as long as the rest of my life, and I will be living with this long after he is gone. But nevertheless, I stop.

He catches up with me and tenders the envelope. It's my father's own stationary, and my name is on the outside. It's light, as though it contains a single sheet of paper.

"When did he give this to you?" I ask.

"Before the hearing. He knew what was going to happen—hell, I think we all did." He looks at me curiously, as though wanting to re-explore the issue of why I would not testify for my father.

I take the envelope. These are the words of a man who will be dead before long. I folded it up and stick it in my pocket.

Clearly the attorney is dying to know what's in it. But he possesses some shred of decency that prevents him from asking directly. He does try to hold me in conversation for minute, tells me he did everything he could. I nod, don't even bother to make the appropriate sounds. It is what it is.

He finally gives up.

Late at night, I opened the envelope.

Twenty-five

It is the same beach I met my father at, but this time the weather is cold. The stars are brighter, close enough to remind me what I missing, how much more brilliant they would be at sea. The light pollution—the ambient light from the city, the smog drifting down from L.A.—all conspired to keep the viewing from being perfect. But at sea, with crystal air and no lights other than those you generate yourself, your view of the heavens is uninterrupted.

I've taken to carrying a gun again, my 9mm. I don't feel completely safe without it. I consider getting a concealed weapon permit then decide not to bother. The last thing I want is anything on the record now. I don't take it to work with me, but every other time, it's either in my car concealed or somewhere on me. Tonight, it's in my jacket pocket.

Hot days, cool, clear nights—the essence of San Diego. The light breeze off the ocean carries just enough chill to justify the jacket. Still, I wonder if it fools anyone who really has reason to care.

There's no one else out here. The beach itself is off-limits after dark, but I had expected to find at least a couple in a car somewhere. The surf crashes against the empty sand.

I hear the other car before I see it, even as it makes the turn onto the road leading to the parking lot. I consider taking cover, waiting to see who it is, but in truth I don't much care. Perhaps I'm unlike my father in that way—whatever comes, I will meet it. We have too much else in common, the old man and I.

A new, dark gray Volvo enters the lot. It stops near the entrance, then slowly approaches to within one hundred feet, then stops again.

Why is it stopping? They must see my car, must see me.

Then I realize that they're as uncertain as I am and are wondering if I have a backup. Perhaps they have reasons to be cautious.

I walk toward them, my hands in plain view, moving slowly, carefully, an excellent target, full frontal. If they want to kill me, destroy the last link in this ungodly chain, then I'll give them every opportunity to do so.

Another test? Am I offering God one final chance to intervene, to somehow magically deflect a bullet, to prove to me at last that He really does exist and gives a shit about what happens? I suppose that's one explanation, but in truth, I really just don't give a damn anymore.

The headlights are blinding and my night vision is destroyed. If I have to run for—and I doubt I will—then I'll be stumbling and tripping like a fool. Like we did in Muralis Island.

The Volvo cuts his engine, and the sounds of the night return. I hear a car door open and then footsteps on the asphalt, coming toward me. A man steps in front of the headlights, takes a few steps forward and stops.

There's something about the way he moves that intrigues me. It's loose-limbed, the walk of a man who's in excellent physical condition, but it still cautious somehow.

I walk toward him, keeping my hands visible. Does he see me move the same way? Probably not—Muralis Island took more out of me than I thought. I still feel a bone deep ache in my legs, the complaints of newly-formed muscle fiber that'll eventually heal up. If I start working out now, I can build on that, get back in excellent shape. I wonder if I'll have the opportunity.

He's wearing a hat, the brim pulled down. Even if he had not been backlit, I wouldn't have been able to see his face. Not until we're close enough to touch each other area does he look up. He's slightly shorter than I am.

"Hello, Lieutenant," he says.

Nothing can surprise me tonight, nothing at all. Not even Forsythe standing before me in the flesh.

We regard each other for a moment, and I'm tempted to ask questions. But there's really not anything I need to know. Oh, there are some details I'm not clear on, but they don't matter.

Forsythe is a traitor, a spy. He worked with my father. He plunged five men into absolute chaos by his acts, even apart from what he did to national security. He's responsible for more than one death, including Maltierre's.

That night in Muralis Island, he was not captured, caught, or trapped. He entered the building and immediately left by the back door. By the time everything went to shit, he was in a place of safety, watching.

Did he make some arrangement to allow us to escape? How could he have known that we would leave, that I wouldn't send the whole team back into the compound to search for him? Because that's what I should have done—that's what every man on the team knew.

He thought you were in on it, one part of my mind supplies. *Your father's son.* Or he didn't care. This is the only point I really want to resolve, but I wait for him to speak first.

"He told me you knew," Forsythe says. "I figured—." he stops, shrugs helplessly. "The other guys might give you a hard time, but you were in charge. They would have done what you said."

"Thomas killed himself a year later," I say. My voice rasps in my throat.

What exactly is the purpose of this entire meeting? Is this my father's final gift, intended to make me forgive myself for something that was not my fault? Is it an act of penance, a request for forgiveness—what?

"I have to go," Forsythe says.

His voice grates on my skin. If I had seen the slightest bit shame, an acknowledgement of what he had done, of what he'd cost others, it might have been different. That he's here, well-dressed, gold hanging around his neck and his wrists, obviously healthy and well fed, is not right.

So I shoot him. Once in the chest, then again in the back as he spun around and fell to the concrete. The final shot to the back of the head. The spray of blood and brains hang in the light of the headlights.

I stand beside him, looking down, watching black blood spread across black asphalt. There's no color at night.

The Volvo just sits there, its headlights blinding. I wait for some reaction, anything, but there is none.

I have no idea how many men are in the Volvo and I can only guess at the substance of their conversation. Finally, I simply walk back to my car, get in it, and drive off. I go home and sleep well for the first time since Caermon's death.

The next morning, I watch the news while eating a bowl of cold cereal. No reports of a body found at the beach, either on the TV, radio, or newspaper. I will check the afternoon editions as well, but I'm fairly certain that the gray Volvo took care of matters.

I suppose I should feel guilty. There were other things that I could have done. Gone to the authorities or to the U.S. attorney who prosecuted my father. But how long would it take them to believe me? Forsythe would simply disappear into whatever shadowy system has hidden him for the past five years.

I've unraveled the strands of duty that kept me bound before. The question now is what the future can hold. Or if there is a future at all.

Twenty-six

I dread facing Bishop Oakes. I've seen him twice, briefly. Each time, I've chattered to fill the silence, trying to avoid what I know he wants from me.

My status with the Navy is still unresolved. The bishop of the armed services told me to call him back after I talk to Bishop Oakes. He reminds me I'm still under the letter of prohibition.

I drive to the diocese that afternoon and am shown in the bishop's office immediately. Bishop Oakes sits behind his desk, surrounded by paperwork, looking more like a corporate CEO than a vicar of Christ at the moment.

I pose two problems for him, I suspect. First, a spiritual one, and second, the human resources one. The second is properly in the realm of the bishop of the armed services, but from the sound of it, he will depend on Bishop Oakes's information before making his own decision. Certainly, I am closer to this man than I am to my direct superior.

He comes from behind the desk, approaches, and takes me into a close hug. For moment, I feel the wall around me shiver as though it might break into a thousand fragments and lay scattered like shards around me.

But then he pulls back, clamps both hands down my wrists, and takes a good, hard look at me. This will not be easy for either of us.

"Please. Sit down." He points at a couch that runs along the far wall, and I do as he directs. Again he surprises me, by sitting next to me. Without asking, he says a brief prayer asking for discernment and guidance. I echo his amen.

"How are you?" he asks. "Physically, I mean. We'll get to the rest of it later."

I shrug. "Bruised, still pretty sore all over. It's been longtime since I've done that sort of thing."

"And emotionally?"

"Okay." I see that he does not believe me and I will have to explain. "His going to prison—that kept me from having to kill him, you know."

He nods, as though he understands perfectly and perhaps he does. I have made the mistake of underestimating him before. It strikes me then that I've made this same mistake about two supervisors—this bishop and Chaplain Haynes. What does that say about my relationship with higher authority?

"And finally to the heart of it—spiritually?" He leans forward, his eyes burning intensely, his hands clasped before him between his knees. For just a moment, I'm reminded of the submarine skipper who picked us up after Muralis Island the first time.

Bishop Oakes wants me to have survived intact. He wants to hear it in my voice, see it in my eyes, not just hear the words. In a very real sense, he cares about what happens to me, unconditionally.

I look away. The kindness is simply too much to bear.

"Talk to me," he says. It is not quite an order—more an invitation. "We can get through this, you and I."

I talk. Not about the facts, not the recitation that everyone in the world heard the last week. He's undoubtedly read the newspaper accounts and anything that's not covered in those is too highly classified to discuss with him.

I lay it all out on the table. What I know he wants to know. Who I was, and what happened.

I talk about how the past came back for me, went over what he already knew about Caermon's confession, but this time with a deeper understanding of it. Then I tell him what happened on Muralis Island. Not the operational details. I talk about what really matters. I don't pretend to have regrets where there are none and don't try to hide the sheer exhilaration I felt being back with the team. It was, as I said, all on the table.

He asks a few questions, not many. I answer them and continue with the story. I conclude with what it's like to watch my father sentenced to fifty years in prison.

Then I stop. If I tell him the rest of it, about Forsythe, then I truly am making decisions about my future, and I'm not sure I trust him that much. Because I myself do not know what I want yet, nor do I have any feeling I know what God wants of me.

But he knows anyway. Not the details. He sees the stain on my soul. The only thing he doesn't know is exactly what happened, but facts aren't what he's interested in.

"There's more," he says. Then he waits.

If I tell him, he faces the same questions I faced with Caermon. It is just as sacred to him, this idea of the seal of the confessional, I think. Will he keep my secrets, absolve me? Will he do for me what I did not do for Caermon?

And so I tell him the rest of it. I marvel that there's no trace of shock on his face. It doesn't take long, and I finish this time with telling him that there's no news.

"I don't even know who was in the car," I conclude. "Maybe they brought him to me for me to kill. Or maybe I surprised him. It took them awhile to react—actually, they didn't react at all. I just left. They must have cleaned up after me."

Finally, he's satisfied. He knows I gutted myself, have not held anything back.

Then he says, "Will you turn again to Christ as your Lord?"

I haven't asked for this, and he's skipping the beginning part of the ritual. I'm not sure I want this, but I've made enough decision about what I want in the last few days. I will trust Bishop Oakes' judgment. "I will," I say.

"Do you, then, forgive those who have sinned against you?"

A tougher question that. I run over the list people, mentally assessing my readiness to forgive them. Most of them are an easy call. I spend some time thinking hard about my father. Finally I say, "I forgive them."

"May Almighty God in mercy receive your confession of sorrow and of faith, strengthen you in all goodness, and by the power of the Holy Spirit keep you in eternal life."

I join him in saying amen.

He places his hand on my head, his fingers curling around to cap my skull, and gives me what I denied Caermon: absolution.

I say, "Thanks be to God." I feel renewed, lighter in spirit, and even though not entitled, I feel at peace.

Bishop Oakes smiles and I know he feels it, too. "Now we can work on the rest of it."

Twenty-seven

A fter my mother died, my father paid more attention to me than he ever had before. He was in so many ways a stranger to me—and I suppose even now—but back then I was simply grateful for any attention, anything to fill the void left by my mother's death, even from this intimidating stranger. Oh, I knew who he was—there was never any doubt in my mind that he was my father. But he was not a part of my life in the way that my mother was. And he didn't even really know me other than through what she told him and an occasional good night kiss.

He approached being a single father the same way he would have planned to invade a foreign country. After her death, he must have sat down and made a list of activities that we could do together. I was granted one week of mourning and then immediately plunged into a maelstrom of Little League, Boy Scouts, hiking, horseback riding, and a variety of sports events. He seemed more comfortable in the organized activities, the one that had guidelines and rules and rituals about how father and son were to be to each other. I always felt that he didn't take easily to being spontaneous.

I remember the horseback riding particularly vividly. Some time in the past, my father had developed a fairly decent seat and he seemed to expect me to have one, too.

My first mount was a gentle old mare named Molly. Molly had a mouth made of wood but her owner would not trust a curb bit in my inexperienced hands. Instead, she had a snaffle bit, although with an additional noseband and a chain link chinstrap. "She's got a bit of mouth on her", the owner had explained, and left me on my own to figure out what that meant. It didn't take long.

I longed for a western saddle, with inlaid leather working and, more importantly, the horn to hang onto. But my father specifically required that I ride English.

He showed me how to measure the stirrups to my size, with my fingertips on the saddle and the iron stirrup hitting me in my armpit, and taught me to mount from the correct side. He discussed neck reining and a few other basics of horsemanship. Years later, I realized that the format was a standard Navy briefing.

Finally, I was mounted and following him down the trail. Or rather, Molly followed. I was too preoccupied with pressing my knees into the hard leather, the chaff of straps against my calves and keeping my balance. My heels didn't want to stay down and I had one hand firmly entwined in Molly's bushy mane.

We went through a short patch of woods, then down along a dusty trail. Once over my initial terror, I begin to get bored, making the transition quickly as children do. My father had scheduled us for one-hour trail ride—fifteen minutes into it, I was ready to return home.

Father rode a tall black gelding named Mike. He looked superb on Mike and Mike understood he had an experienced rider onboard.

Suddenly, just as I was devising excuses to get out of ever doing this again and feeling the first ache start in my thighs and butt, Molly shied. I dropped the reins and grabbed her mane. She reared slightly, throwing me further back in the saddle, then leaped forward and brushed past Mike. Just as she did, I fell off, and narrowly missed being trampled.

My father shouted, and jumped off Mike and was at my side. "Are you hurt?"

I had had the breath knocked out of and couldn't answer. He ran his hands over me, feeling for broken bones, then looked closely the pupils in my eyes. Finally, he pulled me up into a sitting position and said, "Wait here." He bounded back up onto Mike and took off after Molly.

I sat alone in the dirt, feeling the heat beat down. We were in snake country—what would I do if a snake came. Or scorpion? They might be creeping up on me even as I sat there, alone. What if they chased me?

I jumped up and turned around to look behind me. When my father came back ten minutes later, trailing a now docile Molly behind him, I was standing in the middle of the dirt road, keeping careful watch around me.

He led Molly over to me, expecting me to take the reins. I shook my head and looked down the ground. No way. She tried to kill me once—I was never get getting back on that horse. Or any horse for that matter.

My father looked puzzled. "What's wrong?"

I refused to answer.

"You just fell off, that's all. It happens. Especially when you're learning." Still getting no answer, he began to grow exasperated. "Look, she didn't mean to. Something spooked her, that's all. It probably won't happen again."

Probably. As if that was good enough.

"I'm not riding her," I announced, finally speaking. "Never."

Had my mother been there, there would have been no question about it. She always honored my wishes. Mother never made me do anything that I didn't want to. But she was gone and I was left to deal with this stranger.

I could see he was not buying it. I already knew that he would win, one way or another, and that only made me angrier.

He got off Mike and came over to crouch down next me. Still holding both sets of reins, he put his hands on my shoulders and stared me straight in the eyes. The full force of his gaze bore into my soul. The horses moved up to flank us, shutting out the rest of the world.

"This isn't just about a horse, David. It's about more than that. If you don't get back on, you're saying that any time you're frightened, you'll quit. And not just horses—with anything. In school, and in life—the rule is that as soon as you fall off, you get right back on. Understand?"

I shake my head, determined not to get back on her. My mother would have never made me ride a horse who'd been so unkind to me.

At that age, I still harbored the fantasy that one day I would develop superpowers. A spider bite, a visit from aliens: once I was all-powerful, I would never need to be afraid, because there would be nothing or anything in the world that could hurt me. Until then, it paid to be careful.

"It's two miles back to the barn," my father pointed out. He glanced at the sky. "And hot. Come on, I'll help you."

I shook my head again.

My father's expression went blank. I recognize it now as his way of considering a problem, blocking out the rest of the world while he arrives at a decision, but at the time, I thought he was ill.

He stood and scratched Mike absentmindedly behind the ear. Molly crowded over for some attention herself. I moved away from the three of them. "Then I'll leave you here," he said, his voice entirely expressionless. "Last chance." His voice was cold, so far away, just as he had been most of my life.

I had no doubt he would do it, leave me out here for the snakes and the scorpions. When he made the first motion to turn away, I broke. I took one step forward, the smallest of movements, but that was sufficient. Without speaking, my father helped me into the saddle. Then he pulled the reins over Molly's neck and handed them to me. I took them. I hated him.

Without a word, he turned and began walking down the road. Molly fell into step on one side, Mike on the other. We walked that way or perhaps a quarter of a mile. I began to relax again. Yes, Molly might shy again. But right now he walked right beside me, not touching her but ready to keep anything bad from happening. He might be harsh, but he was kind, too.

Eventually, he mounted up again, and we rode side-by-side back to the barn. He remained in position to grab Molly's bridle at the slightest sign of panic.

When it came time to choose our code names in the SEALs—not our nicknames, those were bestowed by our classmates, as Boomer was given to me after an unfortunate incident with a faulty timer—I remembered that last ride. I became Scorpion.

Returning to Balboa, I am getting back on the horse again, but this time I know what I am doing. After three months of retreat, psychological counseling and the support of my fellow priests, I am back on an even keel.

Chaplain Haynes is making coffee when I walk into the office. He glances up, says hello, and continues with what he's doing. After he finishes tidying the area, he turns to me. "Welcome back."

"Thanks." There is so much to say, more than I can get out in hours. Apologies to be made, explanations, although I suspect that Bishop Oakes has done part of that for me.

"I talked to your bishop," he says quietly. "We're glad to have you back—and I mean that truly."

"I couldn't tell you."

"I know. I would have done exactly the same thing." A sardonic look crosses his face. "Well, except perhaps for the swimming part of it. I just barely squeaked by in OCS."

Suddenly, it is all right. A handshake becomes a hug. He returns it with surprising vigor, and when I step back I see tears shining in his eyes. "I wish there was something I could've done," he says, his voice edged with pain.

"I should have tried to talk to you." I'm not sure I mean it. Neither is he. We leave it at that.

I'm surprised how little has changed during my absence. Personal letters, pending files, and all the debris of a normal career are piled on my desk, threatening to slide off. It was a mark of confidence, leaving these things on my desk, "until he returns."

241

I rifle through them quickly, searching for anything particular urgent. Nothing that can't wait.

Except Sarini.

Twenty-eight

Of course, the entire hospital knows what happened. It would be hard not to after all the media coverage.

None of the public reports got the details right. Everything about Muralis Island, before and afterwards, has been officially denied, every file and report stamped "Top-Secret—Compartmented Information". I'm not sure I'm cleared for all the details.

People who work in hospitals sometimes seem jaded to those on the outside. The black humor, jokes, and apparently callous approach to life—those outside this environment see it as sick. In reality, it is the only way to cope with what we deal with every day: the dead, dying and crippled bodies and souls entrusted to us. More than any other profession, doctors and nurses and support staffs swim in black water, deep in the undercurrents. The only way to keep your head up is to pretend you're floating.

I've heard nothing about Sarah Sarini, other than she's back at work. All charges against her were dropped, a public apology issued which she just as publicly accepted, graciously. The shortage of drugs was blamed on an accounting error and the Chief of Staff spoke sternly about new measures in place to prevent it from happening again. I have no doubt she will be promoted as soon as she's eligible, and probably receive a couple of plum assignments to make up for the "inconvenience".

Does she want to see me? I have no idea. I'm not even certain I want to see her.

She may be dangerous to me now. She knows not only who I am but what I was, and who I'm still capable of being. It would be much easier if she didn't know that.

Then again, how can I not see her? The same way that Napier had to see me after Muralis Island, even knowing that I was responsible for the deaths of two of his people. He had to see me because of what we were and what we'd been through together. We were teammates, and nothing could ever change that. Not even hatred and betrayal.

It's much the same with Sarini now. If I tried, I could pinpoint exactly where she was in the hospital right now. That bond, that psychic connection forged between us underwater, is still there. I could reach out through the threading throngs of people, and find her anywhere in the world.

A quick glance at the clock tells me I don't need psychic abilities to know where she is. She's back on her old shift, and she's down in the emergency room, doing what she's always done.

It must be a relief to her, to get back to normal circumstances. To go back to being God, not worrying about people shooting at you or demanding that you jump down mountain shafts or swim in ice-cold water. As frantic as the ER is, it is her home turf and the place where she has always been most alive.

A public meeting or private? I should ask someone, perhaps one of the hoards of young psychologists eager to sustain me through my crisis. Maybe arrange a meeting with Sarini with one of them present to process the experience.

Not a chance. I know where she is.

As I leave the office, Miss Agee steps in front of me. Her face is serious, twisted in some expression I don't exactly understand. She says nothing, simply reaches out to touch the front of my shirt. It is oddly intimate coming from her. Even her constant worry about my soul was not nearly as personal.

She looks up at me, and I see tears in her eyes. She opens her mouth as though she's got something to say then closes it again.

I put both my hands over hers and press it to my chest. Her fingers are warm, slightly sweaty. "Thank you," I say.

She nods and looks profoundly gratified. Neither of us are entirely certain what we are talking about—or rather, we both know but it simply too far beyond words to voice. It has something to do with her relief that I'm alive but it goes further than that.

Finally, she finds her voice. "You'll be okay now." Her voice croaks slightly, as though she can't get the words out.

I nod. "Yes, I will be."

She trots back to her desk, take something out of her drawer and brings it over to me. She holds out her hand, palm down. I stretch out my hand in reflex. She drops a collar tab into my palm. "I thought you might need this. They brought it by, you know. That NCIS agent. It was dirty, so I wash it off. I hope that was all right."

I have a vivid mental picture of Mrs. Angie scrubbing my collar tab with toothpaste, feeling helpless and wanting to do something, anything, to help. My fingers close over the collar tab and I put my hand on top of hers. "That was very kind of you." I know how she feels about the white collar, and she knows how I feel about it. That she has done this for me is deeply touching.

"I'll be back in a little while." I close the collar of my civilian shirt and put the tab into it. I'm not sure that I actually want one on right now. My idea of what and who a priest is so profoundly deeper now than before that I'm not sure I'm worthy to wear it. How little I knew when I was ordained.

"Well." She's nervous now, well outside her comfort zone. "I guess I better—." The phone rings, setting her free. She trots back to her desk to deal with some crisis she understands.

I wonder if I'll ever feel the same way. I envy her.

Nothing has changed. A few new faces, the details of the injured, that's all. It's still life on the edge, every move critical, trying to keep one's head above water in the most dreadful circumstances. The only difference between combat and the emergency room is whether the shooting is over.

Sarini is in one of the treatment rooms, visible from the waist up through the window. Her face is covered with a clear plastic shield, a disposable green gown over her scrubs. The gown is coated with blood, sticking to the scrubs underneath.

She's intent on the man before her, a young black male turning an ominous dusky blue. His face is covered with an oxygen mask and he looks like he's trying to thrash about but is too weak to do so.

Sarini knows I'm here, of that I'm certain. I stay out of the way, not willing to break her concentration for my own sake. What I have to say to her can wait. The man in front of her can't.

A few doctors and nurses drift by, their greetings studiedly casual. Or perhaps not so—perhaps I'm not important enough right now to matter. They've got more to worry about than the lurid details of my latest adventure. Oh, they're dying to hear the details—but not now. Not while people are trying to die on them.

There's nothing I can do here, not without being in the way. I start back out of the doors, feeling both relief and disappointment.

"Father Dalt." Sarini's clear, sharp voice rings out across the room. "Come here—I need you." There's that all-too-familiar note of anger in her voice, the one she gets when she knows she's losing a patient.

I hurry over to the room, pausing only to grab a gown and a pair of gloves. I don't pull the gloves on. I simply carry them as a talisman against whatever blood-borne pathogens are around.

How many times have I stood across a bed from her, seeing the frustration and anger on her face? Anger at this man—barely more than a boy—who's gotten himself shot. Angry at her own helplessness and inability to save him. Angry at whatever God allowed this to happen. It's all focused in her eyes as she looks at me. "Gunshot," she says.

"Conscious?" I asked her.

"Just barely." She shakes her head, her frustration tangible. "He's lost a lot of blood."

"Mr.—" I glanced over at Sarini and she supplies, "Walters." "Mr. Walters," I continue. "I'm Father Dalt. Can you hear me?"

He turns his face towards me and his agitation subsides slightly. His pupils are dull and blank, his face slack. "Am I dying?" he manages, the words slurred.

"They're going to take you up to surgery," I say easily, avoiding the question. "Most people are frightened before surgery."

"Yeah." For all the dullness in his face, he seems to grasp what I'm saying. "My mama—is she here yet?" I glanced over at Sarini who shakes her head.

"No, we're still looking for her," I say. And they will be—I don't even have to check to know that's true.

"When she gets here, you tell her—." His voice breaks off in a groan and he tries to reach for his gut. His hands have been Velcro-strapped to the bed, evidently necessary to keep him from interfering with what they're trying to do—which is to save his life.

"I'll tell her," I say, letting my voice end on a slightly higher note so he'll finish the sentence.

"It wasn't her fault," he says. "Wasn't her fault."

"I'll tell her that. I'll tell her myself. What else?" Because I know there is more, it's just a question of whether he can force the words out or whether I'll have to give voice to what he cannot say. Because to say it now would be to acknowledge just how serious his condition is, how little chance he has of saying those words to her him self. "Love her," he said, his voice fading as his gaze wanders away from my face. "Not her fault. Love her."

So he made it. By entrusting that one final message to me, he's starting to come to terms with just how bad his situation is.

The phone rings and one of the nurses grabs it. She listens for second then turns to Sarini and nods. "They're ready for him in three minutes. "

"Let's go, people. Let's move." Sarini's voice is the same one Napier used on Muralis Island, a voice accustomed to immediate, automatic and unquestioning obedience.

As one, the doctors and nurses take their positions, the movements well-rehearsed. Mr. Walters is rolled out of the room and toward the patient elevator standing by to take him to Surgery. Sarini stays with him as far as the swinging double doors and watches them as they go down the hallway. She turns away, instantly forgetting about him, to face the next challenge.

Judging from the noise level in ER, her next problem is me.

She pulls the surgical mask off, unrolls the gloves, and finally strips away the gown. Physically, she seems much smaller without the trappings of an ER doctor, but nothing can diminish her presence there. She knows what's going on in every corner of the ER, the exact status of each patient as though linked to them with invisible umbilical lines. As long as they are in the ER, they are part of her.

"Welcome back," she says, her voice neutral. In a momentary lull in ER, everyone is trying very hard not to look at either of us. She is aware of that, of course, as am I.

"Thanks, I said. "It's good to be back."

"Coffee?" she asks. She leads the way to the small coffee room set off of the main area. It's the only place there that isn't ringed by windows. If anyone wants to spy on us, they will have to come look. Not that they will. These are her people, her squad, so attuned to her moods that they'll be careful to stay out of the way.

She pours coffee into standard white porcelain mugs, the kind used in the hospital's cafeteria. It's as I expected—dark, slightly bitter—what we used to call midwatch coffee, one cup guaranteed to carry you along on a buzz for at least another four hours. We both pass on the cream and sugar.

"You got back today," she says. It's not really a question. Everyone in the hospital knew when I was coming back. "How does it feel?"

"Different. But the same. If that makes sense." I blow on the coffee—it's not really too hot to drink, but I want a reason not to look at her. She makes a noncommittal sound then takes a sip of her own coffee.

"How have you been?" I asked, filling the silence that's stretching on a little too long for comfort.

"OK. They straightened everything out." She's staring down at the surface of her own coffee as though it holds some answers.

I stared her, my sense of frustration mounting. Is this the way it's going to be? We're not going to talk about it? Just pretend nothing ever happened, going on with life as before? With my trying to convince her to talk to me, her holding me at arm's-length like she does everyone?

It's not fair. I deserve better than that.

I start to say so, when a sense of profound unworthiness sweeps over me. I look at her again and see what I missed the first time.

She's lost weight, and it shows in her face. There are dark circles under her eyes. The muscles of her shoulders are tight, and it's not just from a long shift in the ER. A door bangs shut and she jumps.

She doesn't need me now. Not David Dalt. We've been to hell and back but I've made the trip more times than she has and I know the path.

I back away from her a bit, giving her more space. I looked at my own cup of coffee, searching for the answers. There are none, or at least no easy ones.

What she needs now is a priest.

No doubt when she returned she was offered counseling for post-traumatic stress and I have no doubt she refused it. Now it's starting to show. Before long, I won't be the only one who notices it.

"I've been praying for you," I say, my voice casual. And it's the truth, although I'd say that my prayers were occasionally more of a personal nature than strictly out of concern for her soul. Still, it's not a lie, and that's important.

Her head snaps up and she looks directly at me for the first time. I can feel the intensity her gaze, but I still don't look up. What she needs now is a safe place—which would be the ER, for her—and some distance. A way of thinking about what has happened to her and what she needs to do with it.

I won't be the one to counsel her, of course. Even if I could manage to remember that I'm a priest first, I'm far too involved in what happened to her, not to mention personally interested in her, for that to be in any way appropriate. And yet I'm also the one who knows what happened, and am at least familiar with what she's going through.

"You know, I know you've heard it a thousand times. I imagine the psychiatrists are being a major pain in the ass right now, aren't they?"

Her laugh is short and harsh, with a trace of humor in it. "Them and everyone else. They don't know whether to pretend nothing happened or be sympathetic." Her shoulders slump slightly. "I don't know which one is worse."

"Yeah, I know. At least in the SEAL Teams, you've got each other. At least, those who make it back. The rest of the guys who were there, they have their own ways of dealing with it. And their own people who fix them up."

"It's not like I got hurt," she says, as though I hadn't spoken. "I slept for two days straight, then I was fine."

Oh, but you're far from fine. And you know it. But it doesn't have to be the way you think it has to be.

I take another sip of coffee, letting the silence stretch out. This time, it feels comfortable. We'll dance around the edges for a while and eventually come to the crux of the matter. Maybe not tonight, maybe not even this week. But if I do what I'm supposed to do—if I *am* who I'm supposed to be—I may be able to lead her out of this.

"Trauma is different," I say finally. "It changes the entire programming. The nightmares, the new odd things that bother me—it's the same each time. It hardwires you in a different way. Your reflexes are different." I finally look up and meet her gaze. She's looking a little frantic now, as though someone has discovered a deep dark secret. "It's like that for me every time. Post traumatic stress—it's never what I think it will be like."

Another one of those disturbing laughs. She backs away ever so slightly. "Things like that don't happen to people like me."

I am deeply relieved. To say that, to give voice to the destruction of her assumptions about the world, is a sign of immeasurable progress. And it's a sign that she can be helped.

"It did," I say. "It *did* happen to someone like you. And the only question now is whether you're willing to admit to being human, to recognize that you're going through the same thing that every person on the SEAL team's going through, or whether you're going to pretend you're not human."

"I'm not human. I'm a doctor." She says it without any self-consciousness.

"I know. That makes it harder, not easier. The one thing I always hold onto in the middle of it is this: if the experience didn't kill you, the memory won't."

I feel peace flooding into the room. No, not because I've magically resolved her classic case of post-traumatic stress but because the unspoken is out in the open. The water is clear, all the way to the bottom of the ocean. Now it just remains to discover what's swimming in it.

"Everyone here is too close to you," I say. "Me, especially. But there are a couple of people you need to talk to." She starts to protest, and I hold up my hand to forestall comment. "If your car was making funny noises,

251

you'd take it to a mechanic. You're aware that you're not entirely your normal calm self right now, aren't you? It's like a cylinder's knocking or a spark plug's misfiring."

"I'm not seeing a psychologist." Her voice is defiant.

"I'm not suggesting you do. But there's a guy over at the SEAL Team headquarters—you need to talk to him."

"He's not a psychologist? Or a priest?" Somehow this seems to bother her, the lack of any professional credentials, even though she has a typical medical doctors disdain for someone with a Ph.D. instead of an MD.

"No. Not either of those. He's just a guy. He's the one we all talk to when we come back." I glance at my watch, see the time slipping by. "In fact, I'm kind of surprised he hasn't contacted you yet."

"Then he's just a counselor. A guy with a couple of weeks of active listening school under his belt." Now the scorn in her voice is evident.

I shake my head again. "Not even that. Just someone who's been there. Many times. You won't even have to tell him what happened or why you're there. He'll tell you what you're going through. All you have to do is listen."

"Oh, right. So I can 'process the experience', right? We can talk about the psychophysiology of extreme stress and he can ask me, 'How does it make you feel, getting shot at and swimming in freezing water and almost dying?' and I can say, 'It makes me feel bad,' and he can say, 'That's normal' and I'll be all better, right?"

I drain the rest of my coffee then wash the cup out. "No. He knows what it's like. Better than you do. In fact, he probably won't want you to say anything at all. He's going to tell you what you're going through. And then you can make a decision about how you want to proceed. Think of him as a specialist, if you want to. When you get tired of feeling the way you do, just listen to him."

I put the clean coffee cup in the dish drain then finally look up at her. "It's going to be okay, you know. It will be."

The hydraulic doors in the main room wheeze, the sound of a new patient arriving. Gurney wheels clatter on the tile and someone starts snapping out orders.

Sarini sets her cut down in the sink and heads for the door, already taking in information from what she hears. She's completely focused and has forgotten about me.

I follow her to the door and watch her plunge back into the maelstrom. She'll decide when to get help on her own terms and in her own time. Until then, I've done what I can.

I slipped out of the ER quietly, staying out of the way. Sarini will have to kill her own ghosts. I'll wait.

If my father taught me anything, it's that truth is what you make it. If truth is the first casualty of war, perhaps the past is the last.

The End

The classic that started a nation on the road to healing. *Out of the Night*, by Father Bill Mahedy, broke new ground in treating veterans for post-traumatic stress and offered hope to millions. Recently reissued with an updated foreword, it's still required reading for combat vets looking for hope and for those who care about them.

Available from amazon.com or from radixpress.com.

Coming Soon: Our Common Life, by William P. Mahedy.

Email us to be notified when it's available.

Greyhound Books

available online from www.dogbooks.org

The Airedale Chronicles

Aire Town

When the flu strikes a small town, the Airedale Terriers must take over to protect their people and catch a burglar.

A Very Airey Christmas

An Airedale Terrier pup with a talent for interior decorating is determined to find out if there really is a Santa Claus.

Beagles in Wonderland

Through the Rabbit Hole:

When two impulsive pups disappear down a mysterious black rabbit hole, the King of Beagles and his staff of tactical geniuses must use every trick they know to rescue the pups from a strange underground realm ruled by Greyhounds and guarded by a monster.

The Golden Retriever Chronicles

A Golden Opportunity

Anastasia, the Keeper of the One Song, must find her person the perfect job and resolve dissonance in the world as well.

The Greyhound Chronicles

Greyhound Dancing

Tweeter, a retired racer, faces the greatest challenge of her life when a fox experiencing a midlife crisis attempts to take over Hardin Creek Farms.

Greyhound Singing

The Moon is angry with Tweeter and the stunning retired racer must find out why before it's too late. (Hint: the grasshoppers help!)

Greyhound Laughing:

Tweeter travels to a neighboring farm to solve the problem of a hyena.

A Greyhound Christmas

A pack of retired senior racers escape evil dogsitters and head for the ski slopes to find their people.

050412

Made in the USA
Lexington, KY
22 October 2011